Sophia Watson

Sophia Watson was born in 1962 and educated at Durham University. She has worked in publishing, as a feature writer for the *Daily Mail* and as a ghost writer. Her previous books are *Winning Women*, published in 1989, and *Marina*, a biography of the Duchess of Kent, published in 1994. She is married with four small daughters and lives in West Somerset. Her previous two novels, *Her Husband's Children* and *Strange and Well Bred*, are both available from Sceptre

GW00746218

Also by Sophia Watson

Her Husband's Children
Strange and Well Bred

The Perfect Treasure

SOPHIA WATSON

SCEPTRE

Copyright © 1998 by Sophia Watson

First published in 1998 by Hodder and Stoughton
First published in paperback in 1998 by Hodder and Stoughton
A division of Hodder Headline PLC
A Sceptre Book

The right of Sophia Watson to be identified as the Author of the
Work has been asserted by her in accordance with the Copyright,
Designs and Patents Act 1988.

10 9 8 7 6 5 4 3 2 1

British Library C.I.P.

A CIP catalogue record is available from the British Library

ISBN 0 340 68888 2

Typeset by Hewer Text Ltd, Edinburgh
Printed and bound in Great Britain by Clays Ltd, St Ives plc

Hodder and Stoughton
A division of Hodder Headline PLC
338 Euston Road
London NW1 3BH

For Victoria Clark, my friend and cousin, whose hospitality and enthusiasm one summer's evening helped shape these characters' fates.

With love.

Sometimes they feel like friends, I know them so well. And then it seems to me that I am some kind of spy. I know little things about each and every one that they would probably never even tell their sisters – when they have a hangover, when they've got their periods, when they've taken up or stopped a diet. I have their trust, and that is a very good feeling. They trust me with their keys, their possessions, their treasures – and their secrets.

I'm good, I know that and I hope they do too. Although this cleaning is only for now, until I can change my life for the better, I still want to do it properly. I always see things through to the end. Who was it? Bamber Gascoigne, Magnus Magnusson – one of those telly know-alls. 'I've started so I'll finish.' That's me.

I've been told how stupid I am, how not changing my mind doesn't mean I'm always right. I know that, of course I do. But sometimes I think I've nothing left but my opinions – and Tamsin of course.

When I kept Tamsin everyone told me I was pig-headed, wrecking my life for an idea. But Tamsin was not an idea, she was a baby – a mistake maybe, a stupid mistake to make in 1990, but still a baby. They've invented a new contraceptive, I heard on the radio. It's not new at all, it's called not doing it, but everyone seems very excited by it. It tests your pee and tells you if you're fertile or not. Brilliant. And if you are you don't do it. Obvious. But you've still got to remember to piss, and then remember to Say No. Babies will still be born; nothing is new.

And no, I'm not Catholic. That is an assumption that irritates me. I never did hold with abortion, and when it came to the test

I did not change my mind. But it has nothing to do with religion. It has just always seemed obvious to me that a conception was human – tiny and frail and in all sorts of danger but still human. If anything I'm anti-Catholic. I hate all that gold and incense and sweet-looking plaster statues. I wasn't brought up anything in particular – the Gods of Good Manners and Not Expressing a View were the ones in our house. I think I still respect the first, but the second . . .

That's what this writing is about. I don't know what I'll end up doing, but not this, not cleaning for ever.

I was reading English at university – Reading – when Tamsin happened. Neither of my parents went to university (Dad's a printer and Mum's a secretary at a big law firm) and my older brother left school at sixteen and went to train as a car mechanic. So it was a bit of a surprise to everyone when I wanted to go for a degree and my teachers said I could if I went on working hard. I did English and Sociology and French at A level and passed all three (B,C,C). Everyone was so pleased. And I thought everything would change. I didn't want to be a secretary or a librarian. I wanted to be different. I wanted to change things – my life, my self, my chances. I was given a place at Reading and thought I had made it. It was only the beginning.

It finished almost as soon as it started. I fell pregnant by my second boyfriend before the end of the summer term. I should have known better of course. There was really no excuse, and that's partly why I wouldn't have the abortion. Just because I was stupid, that was no reason for Tamsin – the baby – to be penalised. Pete and I had been going out for a couple of months, I was on the pill . . . the doctor had told me that antibiotics made the pill less reliable but I hadn't listened properly, or if I had I'd forgotten. So I couldn't hold Pete responsible.

He didn't want to know, and I don't blame him. I didn't want to spend the rest of my life with him either: in fact once the shock was over I liked the idea of me and my baby alone together against the world.

You should have heard my parents. They had been so proud when I set off for Reading for the first time, but you would not have believed it to listen to them when I told them I was having Tamsin. First they tried persuasion, then bullying. Then, when they realised I meant it, that whatever they said the baby would be born, they laughed. 'So what's happened to your grand ideas?' they said, 'all that talk of books and publishing?' I had dreamed of that, you see. I wanted to discover the new Graham Greene; I wanted to be Carmen Callil, to start something new, to be someone. I wouldn't tell them about Pete, it was between us. 'At least Steven married Joanne when he got her pregnant' they said. Well, I'd always known my brother was a fool. 'How can you get a job without a degree and with a baby?' they went on. 'You couldn't even be a secretary now.' (I'd been stupid, told Mum I wanted a better deal than she had had and she'd never forgiven me for it.)

They were right, of course. But still – there was the baby.

They did not exactly throw me out, I'll give them that. I had Tamsin from their house, but by the time she was six weeks old they were making it clear that I had lumbered myself and they didn't see why they should have to bear the brunt. She was lovely, Tamsin, lots of dark hair, eyes that turned bright blue very soon, good-natured from the day she was born. Not that that impressed them.

I never had a moment's doubt that I had done the right thing, though, in spite of everything. That first night of her life I woke up in the narrow hospital bed with the baby wrapped up tightly and curled against me. I put my nose against her head and smelt that slightly bitter new-born smell and my heart melted and I cried for love of her and relief that she hadn't been vacuumed out into a kidney dish and thrown out with the leftovers of other people's operations. Bits of gut, diseased breast, little shavings of bits of body that aren't working properly – Tamsin was worth more than that. But I still needed to work out a future for us.

In the books I used to read, families took in single mothers, gave them a flat or a cottage and employed them. At first I thought that was what I would do, and there were indeed some of those sorts of job around. I applied for a few, was even offered one of them, but they were all so far away. One was in the furthest bit of Somerset, another in Cornwall. The one I could have had was in County Durham – miles away from anywhere. I cannot drive and besides a bit of me hoped that Mum would turn out to be a proper Gran. I wanted to

give her the chance, and did not want to cut myself off
entirely.

It was not as easy as I had told myself it could be, finding
a job, somewhere to live. I wanted to go to London; I could
not have the job I had hoped for, but there was no reason
for me to stay in Kent withering away the rest of my days,
seeing Mum and Dad for Sunday lunch once a month, watching
Steven and Joanne playing Happy Families with little Matt. If I
had to do it on my own, I would. It took some manipulation,
but I managed to find myself a Housing Trust flat – well, not
much more than a bedsit really – in North Notting Hill. One
of the Victorian houses carved up into tiny units for the needy
and disadvantaged. Like me. Funny, isn't it? Having Tamsin
made me officially disadvantaged, which in itself gave me an
advantage. And she is not just a leg-up on the housing lists.
She has given me something to hold on to, something worth
a great deal more than a degree from Reading, more than my
parents with their cold care and good manners ever managed.

So there I was, in an all-right 'flatlet' in a part of London I
soon grew to know and love, with various benefits to help me
survive, and Tamsin, and vague hopes of something better in
the future.

The cleaning came later, when Tamsin was two. I saw a notice
up in the post office when I was collecting my benefits one day
and thought why not, easy money, cash in hand. 'Reliable cleaner
wanted. Bassett Road. 968 0841.' Only two streets away. It would
help. So I rang the number and a girl's voice told me to come
round that evening and look at the flat. Which seemed an odd
way to put it, really. I would have thought that the girl would
want to look at me, rather than me look at the flat. I left Tamsin
with Liz who lives over the hall from me and turned up on the
dot of seven. I was surprised at how nervous I felt.

The girl who opened the door for me seemed immediately
familiar, although I could not place her at all. She did not look
as though she had ever seen me before, though – not that she
really looked at me. I doubt she would have recognised me if
she had bumped into me in the supermarket half an hour later.
Still, there was something about her I knew; maybe I had just
noticed her in the street sometime.

She was – is – certainly noticeable. Very pretty, with shiny dark red hair and huge dark blue eyes. She has freckles, and that pale skin redheads often have, but with her it all works. She doesn't look ill-pale, more translucent, shining, somehow fragile. She dresses conventionally enough, expensive well-cut clothes that flow rather than droop.

Her voice takes away from the impression of vulnerability. As soon as she opens her mouth you see her for what she is: confident, quite loud, a little bit affected. The arty type (hence the floppy clothes I suppose). She is called Amanda Quince and I bet no one calls her Mandy.

She talked a lot that first time, waved her hands around, seemed very emphatic and I suddenly thought, how odd, she's nervous too, and that made me more sure of myself. She needed me possibly more than I needed her, I realised.

She showed me around the flat and I could not help but feel a bit envious. She is about my age, perhaps a couple of years older, but what a difference there is in our lives. We live a few streets apart, but it could be opposite ends of the world. Her flat is on the second floor of one of those double-fronted houses in Bassett Road – the Ladbroke Grove end, not further west where they turn into red brick Victorian terraced houses. It takes up the whole floor and the rooms are quite big and even high-ceilinged. Two bedrooms, a fair-sized kitchen, one bathroom and an extra loo, and a really huge (by my standards) living-room. It was all newly painted and clean-smelling, with windows open onto the trees outside. The pictures are framed posters of art exhibitions in posh places – Rome, Venice, New York – and there are a few real pictures. Her furniture is more shabby than you might expect, though, and she told me later that a lot of it was extra stuff her parents had given her. Imagine having a left-over settee – a bit worn, but perfectly good.

She offered me a cup of coffee, although I noticed she had a glass of white wine on the draining board in the kitchen, and she watched me drink the coffee as she told me about herself.

She's a television producer, works freelance on documentaries. This means, she said, that sometimes she's 'very hectic'. '*Often* very hectic', she corrected herself, and so she thought she really needed some extra help in the flat to keep on top of it. I wondered why she was explaining herself to me. It seems perfectly reasonable to me to pay someone to do all the boring things if you can afford it. I would. I will. She had only recently moved into the flat, it was her first, Daddy had helped her buy it, and she did want to keep it nice. 'I'm in love with my flat,' she said, waving her arms around and once again I felt sure I had seen her somewhere before. 'Wouldn't you be?' and it did not seem to occur to her that maybe she was being the smallest bit tactless. So I agreed that yes it was a very nice flat and of course she should keep it as pretty as it now was. 'One other thing: I am thinking of having a lodger to help with the mortgage, so there will be two of us. I hope that won't make any difference,' she said, and I said that no, it did not, and thought how much I would like to be that lodger, and how many hours I would have to work to be able to afford it, and then I thought of Tamsin and how Amanda did not even look at me and I knew I was dreaming.

'How many hours a week were you thinking of?' I asked.

'Well, at least two, preferably three,' she answered, looking at me closely. 'Could you possibly fit me in? And I thought of the long days passed looking after Tamsin and trying not to spend money, and I pretended to consider a little, and said I thought I could manage Tuesday mornings, and three hours would be all right. This was on a Monday and although I did not want to look too keen the thought of the extra money was wonderful.

'I've asked around and five pounds an hour seems to be the going rate,' she said. 'Is that all right?' Five pounds an hour! Fifteen pounds no one need know about! It was much more than I was expecting, and I thought of the little dress I had seen in Woolies and how sweet Tamsin would look in it, and decided that the first week maybe I would use the money on treats, and only be sensible afterwards. I could buy the dress, and maybe a nice piece of meat or a bottle of cheap wine. I had learned to enjoy wine at university – nothing grand, but my parents hardly drank wine at home so anything was new. I do miss that side of student life, the sitting around eating mountains of pasta and drinking wine and talking all night. Not just talking of course. If I had stuck to talking I would not have Tamsin.

My new employer let me out of the flat (and, I expect, returned with some relief to her glass of wine) and I almost skipped back home across Ladbroke Grove. Fifteen pounds extra a week. I could hardly believe it. To celebrate I bought a couple of cans of lager and took them to Liz.

'Thanks for looking after Tamsin,' I said as she let me in. 'I've got the job, so I bought us a drink.'

'You needn't have. She was as good as gold. She's getting sleepy though.' Tamsin was sucking her thumb in front of the television, almost asleep. I do not have one, so she is usually quite bored by it, but the glum faces on some soap seemed to be soothing her nicely. 'She'll be all right for a minute, go on, let's drink these. I haven't seen you properly for ages.'

She's a funny girl, Liz. She has three children by two men (or possibly three, she's not entirely sure about the first one). The smallest, Ayesha, has a black father which is what gave the game away as Tony's father is white and was expecting another child the same colour. To fall pregnant once by mistake is (just about) excusable, but three times is just plain silly. Still, she looks after them really well: they are not at all like the tabloid prototype of deprived single parent families. They are clean and tidy and say their prayers at night (Liz blushed when I found that out, said she couldn't help it, it was her Catholic upbringing and a bit of her is still frightened of the nuns). Her flat, though, is a tip. It is bigger than mine, but really nasty. My mother would die if she saw it. Some chance. She has not been to see me once since I lived in London, although I go to Kent every now and again when I can afford the bus fare. Sometimes, when I am sitting with Liz in her flat, I see the appeal of my mother's type of sterile tidiness. Dirty clothes piled on chairs and trailing on the floor, an unemptied pot stinking in the corner of the room, unfinished plates of food left until the remains form a crust. Really horrible. And yet out of it come these three tidy, affectionate children.

What is even odder about Liz is that she does not seem to mind any of it – the squalor, the hopelessness, the dependency of her position. I put up with my life for now, but I'm still optimistic. She sees no future beyond the children, and does not mind. She says she has learned her lesson about men, and it is true to say she has not had a boyfriend for a while. No one since Ayesha's father, I don't think. She has never admitted it, but I think (despite all the bedtime prayers) that she was on the game for a while – part-time if nothing else, turning a few tricks when money was tight. Which is something I would never do.

'What are you going to do with Tamsin?' Liz asked as my little girl finally tired of the brooding Mitchell brothers and climbed onto my knee. 'I'll have her if you want. I can't see it'll be a problem.'

I hesitated. I had already thought of asking her – we often looked after each other's children – but had decided I could not. However often she had done it for me, it would be different if it was regular and I was being paid while I was away. I would have to offer to pay her – and childminding rates would eat up at least half of my wonderful new money. To think that I had dreamed of running a huge publishing house and now here I was practically wetting my knickers over a poxy fifteen pounds a week. It was pathetic in a way, but in another way it wasn't. At least I was no longer being inert. I was doing something. I had at last taken the first step towards another life.

'I couldn't ask you,' I said. 'Not regularly every week. It wouldn't be fair. You've got your three already.'

'Jackie's at school,' she pointed out. 'And Tony's starting next term. It's only Ayesha and you know she and Tamsin get on.' I wondered if she was thinking about money, but one look at her face told me I was being nasty even considering the idea. She may be an odd best friend for me to have – we have nothing in common, not even our ages – but she is my friend. She is really good, much better than me despite all the dirty dishes and different men. Perhaps it has something to do with the nuns, I don't know. Anyway she was looking at me with her pleased, honest, open face and I knew all she was thinking was how she could do a friend a favour.

'Well, I thought I could take her with me,' I said.

Liz laughed. 'You're mad. I bet you didn't tell Miss Fancy-Pants you were bringing a two year old along with you to draw on her walls.'

'No. But then she didn't ask. Oh, Liz, it'll be all right. Tamsin's a good girl, she'll sit quietly. I'll take a toy or two and she can follow me around and pretend she's helping. Thanks for the offer though – maybe sometimes I'll leave her but it won't hurt her to come too.'

I had finished my drink and put the can on the floor by my chair where it would probably stay for a week or two, or until Ayesha cut her finger on the metal hole at the top. Normally I make a token effort to tidy up after Tamsin and myself at least when we're at Liz's, but now Tamsin was asleep on my knee and I just wanted to pick her up and carry across the hall and put her straight into bed.

Besides which, suddenly I had had enough of Liz and her mess and her goodness and wanted to be alone to think.

I realised that I wanted Tamsin to come with me not because of meanness (although that had been my first, unworthy, reaction), nor because I did not want to put Liz out (my second, nicer feeling). I wanted Tamsin to come with me because, even though she was so young, I wanted her to see a better way of life than the one I could give her.

Even if it was for only three hours a week I wanted her to see pretty things, clean white walls and pale yellow bedspreads. I wanted her to have the chance to take in – however subliminally – that some kitchens are filled with matching china and good food, fresh fruit and bottles of wine. That not all baths are ring-stained through worn-out enamel, not all chairs are just the right side of breaking. I had a vision of her sitting neatly in the middle of that Turkish (or something) rug in that sitting-room looking at framed posters of swimming pools and green doors and the girl lying in the boat who looked a little like Amanda (and I bet Amanda knew it, too). I had not known who these pictures were by (the good thing about posters, though, is that the artist's name is usually printed in huge letters somewhere) but I could see that they were different from – and almost certainly better than – the smiling girls and dogs my mother hung on her walls. I wanted Tamsin to grasp at the idea of beauty. She was not going to find it in a Housing Trust bedsit, that was for sure.

In the end I lost my nerve on the first morning at Amanda's. (I could not – would not – think of her as or even call her Miss Quince.) I remembered the bit about being freelance and just did not want to risk her being there. So in the end Tamsin did not sit staring in awe at the Hockney (I checked) poster but sat in Liz's lounge playing happily among plates of dried-out baked beans. Liz was relaxed about it, and I thought I had better check in future whether Amanda would be there.

In fact she was, hanging around me looking embarrassed and not knowing what to do with herself. She showed me where all the cleaning equipment was kept, made me a cup of coffee, talked a bit about the area. Finally I took pity on her. 'Don't worry about me, I'll just get on,' I said, and immediately worried that maybe she was staying because she thought I might break something or slip something into my bag.

Our eyes met and maybe she realised what I was thinking and she blushed bright red and flapped her arms and slung her bag over her shoulder and disappeared out of the flat. I decided I quite liked her despite her arti-fartiness. I also, sneakily, liked the idea that although she had the upper hand over me in every way, she was still worried about offending me. Maybe we were closer to being equals than I had thought.

It is no good pretending that cleaning up after someone else is fun. I knew it would be a dull, thankless job, but nevertheless it was something different and it gave me and Tamsin that extra fifteen pounds a week. Because I hardly ever knew when Amanda was going to be there it was almost impossible for me to fulfil my imaginary picture of Tamsin sitting like an angel appreciating her surroundings, which was a disappointment. I'm sure being in Bassett Road made a difference to me. Although I was drudging, it was a refreshing change to be surrounded by pretty things, and reminded me of my goals in life. One day I will have an elegant, understated, tidy flat. And then I will pay someone else to clean the bath and wipe my toothpaste stains from my basin.

So that is how I began this work, four years ago. It was not long before Amanda asked me if I could fit anyone else in, and then another person, and another. Now Tamsin is at primary school and I work two full days and three half days a week while she is away. It gives me something to do, and it makes me surprisingly rich. Well, not compared to them of course, but still . . . work it out. Twenty-one hours a week – and the rate has gone up to six pounds an hour. A hundred and twenty-six pounds a week clear. Tamsin and I are in the same flat, at the same low cost. Her clothes don't just come from the Portobello Road market any more, with Woolies as the extravagant high point. I can afford Mothercare now and even, once, bought her a dress at Marks and Sparks. I look tidier, too. I know that some of them, especially Mrs Settrington and Mr Nesbit, expect me to look a certain way: tidy, dull but not dowdy. It goes with the job. I must be prepared to speak up when spoken to, but never initiate conversation. I can laugh at their jokes but be very careful if I go so far as to make one myself. I must be prepared for a long, time-wasting chat on one occasion, and on others remain totally silent. And I must never, ever, refer to anything I have seen in their homes unless they mention it first. It can be tricky.

But I hold a little piece of their lives in my hands and that makes everything worthwhile.

Amanda Quince does not seem to have changed much in the last four years. Maybe she has quietened down a little, is a little less like Fergie in her loud self-confidence. But then Fergie is a little less like Fergie herself now. In the first few months that I worked for her I still had half-flashes of recognition, but now I know her better for herself. I do quite like her. She tries hard to do the right thing – by me, by her family. Sometimes we sit and drink coffee together – or I sit and she leans against her lovely pale blue kitchen units and watches me and never ever finishes her own coffee. She talks to me quite a lot then, about herself mostly. She used to try to discuss television programes with me 'Peggy Mitchell's so brilliant I can even forget she's Barbara Windsor,' 'Wasn't Bianca's abortion awful? How could she have done it?' 'I really will stop watching *Coronation Street* soon, Ashley and Maxine are such an unlikely pair.'

Finally she took in that I do not have television and so barely ever see any of the soaps. That stumped her. In fact I think that was when she really looked at me for the first time. I did not fit into her stereotype, you see. I was much younger than she had expected a cleaning woman to be (she told me that), but clearly she had just readjusted her picture. She could have chosen dole-scrounging layabout, but she went for working-class heroine. 'You are so clever, managing by yourself,' she said once, with a characteristic flap, and she thought she was being complimentary. I knew what she meant of course, she meant she had noticed that I do not have any money or a pretty flat and perhaps it was not that interesting cleaning up – even after her. She does not know about Tamsin or Reading or anything else at all about my life.

I would tell her if she were interested, I am not ashamed, but she has never asked.

Amanda has two sisters, one is a solicitor, although she is at the moment on maternity leave. The other is a television presenter on some regional breakfast show. I think Amanda feels just a little left out. 'I don't want to get married so much as to be married,' she said to me one day as she was opening her post. Another thick white card went up on to the mantelpiece. 'It's to do with my parents, I suppose. Don't you find it hard to stop trying to please your parents?' I had never had that particular problem, but she was not waiting for an answer. She never does. 'I'm the oldest and both my sisters are married and Fiona's got the baby and Sarah's doing so well. I don't want to disappoint them, I always feel I'm disappointing Mummy and Daddy.'

'I'm sure you're not,' I said, moving past her to dust her mantelpiece. Mantelpieces are especially worthwhile if they are good and cluttered. They take a while to clean which gives you the chance to have a good look. And they reflect very well the immediate present, or at any rate the very recent past. Invitations (I had never seen invitations like these before I began cleaning work), photographs, little things just bought or recently given. All of which give me a picture of their lives outside the flat. This new invitation was, as I had guessed, to a wedding. 'Colonel and Mrs Rendle Jones request the pleasure . . .' etc etc. She seems to have a lot of friends with double-barrelled names and military parents. This one, Rendle Jones, seemed like a name I recognised but the thought was so unlikely I put it out of my mind.

'I hope you don't mind my saying so,' I blurted out (I do seem to blurt when my line of thinking shifts), 'but I do like the way your invitations are written. Aren't they old-fashioned?'

Amanda stopped thinking about her marriage prospects for a moment and looked completely stunned. With an obvious effort she took the look of surprise from her face and turned her attention back to the invitation.

'It's not written, it's engraved,' she explained.

Normally I don't answer back but I was not going to let her think I was that stupid. 'I meant the wording.'

She had the grace to look embarrassed. 'Well, I suppose so, but doesn't everyone do it?' she asked, and I almost laughed at the thought of my sending an 'At Home' card to Liz for fish and chips and lager.

I just said 'oh yes' and went on with the dusting. After all these years of knowing her she still has the ability to surprise me with her total lack of tact, or maybe it is not tact she lacks so much as imagination. Perhaps they are in the end the same thing.

Amanda said to me once that the reason she has such a close family is because she is a Catholic, but I think it is more likely that she is still a Catholic because she is so close to her family. Of course I don't know if she goes to church or not – I only know her prayer book or whatever they call it is always in the same place week after week. Those little grass crosses they have at the beginning of Lent seem to crop up year after year so I suppose she goes then. There is a Catholic church on St Charles's Square and sometimes, if I happen to be passing when church is finished, I keep a bit of an eye out for Amanda, but I have never seen her.

Amanda gives dinner parties fairly often (or maybe it is not often at all but she just always gives them on Monday nights so that I will be there to clear up after them the next morning). Her flat after a party rivals Liz's on any day of the week. Coffee cups with fag ends left soaking in the dregs, spilt glasses, puddles of food on plates, and bottles and bottles. They must have two or three different glasses each. What do they do? Put one down, lose it and start another or just drink three different drinks each? It does puzzle me sometimes. I hate those mornings, when I open the flat door and the smell of old cigarettes, stale dope, and red wine hit me in the face. The wine smells like overblown hyacinths and I always leave with a throbbing head. One thing is I can be sure Amanda will not put in an appearance on those days – perhaps she has some shame after all – and I will not be expected to do anything more than clear up.

I was wondering the other day whether shoe-fitters notice feet. Are they either inured to their ugliness or staggered by their beauty? I suppose it is the same as flat cleaning: you muddle along, deadened by the boredom of your job, until something happens to make you sit up and take notice.

The first time Amanda left signs of a boyfriend was like that – I noticed a disposable razor blade in the bin in the bathroom (nearly cut my finger on it) and immediately realised it was not Amanda's. She has one of those funny machines that pull your hairs out (it took me ages to work out what it was the first time I saw it) and uses those orange Bic razors. The very furtiveness of that one razor blade lurking in the bottom of the bin alerted me. Then I noticed that she had made her bed and washed up her breakfast before I arrived, which is unusual. Sure enough, there were two of those huge cups and saucers she uses on the draining rack. I was wondering why she had tried to hide the evidence from me, just her cleaner, when she burst back into the flat loaded down with shopping.

'Oh good, Cindy, I was worried you'd have gone. I've left another load of bags in the downstairs hall – you wouldn't run down and get them for me, would you please? Only Mummy's having lunch with me here and I'm miles behind.'

How odd that 'Mummy' uses a Gillette razor, I thought, disappointed that I had been wrong in my sleuthing.

'Oh, she was staying here, was she?' I said as I went to the door. 'How nice.'

Amanda stopped me with a look. She was the most still I had ever seen her – no affected flapping or silly giggling now. 'Of course not. She has a flat in Edwardes Square,' she said. I wondered her breath could come through her lips to sound the words, her voice was so cold. 'No one was here last night', she added, in case I had not understood the message. 'The bags, please?'

That was when I learned never to comment on anything I had seen.

My second 'client', for want of a better word, was Amanda's great-aunt Mrs Settrington. Her cleaner retired and Amanda offered me up to her. 'It's an easy way for me to be nice to her,' Amanda explained, when she told me about her. 'I told her to ring here on Tuesday morning so that she can book you – if of course you can fit her in,' she added quickly (but too late). Perhaps she was beginning to see through my pretence of a busy working life. 'So I'll leave the answerphone off, and if you could take any other messages and then switch it on again when you leave.'

Of course I took the job. The old lady wanted six hours a week. At this stage I knew I had to start giving Liz something for Tamsin, but she would not take more than a pound an hour and the occasional six-pack of lager, so I was still doing well.

Mrs Settrington is a widow, very small and dainty with big faded-blue eyes and perfect clothes. She lives just the other side of Notting Hill, in Hillgate Village. The front of her house is painted a pale china-blue to match her eyes (she actually told me that once) and three doors down is a lemon-yellow one which belongs to her brother, Vincent Nesbit, now another one of my clients.

In contrast to Amanda's stark comfort, Mrs Settrington's house is cluttered on every surface with her memories. The first time I met her I stood in the middle of her little sitting-room not daring to move in case I broke anything. There would be no question of Tamsin coming here.

'Now, my dear, I'll take you on a lightning tour of the house so that you know what's what,' she said. It was indeed a lightning tour – I have never met an old lady who could move so fast. She talked all the way around the house – about herself of course, but her technique was different from Amanda's. She gives the impression that she is asking about you but then you realise that it is just a ploy.

'Do you live on your own, my dear? Because if you do you will know how precious things are to you? There is no one else to disturb things so of course I know exactly where everything is . . . up here is my bedroom, I know most people prefer the space of a double bed but I would rather have the space in the room. You live near my lovely Amanda, I know, so I expect your rooms are rather larger? You are lucky, well my rooms are small but very easy to look after, aren't they? Has Amanda told you about my husband? Diplomatic corps, painted for a hobby? Do you paint? I've never really had the time, but do look at this one, a view of Kilimanjaro at dawn. I remember him working on that one. Up at first light for days on end.' A surprising, spiteful look crossed her face. 'We were going to live in Kenya after Rory retired,' she told me brightly, 'but unfortunately he died earlier than we had expected so I remain here all alone through these dreary English winters.' Her words were self-pitying but she was smiling sweetly and I was in no doubt that this little old lady was far tougher than she looked.

'Well, dear, I am sure you have a very busy social life of your own, but I do want to make clear that as well as coming in twice a week I would like to know that you can come in occasionally for an evening. I will give you plenty of warning, never fear. I like to have little parties every now and again, and frankly I cannot manage as well as I used. So if I knew you were there to help serve and tidy up it would make a big difference. I will pay you twenty pounds flat fee for the evening work, and you should be home by midnight. All right?'

I was almost dazzled by her smile and her blue eyes, but I found my voice for the first time.

'With a week or so's warning that would be fine,' I said, and then, emboldened by the sight of all her possessions and the three rows of pearls hung around her thin neck, I added, 'but I am afraid if I finish after eleven I'll have to ask for the taxi fare home.'

Her eyes were knowing. 'No problem at all, my dear. I have an account with a mini-cab firm and I will make sure you are always taken home – whatever the hour.' I felt myself begin to blush. I had been bested, been made to look a cheat while she had made herself seem very generous. But to my surprise I saw a gleam of humour come into the old lady's face and she reached out and took my hand in both of hers. 'I feel sure we shall get on famously,' she said. 'Now why don't we sit down and have a cup of coffee and you can tell me all about how Amanda is doing. She's a naughty girl, I don't see nearly enough of her.' And she sat me down – and sat down with me – and poured us both cups of deliciously strong bitter coffee (from a machine, not a jar) and asked me if I knew anything at all about Amanda's career and love life.

Mrs Settrington's brother Vincent was the next on my list. His was another house I knew Tamsin would never be allowed to visit. For one thing, although he is I think just short of retiring age he does not seem to go out to work anywhere and, for another, he collects Staffordshire porcelain ware. It is everywhere – on mantelpieces, where books should be, on little occasional tables.

When I first went to number eight I saw a lot of old china, but he soon put me straight.

'This collection is really quite valuable,' he told me. 'Eighteenth century most of it, which means a good two hundred years old.' I felt myself tense at his patronising words, but nodded and smiled dutifully. 'It is very precious,' he added, in case I had not quite understood. I thought of how my mother had taught me to dust her prized collection of glass animals and said, 'I have never yet broken anything, big or small, in any of the houses I do. I am sure Mrs Settrington will vouch for me.'

'Oh, she has, she has,' he said, 'and of course she knows how precious my figures are to me. I don't want to offend you at all my dear.' Of course he did not: I was beginning to appreciate the value of a good, honest cleaner. 'As long as we understand each other from the beginning I am sure everything will be tickety-boo.' (Tickety-boo, what was the man talking about?)

His house is identical to his sister's in layout, but quite different in character. Where she has water-colours of Abroad he has architectural prints and engravings. Where she has odd knick-knacks of dubious beauty but at least illustrative of her life he has the Staffordshire cows and shepherdesses. Where her walls are papered in dark greens and deep rose pinks, his are painted in clear, light colours. She has chintz floral curtains, he has plain dyed calico drapes. I am not sure I know the difference between curtains and drapes, but I know both Mrs Settrington and Mr Nesbit are very insistent on using one particular word. I did not know people could talk about their curtains so much, but Mr Nesbit certainly does. I have to Hoover them, for heaven's sake.

'Mother lived in Essex Villas after Father died,' Mrs Settrington told me once. 'I suppose as things turned out Vincent – Mr Nesbit – and I could have kept it on, but then Rory was still alive and he and Vincent never quite saw eye to eye.' That fleetingly spiteful look with which I was becoming familiar was back across her face and gone before I could be sure I had really seen it. 'So we sold it and each bought a house in this street. Almost by mistake. Although it's so nice to be near each other,' she said, a little effusively. 'There is no one like a brother.'

'I bought this house because it would make such a wonderful showcase for my pieces,' Mr Nesbit told me another day. 'A jewel to house my jewels, don't you think? And of course I was brought up in this part of London. That is why I began to collect the Staffordshire.' He is nearly always at home when I go to clean, and follows me around, talking, telling me stories about his life, watching that I don't lop off a cow's horn or amputate a shepherdess's arm. 'There's a wonderful shop just down the road, on Kensington Church Street. When I was a young boy I would stand and stare in the window for hours, I knew I had to have them, shelf on shelf of wonderful objects.' He paused. He does sometimes and then I have to say something to show I am paying attention.

'You wouldn't see many young boys nowadays staring at china lambs,' I said, 'More interested in the amusement arcades.' It's the kind of meaningless noise I find easy to say to Mr Nesbit; a little prompt to put him back on his own track so that I can get on with my work and my thoughts. I am not there to give myself away, after all, only my time and my work.

But on this occasion I struck the wrong note. He tipped back on to his heels, grabbed one wrist with his hand and flushed. 'Yes well, dear, I couldn't help that. You had to go to Brighton for a penny arcade when I was a boy and not the same thing at all. We had to find our own entertainment when we were young, you know, and we took what we could find.' He was breathing fast, seemed really cross although trying to restrain himself. I honestly did not know what I had said wrong but it was clearly my fault.

'Well it's given you a lot of pleasure – learning to love pottery.' I said soothingly. He is quite easy to upset, Mr Nesbit, but I have learned it is always better to calm him down than it is to apologise.

'Cindy, my dear, when will you learn. It's porcelain and not pottery,' he said, but he had let go of his wrist and his colour had returned to normal. 'I'll potter down to the kitchen and make us a nice cup of tea,' he said and off he went.

Funny fellow, Mr Nesbit. I often think his heart is sad underneath his sleeveless cashmere cardies.

Then came the Blakes. Glamorous, successful (judging by their things) good looking. I think they have everything. Lynda ('I'd say call me Lyndy but we can't possibly be called Cindy and Lyndy') is a friend of Amanda's through work, although she gave up her career as soon as she married. She told me she needed the time to do up their new house. It is in Cambridge Gardens, so right on my patch. They have the whole house bar the basement, which they want to buy as soon as it is on the market. I can't think why they need so much room, just the two of them (although I suppose they are planning on some little Blakes). Lynda's pride as she showed me around almost made me cry. I didn't need telling how nice it is, for heaven's sake.

'We're knocking the whole of the top floor into one room,' she said as she led me up narrow steps to the top of the house. 'Look, then we'll have light both sides, and all that view over the roofs, and then a little loo in the corner and Randal thought a little kitchenette so that he doesn't have to bother with lunch, you know, a grill, a kettle, a little fridge, maybe a hob. All self-sufficient so I don't have to disturb him, although he thought it would be a good idea to have an intercom so he can call me if he does want something,' (who is this monster? I was beginning to wonder).

'And then, this is our floor.' A big bedroom across the front of the house, another two smaller rooms and bathroom. 'One is Randal's dressing room at the moment,' she said, but of course it will be easy enough to alter if need be,' and for a moment she looked sweet and pretty and unsure and much younger.

'I'm going to be honest with you, I've never had a cleaning woman before,' she said with a giggle as she led me down the stairs to the ground floor. 'So I'll probably do it all wrong. You will tell me, won't you? It would be silly to fall out over a misunderstanding, and it would be much more fun if we were friends.'

Friends! Well there was something new. Amanda is friendly enough but there is never even the faintest doubt about our employer/employee relationship. I was not at all sure how to take the suggestion that we should be friends. Suddenly I felt a surge of something very close to happiness. Apart from Liz I have no real friends . . . could it be possible . . . or was Lynda just taking the mickey? I looked at her distrustfully but saw nothing but open friendliness. She reminded me a bit of Liz, actually. Not in looks so much as in her transparent niceness.

I have only been working for the Blakes for a few months and I have not yet met Randal, the husband. From his photographs he is as handsome as she is pretty. He is a barrister and so has to work very long hours; Lynda is very proud of him. They met when she was producing some chat show on which he was an 'expert' guest. She is completely fascinated by him and by his work: you would never think she had ever had a career of her own. She paints the walls and bakes her bread (honestly) and looks after her man and her house. Sometimes I think she does not actually need me for anything more than company and to reinforce her in her belief (or hope) that she is doing everything the right way.

I hope Randal loves her as much as she loves him.

So there they are: Mrs Settrington, Mr Nesbit, Amanda and Lynda. Mondays and Wednesdays are completely booked, and I work half of the other days. It is not really surprising, is it, that these people take up so much of my thoughts. I see more of them than of anyone else except for Tamsin. And I have just begun to realise that if it were not for them all, I might have gone mad, living alone with Tamsin, always looking inward, never out.

3

I went to my parents for lunch today. I have taken to going more often than I used, partly because I can afford it and partly because I think it is good for Tamsin. I don't want her idea of family to be just me; she must realise she comes from a wider past than her cleaning-woman mother. And after all, if anything happened to me I suppose she would go to them, so she must know them well.

Tamsin was very happy on the way down to Kent. 'I really love buses, Mum,' she said as she opened her packet of crisps.

'Why?'

'Well, we know we are going to Gran's, but we don't know where any of the other people are going. If we had a car everyone in it would be going to the same place. On the bus we think we are, but we're not at all.' She stared out of the window at the dreary autumn rain, completely contented, and I looked at our fellow-passengers, amazed that Tamsin could find anything exciting in them. 'And another thing,' she added, 'is that when you go to the bus station you know that you're going to Kent, but you could, you just could, get on one of those other buses going somewhere else, somewhere foreign. You wouldn't have to tell anyone, you could just get on it and go.'

'And what would Gran think, waiting there with her chicken in the oven?'

She hesitated. She is fond of my mother (fonder than Mum deserves, as far as I am concerned) and hates hurting anyone's feelings. But, 'it wouldn't matter once you got to the abroad bit. It would be almost as though you didn't exist any more.'

I was caught up in the fantasy: I have been saving, we could almost do it. 'Where would you like to go?'

She thought a minute. 'Donna went to Jersey for her holiday and said it was brilliant. And Marcia went to see her Gran in Jamaica. They ate funny fruit and the sun shone all day long. I'd like that.' So would I, but to be honest Ladbroke Grove is the closest I'll ever get to Jamaica.

Dad met us at the bus stop. He had his Sunday jumper on – a V-neck with lots of different blue and grey stripes. Tamsin hugged his legs and gave him a picture she drew for him yesterday. He grunted and pinched her cheek. I think he wants to be affectionate but is not really sure how.

We drove home more or less in silence. I looked out of the window and tried to think of something nice to say. He concentrated on his driving. Tamsin, isolated in the back seat, picked bits of broken crisps off her anorak. I think she knew that Mum would get at me about the mess. Or maybe she just wanted to look tidy for her Gran. I hoped Dad would not notice the little pieces of cheese 'n' onion being scattered all over the tartan rug on the back seat.

'Steven and Joanne are coming over,' Dad said as he backed into his garage. Nine times out ten they do, but it is always announced with a certain amount of pride.

'Oh,' I said, trying to look pleased.

'And Matt? Goody!' said Tamsin, leaning forward.

'Sit back, dear, we don't want you going through the windscreen,' Dad said nervously into the rear-view mirror.

Those are the kind of conversations we have.

Tamsin rushed ahead of us to the house, banging on the frosted-glass door and shouting 'Gran! Gran, we're here!'

'They've got some news – Steven and Joanne,' Dad told me as I waited for him to wind down his garage door. Perhaps they are getting divorced, I thought nastily. 'Good news,' he added, straightening and puffing a little. I followed him into the house with a sinking heart. One thing worse than sitting through a dreary Sunday lunch with Mum and Dad is sitting through one that is meant to be celebratory.

They were all in the kitchen, sitting around with cups of coffee. Mum had her arm around Tamsin and was asking her about her school week while Matt, a big seven year old with a crew cut and a surprisingly gentle smile was pulling on her sleeve and asking her to come into the garden with him.

'Well, keep working hard, dear,' said Mum, releasing Tamsin from her grip. 'You can go a long way with a good education,' and she pretended to be surprised to see me. 'Oh, hello, dear, do you want a cup of coffee? Run along children, we want to talk,' and she withdrew her attention from Tamsin and Matt and put on the kettle.

I ignored the dig and sat down by Joanne.

'Hi Steven, Joanne. How's tricks?'

Joanne giggled. She always does but I can't help but like her. We need some giggles in that house.

'It wasn't a trick, I promise,' she said, and giggled again. 'And Steven's ever so pleased, aren't you?'

My brother looks like a brute – huge, tattooed knuckles, always stained with car grease – but it is all a disguise: it is from Steven that Matt inherited his gentle smile.

'Course I am, love.'

'We're having another baby,' Joanne said, and I was horrified at the envy that overtook me. I had not thought of wanting another child but when I saw their faces I suddenly knew I want nothing more than another baby. I don't want to grow old with nothing but me and Tamsin, no real family around a real table . . . I looked at their expectant faces and pulled myself together.

'Oh, that'll be nice,' I said. 'Really nice,' and I smiled and tried to mean it.

Joanne patted my arm, 'Come on now, Cindy, you should be having another one too. Look how well Matt and Tamsin get on.'

Mum clattered mugs and spoons around. 'Time enough for that when she gets herself settled,' she said ferociously. 'We don't want any more by-blows in this family, thank you very much.' I could see today was going to be particularly tricky. Mum can never just be pleased: instead of being happy for Steven and Joanne she has to start drawing comparisons – always, but always, to my disadvantage.

'You make me sound like a bag lady, Mum.' I tried to

sound jokey but I was furious inside. 'I'm perfectly well settled.'

'I won't count you settled until you've a man's feet under your table – a man who'll put a ring on your finger while he's about it. You can help set the table while you're there, no point in just sitting and looking. And they've some other good news too. Tell her, Stevie.' He is only 'Stevie' when he has done something really wonderful.

I looked at him. 'Well?'

He was looking at my mother in a way I had not seen before. 'Get off her back, Mum,' he said. He spoke mildly but for Steven to speak up to Mum at all was something new. 'She does brilliantly, you know she does.' He turned back to me. 'We're buying a house' he said with enormous pride and added, totally unexpectedly, 'I hope you don't mind, Cind.'

That is how odd my family is. They all expected me to feel put down, or out or something about the house and none of them even considered that I might be crying out for another baby.

It was easy to be pleased for them. Steven explained the finances – how much they had saved, the mortgage rate he was getting, his wage rise at the garage now that he was fully qualified. They live in a flat above an off-licence in Rochester, and for some time (I have heard this record often enough) have felt that it was not a good place for Matt. 'Really rough at the weekend,' said Joanne for the umpteenth time. 'It's not right for Matt to have to try to sleep through that . . . and then the mess on the street . . .' she pulled a fastidious face. 'He's really wanting a garden, too . . . I mean look at him.'

Mum and Dad's close was built in an old orchard and the developers kept as many of the trees as they could. It is the nicest thing about the house, the garden. Tamsin and Matt were swinging on a rope Dad had tied to one of the branches of the apple tree (he can do kind things, Dad, but he won't tell you about them. He waits for you to find out.)

We sat down to chicken and cabbage and Joanne told me about the house. 'We went to the show houses and picked a three-bedroom one; they guarantee you can upgrade to another one on the estate later if you want; it comes with all its carpets – oatmeal or powder-blue all the way through, we thought oatmeal didn't we Steven, and you've a choice of colours it will be painted in. And there's a garden, not as big as here, but a start, and they've promised to build a park for the kids in the next two years. If you put money down now, before they're finished, you get a special deal, otherwise we would only have been able to have a two-bed one. Mum and Nora have been helping me pick fabric for the curtains – oh, if you'd like to help, Cindy, you'd be welcome—'

I pushed back my chair and helped Mum clear the plates. I could be – I was – I am – genuinely pleased about the house for them. But I found it very hard to have Joanne of all people feeling sorry for me. The last thing in the world I want is a new house on an estate on the edges of Rochester. But the rest of it . . . the baby, the man, the *security* . . . All those things I thought I could do without . . . A (tiny) little bit of me would be very happy choosing baby's names and a cot and a living-room suite. I thought of Amanda's huge shabby sofa and Mrs Settrington's chintz and Lynda Blake's dragged or stippled or rolled walls (she is always explaining the difference but I don't take it in) and, I'm sorry but it is true, I felt mean and jealous. It is time I stopped dreaming and got on with life.

After the meal the others sat down to play Old Maid with the children but I said that in spite of the rain I wanted a breath of fresh air. I took Mum's poodle (they don't moult) with me for a quick stride around the rec. A fine rain blew into my face which, I thought, would be a good camouflage for my tears. But I did not cry. I very rarely do. The walk blew most of my spite out of me and I surprised everyone when I walked in by giving Steven a quick hug. 'I'm really pleased about the house. Maybe you'll be doing Sunday lunch for us one of these days, eh?'

And Steven laughed and looked proud and said, 'Your cooking's nearly as good as Mum's isn't it, Jo? You should try her curry, Cindy!' and Tamsin asked if she could go and stay with Matt in the holidays *on her own*, and for once we seemed like a normal, functioning, even happy, family.

'Oh Cindy, I nearly forgot. There's a letter for you behind the telephone,' said Mum. Warm with the feeling of having done the right thing, I sorted through the bits of paper piled on the little table in the hall until I found the letter. The envelope was hand-written, but I did not recognise the writing. Postmarked Torquay, I did not think I knew anyone there.

For some reason I went up to my old bedroom and opened the letter there rather than go back into the kitchen. I sat on the small bed in the cold little room and wondered who had last slept there. They are not great ones for visitors, my parents.

There were two pieces of paper in the envelope, one typed, one written. I read the hand-written one first.

Dear Cindy,

I'm sorry I have not been in touch for so long. I often wondered how you made out after you left us. Your baby (I heard it was a girl) must be six or more now. Maybe you have others, too? No one seems to know what happened to you, you vanished without trace. I don't even know if your parents are still at this address. Still, worth a try.

I work for a big hotel down here in Devon now. For some reason it's been down to me to organise the reunion (you know I was always the bossy one!) But it meant I could pick the venue. Looking at the list of our year, it was surprising how many came from the west, and Exeter's easy to get to from London. I hope you can come. It would be great to see you again.

Love,

Sarah (Nelly)

P.S. I really have often wondered about you. Give a ring either way.

N.

The second letter was a word-processed invitation for the English students of 1989–1992 to a reunion. It was gushing and enthusiastic and did nothing to sell itself to me at all. It too was signed by Nelly.

Sarah Trunk. Nelly. I turned the letter slowly in my hands. My first reaction was almost disgust. I shied away from the idea of a meeting with all those people who had so briefly been my friends, who had once seemed set to be part of my future. Nelly had been a good friend, one made totally by chance. We fell in with each other only because we had been put in adjoining rooms in the hall of residence. We had gone to meals together, discovered we were both reading English, accompanied each other to the Freshers' Departmental cheese and wine party, found that almost despite ourselves we were becoming friends. She was not a type of person I had known until then – public school 'but minor, very minor, I promise you,' she had laughed, as though it made any difference to me. As far as I was concerned boarding school was Enid Blyton and fun and japes and larks in the dorm and ridiculous nicknames: everything I despised, probably because it made me feel like an outsider. And then, just when I thought I had cracked it, when I had begun to make friends without caring where they were educated (although I nearly always knew, especially with the girls) I went and blew it.

So Nelly was in the hotel business. She had always said she was going to be an actress, had done a lot of acting in our first year. She had drawn me in to her enthusiasm and I had found myself helping with props and scenery. Over the years I have kept a vague eye on television credits, half expecting to see Nelly's name. But no, she was Sarah again and in Torquay – doing what in the hotel? Did it matter? She was not the only one whose dreams had failed her.

'Cindy? Where are you?'

I jumped. Mum was hallooing around the place as though I had been gone for hours. 'Cindy? Are you all right?'

I put my head round the door. 'Sorry, Mum. I'm up here. I'll be right down.'

'Only you've to go for the bus soon and I'm just putting the kettle on.'

'Yes. Sorry. I'll be right with you.'

Before she could ask what was the matter with *now* (one of her favourite refrains when we were children) I shut the door. The room is completely bare, you would never know that for all those years it had been my refuge. My place to dream, to work, to escape, and (let's be honest) to sulk.

I wondered what Mum had done with my Marc Bolan and Duran Duran and Queen posters. After Tamsin and I had left everything was just tidied away without a word. I had noticed, felt aggrieved, but never lowered myself to ask. On an impulse I slid open the door of the built-in wardrobe.

And I saw that Mum does have a heart. Box on box, neatly stacked and labelled. 'Cindy's books (school)' 'Cindy's books (college)' and even 'Cindy's posters'. So Marc Bolan was still there. I bet he has survived a lot longer than in most houses. I almost laughed.

I pulled one of the boxes down. 'Cindy's papers'. What could be in there? Essays. Files and jotting pads and file paper. Doodles and notes. My O-and A-level certificates. Nothing of any importance at all. How odd of Mum to have kept them. And then I struck gold. 'Reading University. Department of English. Year One Suggested Reading List.'

The door opened. Mum stood with a frown on her face which dissolved when she saw what I was doing.

'So you've found them,' she said awkwardly.

'I didn't know you'd kept everything.'

'You never asked.'

I could have hugged her but I'd already hugged Steven today and did not want to overdo it. 'Well, thank you,' I said. 'When I saw you'd cleared everything out after Tamsin and I moved out I, well, I thought you'd chucked everything out.'

She almost chuckled. 'You should have known me better. Now come on down, tea's ready and you know what your dad's like about the bus.'

'I'll just tidy up. It's good to know everything's here. Thank you.'

I shoved all the papers back into the box, keeping only the reading list. Because that's what writers should do, isn't it? Read. Then, as I put the box neatly back in to the wardrobe, I could not resist dipping my hand into the box beside it ('Cindy's books, College') and pulling out the first two books which came to hand. A worn-out copy of Hardy's *Tess of the D'Urbervilles* and an unread copy of *Esther Waters* by George Moore. Those would do.

I forgot all about Nelly and the reunion the next day when Tamsin came back from school with a note from her teacher asking if I could see her the following morning. I will mind very much if Tamsin starts fooling around at school, because despite my mother's snide comment I do believe that education will help her out of her background, or at any rate will give her some measure of choice. In fact it turned out that Miss Cox had been told by Tamsin that I do cleaning work and wondered if there was any chance I could help her out. I have never met anyone so shy. There she is, a teacher in charge of a riotous crowd of six year olds, but she can hardly talk to me, let alone look at me. My instinct is to like her. I think she is not so very different from me in some ways, but where she finished the degree and began a worthwhile career I took a different route. Tamsin speaks nothing but good of her and I feel that behind the dowdy, mousy shyness, is a tender heart. Now I am getting soppy. Tender heart, indeed. She is just a dreary school teacher in mud-coloured clothes.

The funny part is that when I asked her if she wanted any references (They never do, but They like being asked) I mentioned Lynda's name. 'I do Mrs Blake in Cambridge Gardens,' I said, and Miss Cox ('Call me Jane' – but somehow that is still, after all these years, hard with a school teacher) looked amazed. 'Not *Lyndy* Blake?' she said, and when I nodded, 'how funny – she's a friend of mine. We were at university together. Well, of course I don't want a reference.' And I could see her thinking, 'if she's good enough for Lyndy she's good enough for me,' and looking at Miss Cox and thinking of the differences between her and Lynda I could not but agree.

I saw Lynda Blake on Wednesday. She was in an uncharacteristically bad mood, but I saw she was making an effort not to take it out on me so did not take offence. She made me a cup of coffee on arrival as normal but did not sit down and have one with me as she usually does. She is covering a footstool with a tapestry she made and although the tapestry is pretty enough she has not the knack of upholstering yet and I heard a lot of hammering and cursing from the next room as I drank the coffee.

'Shall I start upstairs or down?' I asked her through the half-open door.

'Up, please,' she said without looking up. 'But not the top floor as Randal's there this morning. So try not to make too much noise with the Hoover. Oh *bugger*!' she shouted as she bent a nail.

If there is one thing that irritates me it is being asked not to make too much noise with a Hoover. There is a finite mount of noise a Hoover can make, after all, and it cannot be adjusted to suit other people's moods. Especially when they are themselves hammering and cursing energetically.

I went into Lynda's bedroom, wondering how anyone who woke every morning in such a calm, rosy, pink room could ever be cross, and began making the bed. I have to move very slowly in that house to fill in my three hours: Lynda keeps everything so neat and clean there is not too much for me to do. So I always check things like their invitations, and the books by their bed. Randal reads those legal thrillers – Scott Turow and John Grisham, while Lynda is more into Penny Vincenzi and Joanna Trollope. She seems to take ages to finish a book, they just sit beside her bed with tidy spines for ages. If I had all the time she has . . .

I straightened the room and went into the bathroom, admiring as I always do its sleek mirrored surfaces and the expensive jars of face creams lined up neatly.

It was when I bent to empty the bin that I saw something very interesting. Even better than Amanda's razor blade. A cardboard box saying 'Clearblue'. I knew what that was, right enough, and I am sorry but I could not resist it, I tipped the rubbish very slowly into my sack until I saw the Clearblue pen and although I knew I should not, knew I was going way beyond my brief, I could not resist picking it out of the bin and looking.

Not pregnant.

Hence the bad temper.

I remember how desperately I had wished the second line away from its little plastic window, and know how hopelessly Lynda must have willed it to appear. But she has everything, can't she wait just anther month or two? It will not kill her. She is so transparent, Lynda, so eager to please, so bad tempered when crossed, so naïvely delighted with her good fortune and uncomprehending at her bad, that it is sometimes hard not to be irritated by her. Then, looking at the little windows, I just felt sorry. Although it was amazing (and I admit a little disgusting) how powerful I felt knowing her secret.

4

Mr Nesbit was in one of his following-about moods today. He was talking about his holidays, how hard he finds it to decide where to go, how he likes to go alone but is then lonely, 'but I once made the mistake of holidaying with a friend and my dear you can't believe the rows we had! He wanted to sit around in bars watching – watching what? I ask you – and I felt I couldn't leave him alone. And he walked so slowly, I can't tell you. I swore after that that if I had to choose between loneliness and irritation, loneliness would win every time. It's not as though I like beach holidays, after all, those are dull on your own, I mean there's only so much reading you can do, isn't there, and I do like to watch my skin, too much sun is so aging . . .' On and on it went until I thought it was time I made a contribution to the conversation.

'Have you ever gone on holiday with Mrs Settrington?'

You would have thought it a simple enough question, but something about it made him stand more straight and hold his wrist in his other hand as he does when he is upset.

'No. Well yes, of course, when we were children. But not recently. No, we like different things, so it's hardly worth thinking about.'

'I wouldn't have thought Mrs Settrington is much of a beach-holiday lady, either,' I said, perfectly pleasantly, but carefully (I was not at all sure where I had gone wrong).

'No, not at all. But she prefers the type of holiday you take with other people, with lectures and all that laid on. I find that claustrophobic. I prefer to find my own culture, don't you?' Little does he realise that most of the 'culture' I find is in his pottery – sorry porcelain – and in the pictures on all of Their walls. 'Anyway, I always say you can never be alone in a city.' Does he now. Let him try life with a tiny baby in a small flat in a large city where he knows no one and he may change his tune.

He had let go of his wrist now, so I ventured a little further. I don't think I'm cruel, just interested in people, and I wanted to know what had upset him.

'You must have stayed with Mrs Settrington in some of the wonderful places she lived with her husband?' I was dusting the mirror over the mantelpiece, so was able to keep an eye on him and bingo! his hand was once again gripping the wrist.

'Yes, I did. Of course,' he said, and sat down with a puff on the newly plumped-up settee cushions. Almost as soon as his bottom hit the seat, though, he was up again, still wringing his wrist, and walked quickly out of the door. 'I'll just nip down to the kitchen, dear, isn't it time you had a cup of coffee?' he said over his shoulder.

Well, well. What was all that about?

That afternoon was my first at Miss Cox's. The first sight of someone's flat or house is very interesting. Think about it, when you visit a new friend for the first time you see the sitting-room or kitchen or maybe both, possibly the bathroom. But in my job you see everything laid out all at once. And you do not have to look around furtively or casually, it is a part of your job to look into every cranny. Liz told me all about Ruby Wax and how she looks in fridges, and I went over to Liz's to watch the programme with Fergie and what did Ruby do but look in her fridge and everyone made a fuss about it and talked about it in pubs as though it were the final invasion of her privacy, worse than the toe-sucking pictures. But I can look in fridges, bathroom cupboards, kitchen cupboards whenever I want to. I know that Mr Nesbit eats a lot of fish and Amanda has secret chocolate binges. I know that Mrs Settrington gets through a bottle of gin a week (which seems a lot to me) and Amanda drinks eight-pound-a-bottle white wine, but not much of it. (Actually, the bottles seem to have been quite a bit cheaper recently.) I know that Lynda Blake uses Chanel soap and Mr

Blake uses coal tar, that Amanda is always buying mangoes but forgetting to eat them before they rot, that Lynda uses a towel but Mr Blake uses a bathrobe.

And so far all I knew about Jane Cox was that she is a mousy thing loved by children.

Not that her flat gives much more away about her. Perhaps it is because she is poorer than the others I work for. What does a primary-school teacher earn? I don't know, but I am sure less than a television producer and certainly less than Mr Blake.

The flat is in a dark basement in Chesterton Road, just one or two down from the Percy, the pub on the corner. The bedroom is at the front of the house, then there is a sitting-room/eating room and at the back a tiny kitchen and bathroom. It is clean and tidy, has been recently painted in an odd, deadish pale green throughout. The curtains look home-made, but they are made of pretty cotton and lined properly. It feels as though she is trying to make it homely, but maybe she is not there often enough to put her personality on it. Maybe she does not have much of a personality. It has all the essentials – a bed which could be described either as a large single or a small double, a cheap-looking bedside table, a new two-seater settee and one armchair. There is a big pine table which must double as her working and her eating table: it has a second-hand refurbished look. There are only three kitchen-type chairs, so she cannot have people round much. And in the fridge? Yoghurts, one opened tin of tomatoes, milk, a tub of taramasalata and a stale pack of pitta bread. No wine either there or anywhere else, no alcohol at all that I could see. She has no pictures on the walls (not much room for them either) but a few framed photographs in her bedroom.

One thing she does have is books, and until I saw her flat I did not realise how few the Others have. The Blakes have their popular paperbacks, Mrs Settrington her 1950s Reprint Society collection (I have never seen a book out of the shelf in that house, now I think about it), Amanda has shiny new biographies and novels by television celebrities which she once told me she picks up free at work. But Miss Cox – she has shelves and shelves of them. Every spare bit of wall space has been covered with MFI shelves, even in the bathroom, and every shelf is full. I had to look at them, of course I did. And everything is there. A lot of children's books, some I remembered, most I have never seen before, but then I did not have any books as a child, not until I was older and knew that was what I wanted. Then there is quite a lot of poetry, mostly modern, but with all the classics as well. And fiction, from Fanny Burney to Evelyn Waugh and P G Wodehouse, including French and Russian writers. Biography, mostly of writers. Collections, too – of letters, and diaries and by subject – marriage and quotations and food. Everything. The whole world is there. Honestly, her flat is better stocked than the library in Ladbroke Grove.

Suddenly Miss Cox did not seem so mousy. No wonder Lynda Blake despises her, though. 'Oh, Jane,' Lynda had said when I mentioned I was to work for Miss Cox, 'she's very nice, really *worthy* I suppose, but just not . . .' and had changed the conversation abruptly. Lynda is probably frightened to death at the thought of so much erudition (is that the word? I am not sure, but I like it). No wonder there is only just enough furniture and no drink or food or pictures. She cannot have the time, let alone the money to buy anything or do anything else.

I knew I liked her.

I cleaned her flat with twice the care I do for any of the Others. I feel she deserves it more, somehow. She is the only one who goes out to work, after all (Amanda's barely counts, she is so often in these days). I even stayed slightly beyond my three hours, to make up for the time I had spent looking at her books.

And then on the way home I thought that I would follow her example, that from now on I will let myself buy books – not the amount that she does, but say one a week. I have been careful for too long, been living almost as frugally as I did when I lived only on benefits, been saving – but with what in mind? I am going to think of it like this: one of my hours with Jane Cox is going to buy me a book. I wonder if I will ever tell her.

I finally talked to Liz about Nelly. I could not come to any decision on my own, and I knew I must answer the invitation soon. I suppose I need not, Nelly would just think I had never received her letter, but I would know the truth. The truth is that half of me wants to go; to hold my head high and show that I am proud of my decision to keep Tamsin. But the other half of me does not want to have to answer the question, 'What are you doing now?' to my successful peers. She is wonderful, Liz. She goes straight to the heart of the matter. She would have been no good at those all-night student discussions about the state of the world, she cannot stand arguing for the sake of it.

She listened to me tell her the problem, fill her in on Nelly in general and her letter in particular, and then asked,

'Do you want to go?'

'I don't know, that's why I'm asking you.'

'Well, I can't know, can I? I don't know any of these people, don't even know the you that they knew. Is there anybody who might turn up that you'd like to see again?'

'Nelly, I suppose. I was very happy when I got her letter.' I meant that when I said it, but in point of fact I was not happy reading the letter, but having received it made me happy, which I suppose comes to the same thing.

'Any others?'

I thought. Maybe Tim, with whom I had shared tutorials; he had made me laugh. And Clare, and Veronica and Mary – they had all been good friends at the time. And – what was her name. The dark girl who looked so earnest but had the most filthy sense of humour? But I could not even remember her name. Why then bother to go to Exeter on the off-chance of meeting her?

I shook my head. 'Not really, only Nelly.'

Liz looked at me as though she were trying to be tactful but she said it anyway. 'Is there any danger that Tamsin's father might be there?'

'No. He wasn't reading English.'

'Then if that's not what's holding you back, it's easy.'

'Is it?'

'Of course. You don't go. But you do ring up this Nelly.'

'I haven't got a telephone.'

'Don't be silly. That's an excuse, and you know it. You can use one of Theirs, They would never notice.'

'Liz!'

She laughed. 'I knew that would get you. Go on, buy a phone card, give her a ring.' I looked at her, wondering, and she added more gently, 'She needn't even know you're in a phone box, Cindy.'

She is wise, Liz. And she knows me very well.

I went back across the corridor and checked Tamsin. I have bought one of those baby alarms now, so Liz and I can leave the children in bed and spend the evening with each other sometimes. It was a brilliant idea. They are all too old to lug about now that they go to school. In the old days this was all one house anyway and the children would have been miles from the grown-ups without one of those gadgets so I think it is perfectly safe. I doubt the social workers would like it, though.

Anyway it meant that Liz and I had drunk a beer in peace and then I left her to her television and went back home to *Esther Waters*. I am really loving it.

I had not realised that it is about me, sort of. About a girl struggling to keep her illegitimate baby. There are the temptations to dispose of it – abortion in my case, letting the baby-farmer kill it in hers. It comforts me to realise that my story, mine and Tamsin's, is as old as time. There have always been survivors. Esther Waters is one, I will be another.

Lynda was all over me today. More cups of coffee than I could drink, endless chattering about nothing, fantastically cheerful. I looked in the bin in the bathroom for a positive predictor test, but found nothing. Either she is getting more wily or something else is up.

'I think we're ready enough for a party, don't you?' she asked, looking smugly around the perfect kitchen. 'I hate the word house-warming, but you know what I mean. We haven't had a party for ages – not since our wedding, really, and that's not the same, is it. Are you married?' she looked at my left hand. (Imagine never having had the curiosity to look or ask before.)

'No.'

'Oh, well, you wouldn't know then, but your wedding party is not the same as anything else. All the planning goes into the wedding dress and the bridesmaids' clothes and the food and which coloured stripes to have on the marquee. You don't have time to plan the people, if you see what I mean.'

I did not, of course not. My family has never gone in for the kind of entertaining that They like. Sunday lunch is about the extent of it, and then it is only family. Which does not mean that Mum and Dad are friendless, of course they are not. But they are more likely to go out and do things with their friends than they are to invite them in. It is something to do with holding on to your privacy, I think, not that they would ever analyse it. So they might go out to the cinema and have a meal afterwards, or they might go to night classes (Mum is very keen on that). For a while they both joined a country dancing club, but that did not last long. Anyway, whatever they do they do not seem to have this insatiable need to fill their house with people that the Others have. So all this talk of striped marquees and planning people was totally beyond me. I nodded and listened, though: They think I am in their houses to clean, but of course I am there to learn.

'Dinner parties are of course the best way to plan people,' Lynda was going on, diving into the biscuit tin for another chocolate digestive (that one had better start watching her figure, she is not as young as she was and the weight becomes harder to shift after you are thirty, as my mother has always moaned). 'The only problem is that at least one if not two of the ones you actually want to come bring along wives or whatever that you have to put up with. Randal is fantastically hard to please, and if he's in the wrong mood he just won't make the smallest effort. So, I thought a party, and I could *theme* it – say, everyone I know who went to school in Wiltshire, or everyone who has ever worked in a hat shop . . . do you see? And then they all have to guess what it is they have in common. And there could be clues in the food . . . so if we did Wiltshire we could eat sausages, or if it was the hat shop we could all eat whatever Alice and the Mad Hatter had . . .'

'Nothing much, bread and butter and tea,' I said, surprised at myself for remembering. 'I think your guests might be a bit disappointed.' Lynda looked quite put out and I wished I had said nothing. It never works trying to be clever with Them. 'Do

you really know lots of people who have worked in hat shops?'
I asked quickly, trying to change tack, but she only looked more
annoyed.

'Well, no, but you do see the general idea', she said, snapping
the biscuit tin shut (but not before taking a custard cream).

I had never heard more rubbish in one day in my whole life. For
a moment, while she was maundering on about sausages and hats
I had wondered if she had actually flipped. But apparently not. I
thought Amanda was scatty and arty, but this was not arty, this
was plain idiotic.

'Wouldn't a simple house-warming be easier?' I suggested.

'Too bloody right it would,' came a voice from the door and
Lynda jumped, jammed the tin into the cupboard, scooted the
remains of her biscuit over to my side of the table and turned
towards the voice with widened eyes and a big smile.

'Randal! Would you like a cup of coffee?'

'No. I'm on my way upstairs.'

'Randal, this is Cindy. I don't think you've met her, but you
can thank her that the house is so tidy and clean.'

Randal Blake is as good-looking as his pictures, there is no
denying it. He is tall and blond, with an athletic figure and
Weetabix-father chiselled good looks. I am sure his mother
worships him. Lynda certainly does, but more than that she
seems in awe of him in a way I would not expect between
husband and wife, at least not in the twentieth century.

He wiped the scowl from his face and turned to me with a
smile. 'I can indeed thank you. I have never before had a cleaner
who knows what to clean and what to leave. I would never even
guess that you had been up in my study except that dirty cups
disappear and no dust settles. It makes my work much easier.'

It was silly of me, but I was flattered. I was meant to be, I
knew I was meant to be, I despised myself for falling for it, but
I was. After all, if you are going to do something you might as
well do it properly and it is nice to be noticed.

'Thank you.'

He gave a slow smile, a blond lock fell boyishly over
his forehead, and he perched his neat bottom on the edge
of the kitchen table. Lynda's smile did not falter, but she
shifted nervously. I watched, fascinated. I have never seen

such charm so blatantly put into operation – but why waste it on me?

'Perhaps I will have a cup of coffee with you both after all,' he said, not taking his eyes from my face. Before I could move Lynda was at the espresso coffee machine, banging and clanking in her haste. She and I always drink instant.

'Now, this party. I gather my wife's been telling you her plans?' his eyes twinkled at me, colluding in a mockery of his wife.

I nodded.

'I myself hate parties,' he said confidentially.

Lynda actually giggled. She sounded just like Joanne. 'Oh, Randal. No you don't.'

'I said I do,' he said, his voice hard, and then he turned back to me. 'But of course, Lyndy must do as she chooses.'

'Of course.' This man is like a snake. I heard myself agreeing weakly with him and hated myself for being disloyal to Lynda. But she was being so silly.

'So it's settled, then. We'll have a conventional drinks party – champagne, and if you insist a cocktail, and you will be able to come in and help that evening?'

'Of course.' I was agreeing again – and did not even know the date they had in mind.

'Lovely. We'll have, say, fifty and Lyndy can make some of the canapés for which she is so rightly famous, and that will be housewarming done with. Say, today fortnight?'

'That would be fine.'

'Good. Thank you so much, Celia.' And he went out of the room, leaving his coffee untouched on the table. As he left, he turned and said to his wife with a smile, 'You should really watch how many biscuits you eat, Lyndy darling. You've put a bit of weight on your hips recently.'

Now, that is an old-fashioned bastard if ever there was one.

Lynda picked up the coffee cups and carried them to the sink, but not before I had seen the tears in her eyes.

'So that's it then', she said a little sadly. 'Are you sure it's all right for you to come in? It would be a big help.'

'That's fine. As long as my friend can baby-sit.'

'Baby-sit? But I thought you said—' She stopped herself, and you could see her thinking, a Single Mother, my God, and I thought of Esther Waters and wondered fleetingly if I was about to lose my job, but remembered that this is 1997 and people are more relaxed about illegitimacy now.

'I'm sorry, I didn't realise.'

'Don't be embarrassed. I never told you.'

'No. How old?'

'Six.'

'You must have been very young and—'

'Foolish,' I interrupted.

'I was going to say brave.'

'Thank you,' I said and neatly folded a tea-towel.

'Yes, of course, you must go. I'll find my purse.'

I will say one thing for Lynda. She absolutely always has the money she owes me. She never keeps me waiting, fobbing me off with excuses or leaving the house and failing to come back in time accidentally on purpose. There is quite a lot to be said for her, if only she were not so fundamentally silly sometimes.

As she was fumbling though her purse and I was putting on my coat and wondering why Lynda was the first one of Them I had ever told about Tamsin, she said, 'Oh, one other thing, I almost forgot,' and I knew at once that she had not nearly forgotten at all but had probably been gearing herself up to asking me all morning. 'A friend of mine wondered if you had any time free at all. I know you're very busy but he is desperate. His girlfriend's just left him – moved out – and he doesn't know which end of the Hoover does what.'

'Am I being asked to be a cleaner or a girlfriend?' I asked, and wondered if I had not gone too far this time. But to my surprise she not only did not mind, she laughed, and it was not a Joanne giggle, it was a relaxed, happy, almost girlish, laugh. She looked entirely different and I knew that I had no choice at all but to go and work for the person at the very thought of whom Lynda changed so much.

'I don't want to push you.' Lynda handed the money over, looking disappointed.

'Well, seeing as it's you.' I took the money.

Once again her face lit up and she laughed that happy laugh and thanked me. 'You are kind. I did want to help Fergus if I could. He's an old friend – well, an ex-boyfriend to tell the truth – and is feeling a bit mis. Here's his address and telephone number.' She handed me a piece of paper on which the name Fergus Bond and an address in Elgin Crescent had already been written in neat capitals (does she think I can't read properly? and does she suppose that I would not realise that the preparation meant she had been pretty sure of me?) 'Do you want to ring him from here before you go?' She clearly wanted to see the deal set up before I left so I agreed. And left the house five minutes later with a new client and a potential extra eighteen pounds a week.

5 ∫

Meeting Fergus Bond put me in a very bad temper, through no fault of his. I think I am as good as Them – well, I am, just as good, but what I am not is the same. On the whole I am not aware of, and therefore do not mind, the difference but every now and then some minor slight – probably not noticed or meant – succeeds in wriggling through my armour and leaves me low and self-pitying. Somehow I did not mind Randal Blake calling me Celia. I noticed, but it made me laugh. He had spent all that charm on me but could not be bothered to remember my name. It just confirmed my instinct about the second-rate kind of man he is.

But Fergus – he is not as good looking as Randal, not by a long chalk, he is too swarthy and big-nosed with that pitted skin scarred by teenage acne. He made no particular effort to charm me, but was naturally polite and friendly. His flat is a mess – Lynda could not possibly have borne to live with him. Papers and files and overflowing ashtrays litter every surface, dirty glasses lurk under chairs, the bed was unmade and looked as though it had been for days. But he and his flat have a warmth, an immediacy, that I find very attractive. It is almost as though everything, including Fergus himself, is there by mistake. He looks constantly surprised. Surprised that I had come, surprised that his girlfriend has left him, surprised that Lynda lives so close. But all the surprises seem to please him. Even the absence of the girlfriend. Whatever Lynda may choose to think, he does not seem remotely 'mis.' to me.

So what put me into such a bad mood? I suppose it was because I found him attractive, saw that he is the kind of man that in a different, better world I would have liked as a friend, even a lover. And his charm – so different, so much more real, than Randal's, made me realise quite how lonely I am.

I have not had a boyfriend since Tamsin, not a real one. Not even a pretend one, if I am honest. At first it was because I was so involved with her, so desperate to sort out my life, to prove that I could do it, that I was too tired and alone even to meet people. But later, after I met Liz, I had opportunities. We would go out to the pub together with a group of her friends, sometimes go uptown to a club, but I realised I was frightened. One casual relationship had after all turned into so much more – I could not face the lurking dangers of another. There were boys, men, who took me out but after a few dates I always lost my nerve. Liz laughed at me, told me there was nothing to be lost by having a bit of fun, told me to loosen up, feel free to enjoy myself.

After a while you become used to being alone, you even rather like it. I like the theory of marriage, of a good relationship, of shared jokes, rows, real interaction with another adult human being. Yet I have never looked at a man and thought of sharing breakfast with him, of watching him shave, of knowing him inside out, without a shudder of boredom. Mr Nesbit talked of loneliness and irritation, but there is another factor: boredom. That is perhaps the deadliest of all.

Perhaps I just do not meet the right people. But where are they?

Fergus Bond is the right sort of person. I tried my boredom test with him: I looked at him and thought No, I would not be lonely with you. Yes I might sometimes be irritated at your slovenly life, but no, I would never be bored.

He talked to me openly, told me that his girlfriend of two years had moved out a fortnight before, gone off with someone else, but he is surprised at how little he feels. 'Disappointed I suppose – in myself as much as her,' he said, looking surprised. 'I suppose it is partly my fault. You don't go looking elsewhere, do you, if everything is rosy at home. She said I took her for granted, and I suppose I did, but it's rubbish, that sort of talk, isn't it, everyone takes everyone else for granted after a while. I suppose the mistake is showing it. Which doesn't mean I'm going to let that bastard Ronnie (what a name! Imagine running off with a bloke called Ronnie. I mean, would you?) off the hook. Anyway you can see what a mess this place is and I'm very grateful that you can help. *Isn't* Lyndy a clever girl to know you?'

He talked to me a lot. About his work, his girlfriend, his past, his future. He was surprisingly frank, with no side at all. As I cleaned and listened and chatted a little I felt warm inside. Happy to be with such a man, who had so much to say on so many different subjects. He is a news reporter, travels the world, goes to all the trouble spots, never sees a beach. 'My idea of a good holiday is a week in an English boarding house in somewhere like Yorkshire,' he said, looking surprised again. The effect of his constant surprise is that you find yourself believing that in speaking to you he is finding out things about himself for the first time. And this is very flattering in an odd way. Much more so than Randal Blake's folded arms and earnest expression.

On the way home though, hugging this unusual feeling of warmth and contentment close to me, holding on to it as you do on waking from a sweet dream which you will not allow to evaporate, I realised with a shock that perhaps Fergus is no different from the Others. He was grateful and confidential and amusing but had he asked me anything at all about myself? Had I really been anything more than a willing audience for his whimsical self-exploration? Would he, any more than Amanda, recognise me in the street or, recognising me, would he just nod and smile or would he stop to pass the time of day? I doubt it.

In theory, I am quite pretty. My nose is straight, my eyes far apart and a real green, my hair is cheaply cut but has the thick ash blonde of early childhood or Knightsbridge salons. But did Fergus – would he – even look at me? I wonder if his ex-girlfriend is good looking, whether she or I has the smoother skin, the more kissable mouth. Not that it matters. Whatever she is, however squashed her nose or close together her eyes, that kind of man will at least look at her. She will have the right clothes, the right haircut, the right job, the right credentials to warrant a second look. Whereas me – I am as good as Them, but to Them I am a different species.

I had to go straight from Elgin Crescent to pick up Tamsin from school. I was a little late, and only a small knot of children was left standing around Miss Cox in the playground.

'I'm glad I saw you, I wanted to thank you for the wonderful job you did on the flat,' she said, still shy even though she is now my employer.

'Mummy likes doing it. She says it's the one good thing Gran taught her,' chipped in Tamsin.

'Well, if she likes cleaning, she's a very special person,' Miss Cox said, and I looked at her in surprise. 'Well, it's no one's favourite occupation, is it?' and she turned back to me. 'It's not that I don't notice the dust on the skirting board, it's just that I never seem to have the time – what with being out all day, and preparing the lessons—'

'And all those books,' I said. (Mistake. Never comment, never show you have observed anything, never give anything about yourself away.) It was the teacher's turn to look taken aback.

'Are they terrible for dust? I am sorry.'

'No – no. I didn't mean that.' Because I like her I wanted to be sure she had not misunderstood me. 'I just meant – well, it must be hard to do anything else at all when you've all those books staring at you, just begging to be taken down and read.'

Jane Cox looked at me, ignoring another child who tugged at her sleeve to say goodbye. 'Do you enjoy reading?'

'Of course.' The answer was a little abrupt, a little defensive. I was prepared for some show of surprise, but there was none.

'Don't be offended,' she said, 'but if you'd like to borrow anything, you must. Just leave a note telling me what you've taken.'

'Are you sure?' My mind went dizzy for a moment at the thought of all those riches.

'Of course.' Her words were much gentler than mine had been.

'You can trust me to return them, I promise —' and I had not even thanked her yet.

'Come *on* Mummy.' Tamsin was bored. All her friends had left and we were clearly keeping Miss Cox.

'Of course I can. Heavens above, Lynda trusts you with all her precious knick-knacks—'

'But your books are much more tempting than those,' I said

quietly, and this time she did let the faintest glimmer of surprise show in her eyes.

'I expect it's because you feel like that I know I'll see the books back again,' she said, and cut off my thanks with a smile, and a farewell to Tamsin.

My mood entirely changed, I walked back home with Tamsin, thinking only of those bookshelves, longing for Thursday afternoon (six whole days away, how can I wait), until Tamsin's chatter broke through my greedy dream.

'So, Mummy, is Miss Cox your friend now?' she was asking. It would be a dream come true for her if we were friends – we are the two most important people in her life.

'Not really,' I answered, thinking of Fergus, reminding myself of how unreal I am to all of Them.

'You must be, Mummy, if she's lending you things. I only lend things to my friends. Otherwise you might not get them back and you wouldn't want to be the person's friend any more but because they weren't your friend anyway they wouldn't mind and then you'd *never* get them back.' I rootled in my bag for my house keys, smiling at her tortuous logic. She is right of course. I thought of Miss Cox's unpatronising insistence that I help myself, of her shy smile and her farewell, 'and please, Cindy, no more Miss Cox nonsense. You can only borrow the books if you call me Jane' and the warmth I had felt with Fergus earlier in the afternoon returned. I am sure that Jane Cox (Jane – I must practise saying it) does not see me as different. She recognises that cleaning is as dull for me as for everyone else, she wants to lend me her books, she would talk to me in the street . . .

'I don't know Miss Cox very well,' I finally said to Tamsin, 'but perhaps you're right. Perhaps we will be friends.' And she gave a little hop and hugged me and rushed indoors.

I am getting through this week by looking forward to Thursday. I started my *Tess of the D'Urbervilles* at the weekend which will keep me going, although I am not enjoying it nearly as much as I did *Esther Waters*. Perhaps I have become stupid after all, but Hardy does seem to make such a meal of things. Never mind, I am loving the story all over again.

*   *   *

Sometimes I think it is a mistake to work for three members of the same family. Although in a way more interesting – I think you can never know a person well until you know at least half of his immediate family – it also causes complications. They sometimes want to involve me in ways I do not wish to be involved, ask me to pass on messages or fish for information. Mrs Settrington is a great believer in Staff keeping their places and as I am the only Staff she has I am kept fully aware of my lowliness in her world order. Nevertheless she cannot resist trying to winkle little pieces of information out of me about Amanda. I suppose because she has no children of her own (why not? and does she mind? I wonder) her great nieces and nephews are almost her only link with the modern generation. Them and me, and I do not count. But if, unsolicited, I say, 'Amanda has a bad cold,' (I only made that mistake once) I am given a Look to put me in my place. I am meant to notice that the dishwasher needs emptying, but not anything at all about the people who employ me. In *Esther Waters* the posh girl runs off with the father of Esther's baby – a servant – and no one below stairs is meant to know, even though it involved one of their own.

Mr Nesbit is not as bad as his sister. He is a lot less snooty about our comparative status in life, but I think that is because he is lonely and likes to talk to someone. He is much more likely to tell me his views than she is – nothing important, just day-to-day stuff – but Mrs Settrington would feel I was being impertinent if I knew whether she prefers apples or pears.

Amanda is somewhere between the two. She is younger, of course, so you would expect her to be more relaxed, but although always friendly enough I still feel there is a distance between us. She has never opened up to me, even the smallest bit, in the whole four years I have been working for her.

Until yesterday.

I let myself in as usual, calling as I did so. She is nearly always at home these days, and I don't want to be thought to be sneaking up on Them. She was lying in the sitting-room, still in her pyjamas, the curtains drawn, a dirty wine glass and overflowing ashtray on the coffee table in front of her, watching breakfast TV and drinking a cup of coffee. And crying. I was completely taken aback, and I think she was too. She jumped, pushed something she was holding under a cushion, and pulled her pyjamas together at the neck.

'Oh – Cindy – I wasn't expecting you,' she said.

'I'm sorry. It's Tuesday. My usual day.'

'Oh yes. Oh Lord. Oh Cindy, I'm sorry. I'm in a bit of a bad way.'

'Do you want me to go?' I did not move. I did so want to see what she had hidden.

'Yes – no, oh I don't know. What do you think?'

I thought she looked rather pathetic, sitting there with her puffy face, holding her pyjamas together as if her life were in danger.

'I think,' I said crossing the room and drawing the curtains back to let in the feeble winter light, 'that you would feel a lot better if you went and had a hot bath and dressed and let me tidy up in here. Then I'll make you a good cooked breakfast and you'll feel a different person.'

Amanda looked at me in total surprise. 'Yes,' she snivelled. 'Yes, of course. You're very kind.' And, still holding herself together, she stumbled off towards the bedroom.

I waited until I heard the water running into the bath, then I moved to the settee and began puffing up its cushions. Whoops, something fell onto the floor. I bent to pick it up then looked at it, perplexed. It was one of those Catholic necklaces – a rosary – that they pray with. I think. I must check with Liz. But it was very baffling. Amanda, although outwardly scatty and disarmingly inefficient, is in fact one of the most together people I know. She never lets the side down, always looks immaculate, never drops her guard. I have heard her on the telephone to some of her television colleagues and although she sounds as breathless to them as she does to me or her friends, I have detected an undercurrent of steel. She met my eyes once, putting the telephone down on one such conversation and although she was smiling I was alarmed at the coldness in her eyes. 'They make the mistake of thinking they can muck me about,' she said, 'but do you know, it will take him five minutes to realise that he has in fact agreed to everything I wanted. Stupid bastard.' I think that was the true Amanda Quince, not the charming goof-ball the world sees.

So I was amazed, but also very sorry for her, sorrier as I knew how much she would later mind that she had shown herself weak to me. I also felt curious. What could have aroused such a strong response?

I tidied the sitting-room, cleared away the glass, the empty bottles (two, she really had been going it the night before), the ashtray. Then I saw that in the fireplace (one of those gas fake coal ones) was the remains of another glass. Once I noticed it, I saw the splash marks of the wine which went far up the tiled fireplace and out onto the carpet. The glass must have been thrown, and hard, not dropped. Either Amanda had had two glasses and drunk two bottles of wine or someone else had been with her. Well, well. My pity was not lessened by suspecting that there was Man Trouble at the root of her tears, but my interest was intensified. She is so private, Amanda, she clears up behind herself so well, that it is almost impossible for me even to find out when she has a boyfriend. I certainly never meet a man there. Since that first razor in the bin, there has been nothing that obvious. (Invitations are useful – for periods they say just 'Amanda', then it becomes 'Amanda and Robby' for a while, then 'Amanda' again. For some time 'Amanda and Mal' have been featuring on the mantelpiece. Probably no longer.)

I do not know how much she likes cooked breakfast, although sometimes I have seen signs of it, but I do know that it is the best cure for a hangover, especially one that has been exacerbated by heavy-duty crying.

Needless to say there was nothing in the fridge, but I only hesitated a moment, then I let myself back out of the house. I almost ran down Ladbroke Grove to the supermarket by the tube station, bought the makings of a really good fry-up, and was back in the flat cooking by the time Amanda was out of the bathroom.

I looked at her: she seemed better already, her hair washed, her face slightly made up. I did not say anything as I was nervous of her going all grand on me. Actually she was very humble. She sat mutely and watched me as I made us both a cup of coffee and then carried on cooking. She accepted the plate of breakfast without surprise (where did she think the food had come from?) and began eating. At first she just pushed the egg and bacon around, but after the first few mouthfuls of fried tomato and mushroom she began to revive.

'This is delicious. Thank you. You are sweet.' (I hate the word 'sweet' used like that, it is fantastically patronising.) 'I thought I heard the door shut while I was in the bath. Did – someone – come? Was there a delivery?'

Her eagerness made me feel for her again, but still – 'No. I went out to get you some breakfast.'

She had the grace to look ashamed, for a moment at least. 'Oh Lord, Cindy, you went and *bought* it. Well of course you did. You must tell me what you spent and I'll pay you back.'

I wondered if this was a good moment to point out that she has not paid me for three weeks, but before I said anything she burst into tears again. 'But I haven't any money. Oh God, it's all so *hopeless*.'

How can she not have any money? She has her own flat full of nice things, most of which were given her. She works at the BBC. She has a racy red Renault parked in the street outside, and I cannot see why she even needs it. She has posh clothes and well-cut hair and drinks wine every night – two bottles the night before, for heaven's sake. I looked at her, trying to keep my face neutral, trying not to despise her for having so much and thinking it so little.

'You must think I'm silly,' she said after a moment. 'Probably I am. I broke up with my boyfriend last night, I don't quite know why, but it was very nasty. I think he was frightened I wanted to marry him.'

'And did you?' I dared to ask.

'Yes. But I thought I was playing it cool. It is time I got married – or so Mummy and Aunt Patricia keep telling me. My sisters are worse, they spend all their time being tactful.'

She seemed softer now, for the first time talking to me almost as though I were her friend, so I bravely asked another question. 'Did you want to marry him or do you want to be married?'

'Is there a difference? I suppose you're right, there is.' She took a sip at her coffee, pulled a face, 'I've let it get cold,' let me pick up the cup, rinse it out, put the kettle back on. 'I want to be married,' she said finally. 'I want to feel safe. And have children, I suppose. At least I think I want them until I spend any amount of time with someone else's. I suppose I want not to have children because I've made that choice, not because no one's asked me.' She still does not know about Tamsin, and I nearly told her then, but something stopped me. I think I felt that if I reminded her that I exist as a person outside the walls of her flat, she would stop confiding in me.

She sighed, stood up, put some bread in the toaster. 'I suppose there's time. I'm not quite thirty, after all. But I'm coming up to that big birthday and it does make you think. How old are you?' She looked at me, really looked into my face. It is not often she shows that much interest in me.

'Twenty-six, nearly twenty-seven.'

'Oh, so you're not so young yourself,' she said carelessly, and went back to thinking about herself. (No, but I have Tamsin. I would like more children, but I have Tamsin. I am not going to be like Mrs Settrington and possibly Amanda, relying on nieces and nephews for my future.)

'And work – Malcolm – my boyfriend – my ex-boyfriend I should say – works at the BBC. He commissions ideas, puts the packages together. He won't employ me now, he'll choose other people, winsome little graduates from Balliol, probably,' she said viciously.

'But I thought you worked at the BBC?'

'I did. But my contract wasn't renewed and I've been freelance since. Which is much harder. Oh, you're paid better when you work, but it's a question of when. I respect the joys of a salary now.'

'I see,' I said, and I did. Those bottles of white wine which used to have £8.99 stickers on them have for some months become nearer £4.99 or even £4. The bottles of shampoo which used to say Toni & Guy now say Sainsbury's own. They used to be thrown in the bin with a good half inch left in the bottom, the new ones are jammed upside down against the taps so that every last drop can be used.

'I know I haven't paid you for a week or two and I'm sorry,' she was saying. 'It's awful of me. But I'm up against every limit going. I daren't ask Daddy for any more. I've used up all the money in my deposit account which was meant to pay the tax man. My overdraft is in the thousands, and I haven't a job in sight . . .'

I thought I had learned a lot while working for Them. But this is the biggest revelation of all. I do not have much, but I live well within my income. In the small hours of the night I have many worries but never about money. I know I can pay my bills, I have not been overdrawn at the bank for three years, I have a deposit account which is quietly healthy. I do not have a pretty flat or a car or nice clothes (neither, I have to admit, do I have a tax man), but I have independence and pride. *I am richer than Amanda*. I nearly laughed out loud at the realisation.

Amanda was sitting there looking at me blankly, as though she was waiting for me to come up with an answer to all her problems.

'What about lodgers? I asked. 'When I first came to work here you said you would take lodgers, but you never have.'

'I know, but I can't, I'm used to living on my own now. I need the space.'

'You could sell your car,' I suggested.

'How can I sell it? How would I get about? I thought of it, but honestly it wouldn't pay. I'd spend more on taxis in a month than the road tax costs a year.' Sometimes I think we speak different languages. How can you deal with someone who thinks the only alternative to running a car is to go everywhere by taxi? I was overcome by a flash of malice and my new role as confidante emboldened me to say,

'What about getting a job?'

'Cindy, don't think I haven't tried. I've approached every station – even the extra-terrestrial ones. There just does not seem to be anything going.'

'I don't mean in television,' I said patiently (but already smiling to myself at the thought of her reaction when she finally understood). 'I mean some other kind of job. You know, part-time work. I bet you could get waitressing work easy as anything, and you wouldn't have to go far. That French restaurant at the bottom of Portobello Road was advertising for a waitress a week or so ago, or if that job's gone there are all those restaurants in Kensington Park Road – that's only a ten minute walk away.'

The reaction was even better than I had imagined. '*Cindy*! I haven't waitresssed since I was a student!'

She was absolutely horrified, so I could not resist pushing the point a little further. 'I'm sure you would pick it up again quickly,' I said seriously.

'No, but Cindy, I *couldn't*. My friends go to those places!'

'Then I'm sure you would get good tips.' For a moment I thought I had gone too far, that I was about to be thrown out of the house without my three (and a half) weeks' wages, never mind the £3.42 I had spent on breakfast. Then to my surprise Amanda's face changed. She gave me a huge smile and, reaching across the table, patted my hand.

'Cindy! You're teasing. I *am* relieved,' she laughed. 'You're right, it would be funny to see their faces when they noticed it was me bringing them their *rognons à la crème*! Best of all would be if I got a job in one of the restaurants Daddy goes to,' Amanda burbled on, hugely enjoying the joke. 'He would be horrified! And I bet he'd give me a tip big enough to let me retire.'

Her laughter stopped as suddenly as it had started. 'But seriously, Cindy, joking apart, what am I to do?'

I stood up and began clearing away the breakfast. 'Cheer up, something will come along. I probably shouldn't say anything, so please don't let on I told you, but your aunt's inviting you to dinner next week. I'll be helping. She's got some man – a godson or something – who she wants to introduce you to. Maybe he'll be the man of your dreams.'

She laughed again, and there was less tension, more real humour, in it this time. 'I doubt it. If you knew the amount of worthy young men that Aunt Patricia has introduced me to in the last six years – dull as ditch water every last one. I'll bet you one thing, the man of my dreams is unlikely to spend much time going out to dinner with seventy-somethings. Anyway, there's another party coming up I've been asked to – Lyndy and Randal Blake are giving one the week after next. House-warming, I suppose.'

'Yes, I'm helping there too.'

'Oh *good*.' And she really did look pleased. 'Well, I bet there'll be more likely men there than at Aunt Patricia's. You might even pick one up yourself.' Her voice was teasing, as though we were friends, but the amusement in her eyes was at the improbability of the notion that I should meet a man through her friends.

Fair enough, I suppose. I had my joke at her expense. And you never know she might be right in spite of herself . . . it is time I met a man, somewhere.

I'm trying to finish *Tess* before I go to Jane on Thursday, but I doubt I will. It is much longer than I remembered. I will still choose something for afterwards, though. I just cannot think where to begin.

It was a funny coincidence that I should have chanced upon *Tess* and *Esther Waters* when I pulled two books from the box at Mum's, because of course Tess also has an illegitimate baby. I do not remember being shocked at Tess's attitude to her baby when I first read the book, but I am now. I wanted to dismiss it as having been written by a man who could not be expected to understand, but then George Moore was a man too, and he allows Esther to love her baby. Whereas Tess – she gives her baby no name until it is dying, and then she calls it Sorrow. She is 'gloomy and indifferent' towards it – only being really passionate when it is dying.

I suppose it is obvious that I should be interested in this illegitimacy subject, and maybe I am becoming morbid about it. Everywhere I look there are children without fathers, and neither they nor their mothers seem to mind. Yet such a short time ago it was shaming beyond measure to have a 'bastard' in the family, something unmentionable. I think Mum still feels it a little with her talk of 'by-blows'.

Those men – Hardy, Moore, I wonder who else – were, I suppose, brave to write about the subject. But where are the middle-class girls who did not wait for a ring? Where are all the children fathered by younger sons of dukes? Moore and Hardy do not dare to mention them.

To the novelists, it was a story, an exercise, social observation with a moral.

But Tamsin and me, Liz and her three, we are real life.

Sometimes I wish it were different. Tamsin needs a father.

Not her real one, wherever he is, but someone. A man in her life who does not wear diamond-patterned jumpers and worry about catching buses on time.

It has taken me a long time to care. Maybe Amanda has opened my eyes, maybe it is Steven and Joanne expecting another baby, maybe I am just getting older, but oh dear oh Lord I would like to find a man.

The Blakes – or at any rate Lynda – can talk of nothing but their party. She has a pile of cards printed in purple (I think she thinks purple is an artistic colour). 'Mrs Randal Blake At Home.' All very smart. Mr Blake was there again yesterday morning and he was very snappy, told Lynda she has invited too many people, that she must cut back. 'Am I made of money? Do I even like these people? Why should they come to my house and pour champagne down their throats? Why couldn't you have gone to Oddbins and bought some cheap white? Why must you always be so extravagant? It's just another way of showing off, pure selfishness.' On and on he went until she was almost crying. She did dare to point out that champagne had been his idea, and she looked at me appealing for corroboration, but I am afraid I was too cowardly to say anything. I feel a bit ashamed about that.

Mr Blake still bothered to flash me his handsome smile, checked that I was able to help at the party, called me Sammy. I did not bother to correct him and Lynda looked mortified but too frightened to speak.

Finally he left the house in a cloud of self-righteous bad temper, and Lynda cheered up.

'You mustn't think badly of him,' she said, following me up the stairs to his study. 'He is under tremendous pressure at work, and you know people always take it out on those they love most.' I wondered why he did not vent his bad temper on himself, then, rather than Lynda.

'Did you ever ring that friend, the one who wrote to you?' It is funny how life works. I had just come to the realisation that

I need more people in my life, people of my own, who look at me for what I am, not what I do, when Liz decided I needed a little encouragement in the same direction.

'Who do you mean?' Stupid of me, I know, but I needed to stall for time.

'The university one – with the silly name. You know.'

'Are you ready?' We were meeting some friends in the Percy, thought we might go dancing later, one of Liz's many younger sisters was passing through London and we had decided to take advantage of her stay and use her to baby-sit.

'Cindy, don't be daft.'

'No, I haven't. I will.'

'When? Come on Cindy, if you leave it too long you never will. When's the reunion thing anyway? Has it happened yet?'

I carefully painted a new lipstick on to my mouth and admired the effect. It is a pale pink, very sixties, rather glamorous. I have taken to using make-up more often recently. I like that smoky-eyed, slightly-ill Biba look. Seventies maybe. Before my time anyway. Before all of this.

'Cindy.'

'No, I don't think it has. I think it is at the beginning of next month.'

I knew exactly when it was, of course. The date – 5th December – kept popping into my head, drawing me towards it.

'Come on, girl, it's not like you to have bad manners. What would your Mam say to you?'

'I don't do anything to please my mother. I haven't for a long time.'

'Then do it to please yourself. No harm can come of it, and you'll always wonder if you don't.'

'Liz—'

She had a mulish expression which I do not see often on her face, although I know it well on Tony, her middle child. 'I'm not going to drop it, Cindy. You're getting into a rut, you're doing yourself no favours. I had to work too hard to get you to come out tonight, you work every hour you can, but you've forgotten how to have a good time. It's nice when you come in and we have a beer or two in an evening, but that should be a quiet night in, not your only night out. That girl got in touch with you, she was a friend, she made an effort. Okay some years have gone by and your life has changed, but she knew that when she wrote. She knew you'd had a baby – and kept it – and it didn't put her off. If you don't get in touch with her it will be pathetic, Cindy, and I never had you down as a mouse. You're tougher than that, you're probably tougher than she is. So get a grip and ring her.'

I stared at her. I think that is the most I have ever heard her say, and even in my bewilderment that touched me. She stood there, facing me, glaring at me, willing me to obey her. Then, just as I was trying to answer, she relaxed, and softened. 'For what it's worth, you're looking really good,' she said, and added with a smile, 'if you want I'll hold your hand in the phone box. But I'm telling you one thing, you'll be doing it before you've had your first drink tonight.'

I did. How could I resist her? I did not even pretend I had lost the telephone number. I meekly went to the drawer where I keep my writing and took out Nelly's letter. I kissed Tamsin good night, checked the baby alarm was working through to Liz's, gave her sister Maureen the beer I had bought for her, and followed Liz down the street to the Percy. The telephone there is on the wall, and you have to pull the receiver into the ladies' and shut the door to have any chance of hearing. I started to say it was not good enough, but Liz gave no quarter. 'Just do it, now,' she hissed when I began to speak.

The telephone was answered on the third ring and for a second I hoped it would be an answering machine.

'Hello. Hello? Sarah Trunk here. Hello?'

'Hello.' I had to clear my throat and try again. Her voice was suddenly so familiar I felt as though I had heard it last only a week ago. 'Hello, Nelly. I mean Sarah. It's Cindy. Cindy Martin.'

'Cindy? Cindy, how brilliant, it's not true! How are you, I can't hear you very well, Are you on a mobile?'

That question alone made me realise – if I had not known it before – the difference in our lives. I nearly hung up in a panic, but forced myself to cling to the receiver. 'No, I'm in a pub.'

She laughed. 'Lucky you. I'm stuck in this evening with a mountain of paperwork. So you got my letter. Are you coming?' She sounded so easy, so pleased to hear me. I began to relax, to bask in the warmth of the old friendship.

'No, I'm not. I don't think I can.' I did not say it was lack of will, not opportunity, that hindered me.

'Oh, Cindy, what a shame. But look, we must meet. Where do you live?' The monitor started flashing at me and I mouthed at Liz for another ten pence piece. She pushed a fifty into the box. Why is she so keen for me to make a go of this friendship?

'London. Ladbroke Grove.'

'That's sort of Notting Hill, isn't it? Brilliant. Cindy, I'm coming up to London next week – no, it's the week after, I'm going to some meetings in the day – it's the fourteenth, Wednesday. Could we meet for a drink that evening? Maybe some dinner.' Again, a wave of panic came over me. I would not be able to afford her kind of dinner, but her friendly voice stopped me from refusing. Why else had I rung her, after all? Of course I can afford it, Liz has been encouraging me to have a splurge. There are all those pounds sitting in a deposit account . . . I have earned them to pull me from my rut, now I must learn how to spend them.

'Yes. Yes, why not. I'd like that.'

'Where shall we go? It's your patch, tell me where to meet you.' Of course my mind went blank. All I could think of was the Percy, and that would never do.

'Why don't we meet at Notting Hill tube?' I suggested. She obviously rates Notting Hill higher than Ladbroke Grove. 'Then you can see what you like the look of.' And please let it be Pizza Express not the Pomme d'Amour.

'Brilliant. See you then. Oh, Cindy how exciting. Seven o'clock on the fourteenth at Notting Hill Gate underground station.'

'South side.'

'South side,' she repeated, sounding a little mystified. 'And Cindy, I didn't ask you – your baby?'

I laughed. 'She's not a baby any more, Nelly. She's six. She's called Tamsin. See you on the fourteenth. 'Bye.'

I was so relieved after the telephone call which had been haunting me for so long was finally made that I drank far too much, stayed out far too late, and woke up the next morning with a fully fledged hangover. My first for ages.

'Did you go dancing?' asked Tamsin, prancing around the room to the Spice Girls tape Liz gave her for her birthday.

'Yes.'

'I can always tell. You get up slowly and eat a lot of breakfast.'

'Don't be cheeky. Sit down and eat your toast.'

'I'm not. Anyway it's true. D'you like dancing?' She came and sat down at our small table and looked longingly at the plate of food I had just put down in my place. 'Oh, Mum, can I have some?'

'You said no.'

'But, Mum, it looks so good.' I pushed the plate towards her and wearily set about frying some more egg and bacon. It makes the room stink but sometimes it is worth it. 'Do you?'

'Do I what?' I tried not to be too irritable. It was not Tamsin's fault I felt so ill.

'Like dancing?'

'I suppose so.'

'Good. I like having a groovy mum. Rhiannon's mum hasn't been dancing for five years. She told me yesterday.'

The idea that I am a 'groovy' mum made me smile. I did not realise children that age had any concept of 'groovy', nor that 'groovy' itself was back. I have learned a lot since Tamsin started school. I am sure that at her age I was not half so conscious of pop music, or the dance between the sexes, nor do I remember any desire for a 'groovy' mother. (I would certainly have been disappointed there.) I suppose mothers have been saying that for years.

We mopped up the last of our egg yolks with fried bread. 'Come on Baby Spice, time for school.'

She stood up and danced towards her satchel. 'Did Miss Cox go with you?'

'Miss Cox? Of course not (have you got your packet of crisps?) why should she?'

'I thought you were friends.'

'Oh, Tamsin—' I wish she did not have this bee in her bonnet about Jane and me being friends. I am nervous of what she will say, she might make Jane think I have been saying things I have not and make a fool of me. 'I'm friendly with her,' I tried to explain, 'but she's not the kind of friend I go dancing with. Or out to the pub. I went with Liz, you know that, and Sally and Jim and Dave and Ed.'

We reached the school gate and I bent to kiss Tamsin good-bye. 'Ayesha says Liz is always seeing Dave these days,' she said, returning the kiss and taking her lunch box from me. 'He came round really late the other night, Ayesha woke up and heard him come in, but Liz told him he had to go away and Ayesha heard him arguing. I suppose it would be a bit of a squish if he stayed there too. 'Bye.'

I watched her crossing the playground, fear making my insides cold. Is Liz seeing Dave? She can't be, I am sure she would have told me. I thought back to the night before and I could not then and can not now think of a single look or touch or aside passing between them that could have been anything more than friendly. And yet . . . Dave's a nice man, Irish Liverpudlian like Liz. He works on the sites, seems to have a lot of work. He knows how to have a good time all right, is always generous on Friday when he is paid but unlike the rest of them does not run out of money by Thursday. I should think he is a bit younger than Liz, but not much. I have never seen him at Liz's flat, in fact I am surprised he even knows where it is.

Why would Liz not tell me if she is going out with him? She has been telling me for years that she is finished with men, but there is no reason why she should not change her mind. Either Tamsin and Ayesha have cooked up this story based on nothing – which is possible – or Liz is seeing Dave. If she *is* seeing him she is either not telling me because it does not count, which is unlikely, or because it is serious. Which frightens me very much.

I cannot afford to lose Liz. I would be totally bereft. What am I to do?

What with my hangover and my state of shock at the thought of Liz disappearing from my life I arrived at Mr Nesbit's in a bad way. Luckily he was busy himself, fussing around in the kitchen and being mysterious about his lunch guest. If he thinks I care at all about his social life, he is quite mistaken, but it was rather pathetic to see how pleased the old boy was to be having a guest. His preparations seemed to be aimed at pointing out to me what a busy, popular chap he is. I had my cup of coffee with him (I could not have refused, I was desperate for one by then) and watched him fidget around with some chicken breasts and an elaborate (or maybe he just made it seem elaborate) marinade involving messily squeezing a lot of limes. It is all very good fun cooking when you can afford eight limes and someone to tidy up after you.

On the other hand – there were some questions I needed answering and perhaps now was the moment. People are always more likely to talk freely when they are busy with their hands. 'Do you want help, Mr Nesbit? That dish looks interesting.' Somehow I dislike being sly with Mr Nesbit, but when he looked pleased I felt happier.

'I'd love you to, thank you. Do mind just being my kitchen-maid?'

'Of course not.'

We worked in silence for a while and I thought about the best way to broach the subject I had in mind. I peeled and diced some potatoes, he went on smearing lime juice around. He looked happy.

'Do you mind my asking you something, Mr Nesbit?'

'I'm always happy to help you out, Cindy,' he said, dripping juice onto his recipe book as he squinted at it.

'Are you a Catholic?'

He looked up at me for a moment, sharp surprise in his eyes. 'Yes, of course.' (That's another odd thing about Catholics, it's always 'of course'. Why?)

'I just wondered – those rosaries, what are they for?'

'Rosaries?' His face relaxed, I had obviously not asked a threatening question. 'They are a way of praying. For each bead you say a prayer, the decades – ten beads together – are for the Hail Mary, then you say the Glory Be and the Our Father. Oh dear, it's a long time since I've used my rosary, I fear . . .' he sighed and returned to his coriander.

'But why do you need the beads?' I persisted. 'Why can't you just say your prayers, or use your fingers or something?'

'You can, but I suppose the rosary is a discipline, a

comfort . . .' He tailed off and looked as though he were thinking the question through properly at last. 'The thing about Catholics – or most Catholics I know – is how deeply entrenched their religion – not just its form – is in them.'

'What do you mean?'

He shook his head. 'I don't know why it should be. Maybe because for centuries we have been in the minority in this country, so at some atavistic level we feel we have to prove ourselves. But I've seen it time and again. Especially in the young. They fight against it, rebel, stop practising, truly believe that they have it out of their system, but then something happens and they feel the pull again. The comfort of the Church, the reassurance of Her discipline. The Jesuits say, you know, that if they have a child for the first seven years of his life they have him for ever. There's something in that.'

I was not sure what the Jesuits were, but wanted to keep him on track. For some reason Amanda and her missals and her rosary were suddenly very important to me. I had to get to the bottom of it all.

'So what kind of things are important?'

'Oh, you know, prayer, and Mass, and kindness, and respect for life . . .' He looked uncomfortable again, and I sensed I was not going to learn much more. 'Why do you ask, anyway?'

'Oh, my neighbour is a Catholic – or was. She's had a rackety old life of it, and I thought none of it mattered any more. But she told me once that she still taught her children to say their prayers, felt somehow they must.'

'You see? And it's not just habit, that's the mistake other people make. It goes much deeper than that, it's a real feeling for something greater than yourself, something you cannot in the end argue with. You watch, your friend will be praying again herself one day. When something truly awful, or joyous happens to her. She will turn to prayer again.'

Liz, Amanda – I wonder if he is right. I might envy them if he is. I left the kitchen, hauling the hoover and polish up to his room to begin cleaning. Two hours later I was about to leave the house when the doorbell rang. Mr Nesbit had nipped (or popped – he always seems to 'pop' out, never to 'go' or 'walk') – out to buy some flowers from the shop by the tube station and he had asked me to wait in case his guest came while he was out so I put on my coat as I answered the door.

Some mystery guest: it was Amanda.

'Cindy, I thought it was your day here today, I'm really glad to see you.' I was surprised. Usually people hate the person they have confided in; I have been dreading next Tuesday for that reason. 'Where's Uncle Vincent?'

'He's just popped out for some flowers.' I had not meant to imitate him – heavens above, my job is worth more than that, but there must have been an echo of him in my intonation. Something made Amanda laugh and flash a blue gleam of pure amusement at me.

'Cindy, don't! He is a peach, isn't he?'

I began pretending not to know what she meant, but her look was so conspiratorial, so *equal*, that I just laughed. 'I'm sorry, I—'

'Don't be. He thinks the world of you, says you're so *gentle* with your hands. If I didn't know better . . . He calls you his "perfect treasure".'

'I thought his porcelain was his treasure.'

'Yes, but it takes a treasure to guard a treasure.' Her mimicry was excellent, and I had a funny flash of an almost-recognised memory. 'Or something,' Amanda smiled. 'Anyway you're obviously kind to him and I know that can be hard. He's a fussy old stick, but a good man really.'

'I had better go,' I said, looking at my watch. 'I've got to get to Chesterton Road and I'm running late today.'

'Oh, but I've got to talk to you. Just a minute, please, I won't keep you long.'

I was not sure if I was strong enough for another crisis of Amanda's soul, but I could hardly refuse. I made no move to take off my coat, though, nor to go back into the house. I just stood there in the little hall (more of a corridor really), arms folded, trying to look friendly but not overly encouraging.

'I wanted to thank you for the other day.' She reached into her big sack of a bag and brought out a bottle. 'I don't know if you like wine, but . . .' Funny how hesitant she sounded, and I realised with a little jolt that she was worried about offending me. 'You were very kind, and I was being nothing but self-indulgent.

I'll be all right, get myself another job, sometimes it's just very frightening being self-employed.' She hesitated again, then added awkwardly, 'as I'm sure you know.' Well, well. Far from hating me for having seen her in her puddle of despair she seems to have crossed some kind of barrier, to understand for the first time in all these years that we are the same species after all.

I took the wine with a smile. 'You needn't have, but thank you. It'll be a treat for me. And of course you'll find another job before long. Another man, too, if you ask me. It's never as bleak in the middle of the morning as it is in the middle of the night.'

She laughed 'I think Uncle Vincent may be right – you are a perfect treasure.' Somehow I did not like the phrase so much coming direct from her. 'But seriously, I mean it. Thank you.'

I tucked the wine under my arm and picked up my bag. 'It was nothing—'

'There is one other thing.'

Of course there was. These smiles and presents and jokes would not come unattached. How could I have imagined it possible. 'Yes?'

Perhaps she sensed my resignation, but I doubt it. She is not very interested in other people's feelings, after all. She did seem nervous though. 'It's just – well, it's Lyndy. I know it's a lot to ask, but please, if you don't mind – I'd rather you did not say anything to her. About the other day.'

'It wouldn't occur to me.' I was cross and I let it show.

'Oh, Lord, Cindy, now I've offended you.' She was being actressy again, but to give her the benefit of the doubt I do believe it was from genuine embarrassment. 'Cindy, I'm not saying you're a gossip, I know you're not, but I just wanted to be sure . . . you know, if she asked you might just say "oh she's a bit low" or something. Of course, I'll tell her about Mal, after all he won't be going to her party now, but you see, she knows people in the business, and if it gets out that I'm desperate . . . you know, the cycle of failure . . . Mal won't be doing me any favours, I just don't need to be undermined . . .'

I softened a little. 'Amanda, you can trust me,' I said, which I suppose is true, but I was thinking how odd it was that she was so secretive towards Lynda, who is supposed to be a good friend.

'I know I can, and I'm sorry I couldn't stop myself from asking you. But Lyndy, of all people . . . I shouldn't say this, but she's really become a bit smug since marrying Randal. You know, all that perfect china, perfect paint work, perfect cooking . . .' And a far from perfect husband, I wanted to add, but did not. I think Amanda would be a little too pleased if she thought that all was not quite right in Lynda's little utopia.

'People change.' I knew I was being banal, but I was desperate to leave. 'Trust me, and I'll see you next week, Amanda.' I did not thank her again for the wine. She had taken some of my pleasure from the gift, which now seemed closer to a bribe.

She stood aside to let me pass. 'On the other hand, if Uncle Vincent or Aunt Patricia express any concern for my welfare, you have my full permission to tell them I'm feeling broke. Perhaps they will come up trumps.' She laughed, but I do not think she was joking. How odd it must be to feel poor, yet to be surrounded by rich relations who think inviting you to lunch takes away from your worries. Amanda is beginning to make me realise that I am in fact very lucky.

After all that I could not really do justice to Jane's flat. There was Tamsin to be fetched at three thirty, and I have been looking forward all week to choosing something from those laden shelves. I gave them a good dusting while I looked but the skirting boards were certainly left to fend for themselves.

I had been imagining the pleasures of those shelves so vividly that when I was at last faced with them it was something of a let-down. I gazed blankly at the rows of books filled with familiar and unfamiliar names. Amis, Collins, Hardy, Huth, Inchbald, James, Meredith, Powell, Trollope . . . where should I start? In the end I took *The Woman in White*. I think the thing to do is to go back to the university reading list which I picked up at home. I need some guidance and I do not dare ask Jane. Maybe I will one day, when I feel a little less ignorant.

I gave the flat the sort of cleaning of which my mother would be thoroughly disapproving. Very much on the surface, and using far too much of the cleaning products so that Jane would notice the clean smell of the flat as soon as she walked through the door and with any luck then not notice the dusty corners. Hers is an easy flat to clean – no ornaments, no invitations (which is odd, she should have one from the Blakes by now), no dainty candlesticks or precious decanters to work around.

I left a note 'I owe you half an hour' (actually slightly over three-quarters, but still). 'Sorry. I have *The Woman In White*. Thank you. Cindy' and let myself out of the door. Before I had reached the end of the road my thoughts had turned to Fergus, who I am due to clean for tomorrow. I have not been able to work out if I like him or loathe him, and am looking forward to finding out.

Fergus has his invitation from the Blakes. He has had a clear-out since last week, shuffled all his papers into three more or less neat piles, thrown away all the cards and photographs on the mantelpiece so that the ridiculous purple lettering shouted at me almost as soon as I walked into the room. I think he saw me noticing it, which must mean I am slipping.

'I must admit I'm looking forward to that party,' he said, handing me a cup of coffee. 'I feel like a party – haven't been to one since the split. And let's be honest, parties are much more fun when you are seriously single.' I think the whole of west London is in a mating frenzy over this party, and I must admit I am very glad to be helping at it – it will be interesting to see Them all at play.

'Do you like flirting?' Fergus suddenly asked me, and to my shame I felt myself blush.

'Me? I don't know, I don't suppose I'm very good at it.'

'Of course you are. Everyone is, aren't they? I used to get in terrible trouble from Lottie about it, although she was just as bad. Worse, come to think of it – look where her flirting with Ronnie ended up.'

'I hope the spice won't have gone out of it then.'

'Out of what?'

'Flirting. Will it be as much fun when there's no one there watching and feeling jealous?'

He looked crestfallen. 'Perhaps you're right. I hadn't thought of that,' and then, seeing my face, realised that I was teasing him and laughed. 'No, it'll be all right. I haven't let myself lose the knack and I must admit I am getting bored of eating take away on my own. I had not noticed until Lottie left how many of my friends are married now.'

'Perhaps you should begin flirting with intent, then.' (Was I flirting? I don't know. Perhaps. Does it matter?)

'With intent?'

'To marry. You know, like in the lonely hearts column. The ads always make it clear whether the person is looking for a bit on the side or for a long-term relationship.'

'Do *you* read the lonely hearts?' and, although it is so much part of his character, I was flattered by his surprise, and blushed again.

'Well, sometimes, in the *Standard*. Out of curiosity.'

'We *all* read them "out of curiosity".' And it was my turn to be taken aback.

'So you read them too?'

'I read them because I wonder if I will ever be lonely enough to need them, and I want to know what will be on offer when that day comes.'

'And?'

'And I will be offered professional women who are panic-stricken at the realisation they may have left it too late to have a baby or divorced women panic-stricken that no one will want them because they have too many children.'

'Which is better?'

'I decide to stick to flirting at parties.'

We both laughed, and I wished I was asked to more parties.

He left me alone after that, and I gave his kitchen a clean such as it has almost certainly never seen before. I washed down the walls, scrubbed the floor, turned out the cupboards, cleaned the oven. It was an enjoyable job – it is always satisfying to tackle real filth. I hoped he would notice, and to his credit he did.

'This makes me see why people are prepared to spend so much time being tidy,' he said, handing over the eighteen pounds. 'Although I doubt I will ever arrive at Lyndy's extremes. She's a good girl, Lyndy, but I don't think cleaning should be the first thing in your life, do you? Except professionally, of course.'

I smiled: I liked his tact. 'Oh, it's not the first thing in Lynda's life, either. That is Mr Blake. All that cleaning's for his comfort.'

His face clouded over. 'I suppose you're right. Well, see you next week.'

7

The highlight of this week will be Mrs Settrington's dinner party. They are usually dull affairs, but it will make a difference to see Amanda on parade and maybe this godson will be the man of her dreams.

This morning (Monday) Mrs Settrington asked me to help with the cooking rather than clean upstairs. I quite like cooking, especially in other people's kitchens with their expensive ingredients, so from that point of view I was more than happy to be doing something different. On the other hand I like Mrs Settrington the least of all my clients and did not relish the prospect of being shut in that small kitchen with her for three hours. She is very bad at delegating: she will ask me to do something and then stand over me and criticise as I do it, rather than letting me get on with it and do something useful herself.

She was all keyed up about this dinner party, although she entertains so regularly. She wants to impress the Allbright-Markhams, her smart young(ish) neighbours, wants to show off to her godson, wants to be the one who finds Amanda a husband. She does not care much about Mr Nesbit, and I am surprised she asked him. Usually he is asked to the low-key affairs – two courses and no card-playing. Most often she just asks him on his own, and then complains about it. He is her duty, she sighs, 'and we all have a duty to someone, don't we dear?' I cannot imagine thinking of my brother as a 'duty'. I am quite fond of him really – more than of anyone else in my family. Sometimes he irritates me, and we will never see truly eye to eye, but I would never see him out of duty and would never lose touch with him.

But I nod and agree and smile and wonder what is in their shared past which binds Mr Nesbit and Mrs Settrington together and yet keeps them so separate.

I also wonder why the Colonel was not called up for this party. The Colonel is a doddery old fool, but sweet in his way. He has runny blue eyes and smokes a pipe. He never talks much, and when he does it is usually to agree with Mrs Settrington. He drinks weak whisky and soda by the bucket at all hours of the day but I have noticed that on their card evenings it is nearly always the Colonel who is collecting money from the others. I suppose I should describe him as a friend of Mrs Settrington's – he is quite often at lunch, goes with her to the Gate Cinema, is nearly always the spare man at her dinner parties – but I do not think you can have a true friendship which is so unequal. It may be different when I am not there, but I have never heard him put forward a view or suggest a course of action. I have never heard them laugh together, or even have a real two-handed conversation. I have only ever heard her lay down the law, and him agree, and seen him nod and smile and pocket his card winnings and drink whisky.

Perhaps Mrs Settrington thinks he is not up to the Allbright-Markhams, or perhaps she has finally realised how much money he has taken from her over the years, or perhaps (but I do not think this can be the case) she has tired of only hearing her own opinions repeated back at her and wants a friend with the nerve to disagree.

She was in a much better frame of mind than normal today, probably because she is looking forward to the dinner. She is in some ways easier to deal with than most of Them because her attitude to me does not lurch about in the same way as the rest of Theirs. She knows my place, it would never occur to her to be in any way interested in my life or expect me to play any part in hers other than that defined by my job. So today we sat together and went through her recipe books for ideas and decided on the menu, and we chatted perfectly amicably while I made salmon mousse and she rolled out ready-made pastry and peeled apples. She even complimented me on the mousse when it was finished, which surprised me.

By the time I left, the first course and pudding were ready, the potatoes peeled and carrots scraped and chopped and waiting in water. The dining room table was laid with silver and shining glass and stiff white linen. The flowers were arranged, the gin and tonic glasses laid out on a tray in the sitting room.

The dinner party is on Wednesday, and I go to her on Wednesday afternoon. Aren't old people odd?

Mr Nesbit is almost as over-excited as his sister. He was laying out his clothes for Wednesday night, holding one silk foulard after another up against his green velvet jacket. 'I know it's not a dinner jacket evening, but what is the point of not dressing up when you go out. Don't you agree?' he fussed, looking critically at a multi-coloured peacock-print necktie. 'Now that might be a little *too* much. I know I'm being the tiniest bit previous to myself but I wanted to be sure I had everything I need in case I wanted you to iron anything. Now what do you think?'

I thought that there is no point behaving like an old queen if you do not look like one, so I guided him towards a turquoise silk shirt and the peacock-print neckerchief.

Don't you think that's the smallest bit bright?' he frowned, but I pointed out how the peacock colours included turquoise as well as the green of the jacket and how artistically the tie brought the two together.

Mrs Settrington does not like men in bright colours – I heard her nagging the Colonel about some yellow socks once. I wonder what the Allbright-Markhams will make of Mr Nesbit. Sometimes life is great fun after all.

I was exhausted by the time the first guests arrived at Mrs Settrington's house on Wednesday night. I had spent the morning at the Blakes', where Lyndy was agonising over endless tiny details for her party. Thank heavens Mr Blake was out – he is prosecuting a big paedophile case at the moment, Lynda showed me *The Telegraph* where half of page three was given up to the story. I think the combination of the party and Mr Blake almost certainly being foul to her because of the pressure he is under is driving Lynda half mad. After leaving her I went up to Mrs Settrington, where I had to tidy up all the fallen petals from Monday, change the water of the carrots and potatoes which were beginning to look a little slimy, and clean as normal. Then back home to pick up Tamsin and give her tea, and up the hill again to Hillgate Village by seven. Mrs Settrington only pays for the taxi home and the buses just were not coming so I had to walk.

Mrs Settrington let me in and went upstairs to change. Her lipstick is always a little too orange on these occasions, and I think she must be long-sighted as her powder is never even and she has great splodges of it across half her face.

The godson arrived first. He was not at all what I had been hoping to see, for Amanda's sake. Seth Hardwicke had sounded rather romantic, but what stood on the doorway clutching a bunch of yellow roses was nothing like the tall, dark, sneering heroes of second-rate fiction. He is short, five eight if he is lucky, and paunchy. His hair is an expensive mass of Hugh Grant floppy blackness (and I think it is dyed although I would have to see it in daylight to be sure). His upper lip is very long, with a small moustache which may be meant to disguise this fault but only makes it the more obscene. And I am absolutely sure there is a hole for an earring in his ear. He was not wearing any jewellery, but he looked as though he usually does. I don't know, something to do with the way he moves his hands. Amanda uses her hands a lot, but very energetically, very illustratively. His are wafted around more languidly. Perhaps I was thinking of Elizabeth Taylor talking about the huge diamond ring Richard Burton gave her, 'It's amazing how left-handed you become when you wear a ring like this.' There is that sort of feel to him. So much for the romantic nook Mrs Settrington had set up at the end of her living-room; I thought the chances of Seth and Amanda being cosied up together there were slight. His type usually prefers long chats with the older woman.

Mrs Settrington did look taken aback when I showed Seth in to the living-room (that is the way she likes things done when she has these evenings. I am cook, parlour maid, waitress and butler all in one), but she recovered quickly. She handed me the roses and asked Seth what he wanted to drink.

He smiled. 'The heaven of being back in England is people understanding drinks. In the States it's nothing at all or endless cocktails which make you frightfully drunk. Hong Kong is honestly the more civilised. I'll have a glass of white wine please – as long as it's not Californian!' (Why could he not just say, 'White wine, please'?)

Mrs Settrington nodded at me. 'Would you, Cindy? And a gin and tonic for me.'

I had to go downstairs to the kitchen to fetch the white wine from the fridge, and when I came back they were still standing awkwardly on either side of the fireplace, making stilted conversation. Little silences followed nervous rushes of inane questions. I felt almost sorry for them both.

'Silly of me, I know,' Mrs Settrington said as she took her drink from me, 'but I did expect you to look more like your mother.'

'And isn't it a shame I don't,' he answered, taking his wine without looking at me (but he must have known I was there, he put his hand in exactly the right place to receive the glass). They both laughed, but I sensed embarrassment in Mrs Settrington and bitterness in Seth. Perhaps I read too much into people, but I have so little time in which to form my impressions.

'Well, your mother was certainly the great beauty of our day.'

'I am sure everyone was very surprised when she married my father.'

'She could have married anybody so we knew it must be love.' I could not busy myself on the edges of that small room any longer and left, smiling to myself at Mrs Settrington's lack of tact. What could have been wrong with Seth's father, apart from the fact that he looked like Seth?

Amanda was the next to arrive, just as I was bringing the yellow roses up to the sitting-room. I wish people would not bring flowers to dinner. The last thing you want to do when you are cooking and trying to juggle everything is to find a vase. Send them the next day, when they cheer you up during the clearing up. (On the other hand, new vases of flowers do give me an excuse to make an appearance in the sitting-room.)

'Am I last?' asked Amanda.

'No, only Mrs Settrington's godson is here.'

'And?'

Aren't we pally these days? Of course I knew exactly what

she meant. 'Not a chance,' I said, grinning. 'At least I'd be very surprised.'

'Oh Lord, I might as well go straight home then. I don't feel like this at all.'

I took her coat. 'Go on, I could be entirely wrong. Miss Quince is here, Mrs Settrington.' It was the first time I have ever referred to her as Miss Quince, and I heard Amanda give a surprised snort of laughter as she followed me into the room.

'Amanda, how lovely to see you.' (Why did Mrs Settrington sound so surprised, she had invited the girl after all. Maybe she was just relieved, conversation had not eased between herself and her godson.) 'This is my godson, Seth Hardwicke, whom I have not seen for years,' (was she trying to excuse him?) 'Seth, this is my niece, or I suppose I should say great-niece, Amanda Quince. Amanda, a drink?'

Amanda turned her back on her aunt and faced me. 'I would love a glass of wine, please, Cindy, white if there is some.' Her tone was level but her eyes were rolling around in her head like a mad cow's and I was finding it hard not to laugh. When she turned back to Seth, though, she was all courteous interest. 'So, Seth, Aunt Patricia tells me you've been working abroad.'

Unhappiness certainly improves Amanda's manners.

By the time all the guests had arrived Mrs Settrington was halfway to being pickled. She had had at least two gins and tonics before I arrived (I found a dirty glass in the kitchen and a half-empty one in her bedroom). Mr Nesbit arrived at a quarter past eight, but the Allbright-Markhams did not knock at the door until ten to nine, by which time I was in a quiet panic about the leg of lamb which was shrivelling up before my eyes.

I led the Allbright-Markhams into the sitting-room. He, like Randal Blake, is a barrister, and you can see they come from the same mould. Both wear beautiful but conservative suits and bright, pretty ties. Both are conventionally very good looking and Mr Allbright-Markham also has that air of being sure that everyone will be pleased to see him when he walks into a room. His wife looks a little stern, like those well-turned out Frenchwomen you see shopping in Knightsbridge. She was also in a smart suit, and is obviously quite vain: her legs are excellent and not at all business-like in sheer tights and high court shoes. Unfashionable maybe, but they certainly showed off her legs to their best advantage.

'I'm so sorry we're late, Mrs Settrington. I was held up at work.' She shook hands and smiled.

'Oh don't worry at all. I expect it of the young.' Her hostess answered, clutching her glass tightly.

Mrs Allbright-Markham looked a little surprised and glanced at her husband for support.

'I wish we could claim that excuse,' he said, with a smile as self-consciously charming as Mr Blake's. 'No, poor Melinda was kept unconscionably late sorting out a young girl's problem. She was caught between being rude to you and being hard-hearted to the employee. Melinda is the Personnel Director of a large city law firm,' he explained to the company at large. 'Sometimes I think she is used as an agony aunt more than anything. Please, Mrs Settrington, accept our apologies.'

Mrs Settrington nodded, mollified in spite of her irritation. I saw her look from Mr Allbright-Markham to Seth and back again. It was not hard to see how she wished her godson had been more like this man. Then she pulled herself together. 'Drinks, Cindy?' I took the orders and left Mrs Settrington making introductions. I was relieved on her behalf: Amanda had been trying valiantly but her glances at me as I went in and out told me that there was no point of contact between her and Seth. Mr Nesbit and his sister had been bickering in low voices about his clothes: she had practically ordered him to take off his cravat and he had flatly refused. The newcomers may have arrived late, but at least they were prepared to sing for their supper.

Everything seemed to improve over the salmon mousse. Mrs Allbright-Markham's tense face relaxed a little (I wondered if the real reason for their lateness was an argument before they left home) and her husband appeared to charm everyone easily. He told long stories in a slightly theatrical way, stories which made everyone else roar with laughter but which I never heard enough of to understand. It is horrible looking at a roomful of red, roaring mouths and feeling left out. You do not know how to arrange your features – what is appropriate? And it does not matter really as no one is interested in your expression or even knows you are there.

They were all drinking fast except for Seth: two bottles of white wine were drunk with the first course, and I opened the third red one as they began the apple tart.

I served out the tart and tried to gauge who was liking whom. Mrs Settrington was clearly disliking everyone, including Seth. She was not really joining in the conversation, just occasionally interjecting nasty little remarks in a reasonable voice.

By the time they went back upstairs for coffee it was clear to me that Mrs Settrington was more than a little drunk. She had to hold on to the banister and haul herself up the stairs, then bumped into the table lamp in the hall and nearly sent it flying. Reaching the living-room she sank ungracefully but thankfully into the best armchair.

I had had enough by then, on my own account certainly but also on behalf of her guests. Mrs Settrington is a vicious old bitch with no manners, I thought as I made the coffee and cleared away the last course. It is no good thinking you are better than other people and then being so graceless. She cannot control other people, although I suppose she is too old now to accept that painful fact. I slammed my way around the kitchen in double-quick time. I wanted to get that coffee up to the guests as soon as possible so that they could decently leave. Those of her guests who were not under attack must be bored and faintly embarrassed by her antics.

Usually I take the coffee pot and cups upstairs for Mrs Settrington to serve, but this time I poured the coffee out before carrying the cups up on a tray. There was no point in allowing the drunken old bird to pour scalding coffee all over herself.

'Cindy, you know I like to pour it myself,' she said crossly when she saw what I had done, although she was slumped back in her chair and looked as though she would have difficulty in sitting up straight, let alone handling a pot and cup and saucer.

I murmured some sort of apology, and as I handed Amanda her cup she gave me a small nod and smile. 'Oh, well, Aunt Patricia, it saves you the bother,' she said.

'And makes the coffee cold,' her aunt snapped back.

'So we can drink it all the more quickly,' answered Amanda.

This was beginning to sound like Red Riding Hood and the wolf. I went back downstairs, thinking there was no more mileage to be gained from this party.

I was wrong. I finished clearing up in the kitchen and rang for the taxi, then I went upstairs to the sitting room to tell Mrs Settrington that I was on my way. The last of the guests had gone and she was slouched in her sofa, staring bleakly at the fire.

'Have a cup of coffee with me while you wait for the taxi,' she suggested, which was a surprise in itself. She occasionally has a coffee with me during the day, but never after one of her dinners. I did not want to at all, but there was no reason not to, so I fetched myself a cup from downstairs, praying the taxi would soon arrive.

'I suppose it went all right,' Mrs Settrington said as I sat down opposite her on the upright velvet chair that her grandfather had used at some coronation. 'At any rate I've done my duty to the Allbright-Markhams. It's all very well having *jobs* and being *important* but I can't see that's any excuse for having no manners. Pour me a whisky, there's a good girl.'

I was sure I should not: she was slurring dreadfully and her eyes were barely focusing but I knew My Place was to do as I was told. I poured it weak with plenty of soda while she rambled on.

'Still, it is always worth knowing a barrister. They keep the conversation going when all else fails. And one never knows when one's going to need a good legal brain.'

Finally she stopped and I wondered if she had fallen asleep, but she was staring at the fire again, brooding.

'Everyone seemed to be laughing a lot,' I said to fill the gap. (Where, oh where was my taxi?)

'All my life I've been surrounded by them, you know,' she said quietly, almost as though she were talking to herself. I had no idea what she meant, did not know what to say. I looked at her, but she seemed to have forgotten me. 'I suppose it's to be expected Abroad. They were refugees from decent society, had to take their pleasures where they could. I had to learn to put up with it. It was that or no social life at all. And everyone behaved differently, the sun I suppose. Drunkenness, adultery, I've seen it all and then they come home and butter wouldn't melt . . .' Was she raving? Hallucinating? Should I suggest she go to bed? I suppose that would have been kind, but I could not. She was slurring so much I could hardly understand her, but I was fascinated. I felt sure that out of the wanderings would come something seriously interesting, so I sat very still and waited.

Anyway, I doubt I would have succeeded in persuading her into bed.

'It's a bit too much, now, though. We're in England for heaven's sake. There's no excuse. Although Hong Kong I suppose . . .'

She tailed off again while I struggled to make sense of it all.

'Perhaps if I had seen more of him when he was a child, but that wouldn't have done either, not at all.' She shuddered. 'I suppose I should be charitable. His mother sent his father packing, very wise in one sense, but it meant he never had a father figure. And she was dreadful, little better than a tart by all accounts. I can't think what I ever saw in her, but friends do change, there's no shame in that . . . no, I'm not to be blamed. . . .' She slurped at the whisky, missing her mouth slightly. Some dribbled down her chin and spotted the front of her dress, but she did not seem to notice. I finished my coffee, watched her with interest, waited for more.

'I did want to do the right thing by Amanda, though, I don't want her to end up like Gloria, forcing herself into marriage with a nasty little—'

Finally. The doorbell rang and Mrs Settrington jumped, looked about her, looked at me in surprise, came to herself.

'You still here, dear? Well, off you go, there's a good girl. I'm a little tired now. Thank you for your help.'

She made no move to stand. I think she realised she would find it hard and did not want to give herself away. It was not until I was in the taxi, trying to make sense of all that she had said, that I realised that she might have been tired and drunk enough not to realise she was speaking aloud.

If she does realise, next Monday will be embarrassing. If not, it might be rather interesting.

*   *   *

The next morning Mr Nesbit was not looking well. 'It's not the wine that disagrees with me,' he said, sipping an Alka-Seltzer, 'so much as the malice.' I kept my face blank. 'I probably should not say so to you, but my sister can be a little cruel. When I think of the dear boy's face while she was talking about his mother . . . I mean, no one should have to hear people talking about their mothers like that . . . she would not like it. Actually she would probably not mind . . .' I stood with my back to him, squeezing the oranges he needed 'to lift me up a little, dear. It *was* a late night and I'm feeling the tiniest bit fragile.'

'I think Mrs Settrington was feeling tired,' I said evenly. 'And the Allbright-Markhams did keep you all waiting.'

'I know, the kind of excuse Father always used. Blind drunk by the time we'd sat down to dinner and always somebody else's fault. Not that Mother would let him sit down in that condition, and quite right too. She said it was an insult to her. To be fair, Patricia's not in Father's league, or anywhere near. No, Patricia could never come first in any competition, always a close run second, little Patsy.' He pressed fingers which trembled to his eyelids.

I handed him the orange juice and sat at the table opposite him. He looked a hundred years old, sad and defeated. I almost felt sorry for him. 'Are you all right? Can I get you anything else or shall I start cleaning?'

He shook his head, his fingers still at his eyeballs, and I did not know what he meant. I began to move but then he began talking again. 'She shouldn't have asked me, you know. I can see why she did. She hoped Seth would put me in my place. Make me realise all the things I had missed.'

'I think she just wanted to introduce him to some people,' I suggested. 'Amanda—'

'Of course that's what she *said*.' He flashed me a scornful look. 'It might even have been what she thought she thought. I was friends with Seth's mother, you see. People thought we would marry, but I knew we never would and I think – I'm sure – she knew it too. We were friends, just friends.' His hand was shaking as he lifted the glass to his lips. I wondered who his friends are now. I never see them. I suppose they exist.

'But it all backfired, of course. Seth is the kind of man she hates, is almost frightened of. She sees them as a threat.' I remembered the drunken maundering of the night before and knew he was right. 'She has good reason to, I suppose.' He smiled and for the first time I saw some of his sister's malice on his face. 'And so she had to take it out on him, the dear boy. A guest. Her godson. Dear boy, he does not deserve it.' How could he know, I asked myself. He knew no more of Seth than did Mrs Settrington. How could that harmless, ugly little man have provoked two such differing, yet strong reactions in the course of one evening?

'We sat together after dinner. Patricia had done something odd with the furniture. I don't know how it happened, but we found ourselves on our own at the back end of the room.' The corner planned for Amanda and Seth. Poor Mrs Settrington. It must have half-killed her. 'He hasn't had a good time. His father left home when he was a baby and he only saw him two or three times a year. Gloria seems to have led a rackety enough life since, although the boy was loyal, touchingly loyal. The family lost the money, I don't know how, when he was ten. But he's done well for himself, the clever boy. Works hard by the sound of it.'

Why was he telling me all this? Watching him fingering his glass, calmer now than he had been, I remembered Mrs Settrington the night before and wondered if he knew I was there. It is interesting, not existing. They do not seem to mind what They tell you. I think it is a little like a child's attitude to a teacher: outside the classroom the teacher ceases to have a life. The idea of a teacher's family or home is treated as a comic impossibility by most children. The teacher exists in a vacuum created by the child's need. As I do to Them.

'I'll have to make it up to him,' Mr Nesbit said, and brightened at the thought. 'I'm sure he really wants to meet young people, his own age, but I would like to show him that not all of my family is rude. I shall ask him here for dinner, or perhaps lunch would be more appropriate. Although he works, doesn't he, perhaps he wouldn't have time . . .' The thought seemed to discourage him, then he stood, finished his juice at a gulp and handed the glass to me to wash up. 'Never mind, I'll ask the boy to dinner. Maybe I'll take him out, that would be easier. There's the Italian down the road or maybe the Indian. Or Jeals of course, that's very English, fish and chips, perhaps he would like that. But I would not. I can't bear the smell of their frying, something should be done about it. Well, what are you waiting for, dear? Off you go, work to be done. I've bought a new cow, she's in the cabinet in the study. Not one of my finest pieces, but I could not resist her crumpled horn. Like the nursery rhyme, don't you know. See if you can't think of a name for her, but mind you're gentle. I'm sure the boy would be interested in my collection, he has an artistic air. And I'll see if I can find some old pictures of his mother, I'm sure I've an album somewhere . . . That's the ticket, have the boy here . . .'

I gathered up my dusters and polish from the cupboard. I have been stupid, haven't I? Despite the pottery and the drapes and the fey tone and the peacock clothing I somehow had never realised that Mr Nesbit is not just *like* an old queen, he *is* one. I suppose I have never known anyone like him before, so all his mannerisms I took as eccentricity. Seth I had spotted a mile off, maybe because he is closer to my age. It may be odd, but I have no gay friends. Not close friends. The London Lighthouse is just down the road, and we get quite a few lads who turn up in the Percy – Earls Court types with little moustaches and leather chaps over their jeans and huge buckled belts. Seth was being respectable at Mrs Settrington's, but I think he may be one of those. Mr Nesbit, though, is something else.

It took Seth to make the scales fall from my eyes. Why had it never occurred to me to ask who the Earls Court types go to bed with? Who they are hanging around for outside the pubs up and down the Earls Court Road? Each other, perhaps. But not just each other. Poor, lonely, respectable Mr Nesbit has been waiting for someone to come into his life. Like all of us I suppose. But not a respectable widow or a gay divorcée. Gay divorcé more like.

And now he has seen that little runt who was meant to be the man of Amanda's dreams and he has fallen for him. And it is perfect, it makes his life so tidy. He could never be more than a friend to Seth's mother. I wonder if he wanted to be in love with her, if he tried and tried to want her and love her but failed. So she went off to America and married this unsatisfactory type who all her friends loathed (but then she had not succeeded with the one they chose for her, had they, so why not try something different?) and had a little son. A boy (a 'dear boy') who did not look like her but was half her. And then she sent him back across the ocean to her old friends the Nesbits. I wonder if she is still alive. I wonder if she knows about Mr Nesbit. About Seth. She must be a very understanding woman.

Am I letting my imagination run away with me? Am I?

Looking at Mr Nesbit's busy, happy face as he rummaged in a cupboard looking for his old photograph albums I decided that no, I was probably not imagining too much. I think I am more or less right.

I wonder how Seth will take it.

I wonder how Mrs Settrington will take it.

I wonder what Amanda will think.

8

I do not think Mrs Settrington remembered anything about the end of Wednesday night. She would have been embarrassed, or awkward, or something. She was just as usual, though. She asked me if she had paid me for the evening or not (she had not) but seemed to think it normal that she did not know. Perhaps she is always drunk at bedtime. Perfectly possible, I suppose.

'I think the evening went rather well,' she said over our cup of coffee at the end of Monday morning. 'Too dull how none of the young knows how to play cards, but otherwise . . . Charming man, Ralph Allbright-Markham. Wife a bit tiresome, but that's career women for you. Smart with no heart.'

'Do they have children?' I asked, more for something to say than out of any interest.

'No. Never trust a marriage with no children,' she said. Startled, I looked at her and she, catching my look, flushed that ugly hard red, realising what she had said.

'Although there may be a very good reason,' she added. 'Have a biscuit?' I was not stupid enough to be fooled by that, but I dropped my gaze and took a café noir and reminded myself to brood about her comment later.

'And my godson, Mr Hardwicke, is a charming young man.' How can someone change their tune so radically? Looking at her, I could almost believe she meant what she said. Anyone else, who had not heard her confused, bitter nonsensical outpourings, would have.

'I wonder if he has called Amanda yet.' She gave me that fishy, sidelong look that she gives when she is hoping for some gossip. But, you see, I Know My Place.

I stirred my coffee thoughtfully and smiled. 'That would be nice, wouldn't it?' I decided to play the fool. 'Wouldn't it be romantic – your great-niece and your godson. Think what fun the wedding would be – you'd know everyone.'

She was not entirely fooled. 'Don't be silly, dear. They've only met once. It would be nice, though, if they were friends. Just friends.' (Where have I heard that recently?) 'Anyway, there's plenty of time for Seth. No reason for him to make up his mind for a while.'

I stood and began clearing away the coffee things. 'I wonder if he's called her though.' She was going around in circles.

'Goodbye, then, Mrs Settrington. I'll see you on Wednesday.'

Goaded into desperation, she handed over my money and then asked, 'Do you know if he has? Has Amanda mentioned him?'

Now it was my turn to feel driven. 'I really don't know, Mrs Settrington. I don't go to Amanda's until Tuesday, and I doubt whether she would confide in me anyway.' That last bit was no longer true, but I was not going to give anything away. Then, prompted by some unknown malice (perhaps it is catching) I said, 'Mr Nesbit has, though. He seemed quite taken with Mr Hardwicke. Quite concerned about his social life, he was. 'Bye then. Must go.'

I felt a little guilty as I walked down Farmer Street. Her face had looked so stricken. But only a little.

I met Nelly as planned, standing outside the Notting Hill Gate tube station. I was absurdly nervous, as nervous as I used to be when a teenager, waiting to meet a new boyfriend. I had even found it hard to decide what to wear. I did not want to look as though I were making too much of an effort, but neither did I want to look scruffy. Apart from anything else, I did not know what we would end up doing. We could take one look at each other and decide mulling over the past over a half of lager would be enough, or we could end up dancing the night away at a Soho nightclub.

Of course we did something in between. I was at the station first, and spotted Nelly as she walked up the stairs towards me. I think I would have recognised her even if I had not been expecting to see her: her clothes were smarter, her hair slightly blonder, but the big hooked nose and bouncing stride seemed unaltered with the years. For a moment I wondered if I could just turn and leave. I felt too shy to step forward, too shy to say her name. Then she caught sight of me, looked more closely, hesitated only a second and then 'Cindy! My God, you look *exactly* the same! I thought children were meant to be aging!' and she sprinted up the last few steps and flung her arms around me and hugged me. She always was effusive.

I stepped out of the hug and looked at her. 'Nelly. I can't say you've changed much either. Except for your name. Should I call you Sarah now?'

She laughed. 'God, no. But I couldn't start a career with a name like Nelly Trunk, now could I? I like having two names, anyway. When I hear "Nelly" I know I'm with friends, "Sarah" and I'm in grown-up mode.' She always did talk a lot, but I sensed that she was nervous too and had probably had as many second thoughts about this meeting as I had. The realisation reassured me, made me feel more confident.

'So, what would you like to do?' I put the onus of decision on to her.

'A drink! It's obvious we must have a drink!' She was right of course. There was no point in our standing in the street feeling awkward.

I do not drink in Notting Hill much, but I had scouted around a little in the days before our date. I did not know what Nelly had become, but was pretty sure the Percy would not be her kind of pub. It is fine for a local, but not really the sort of pub you go out of your way to visit. And Torquay is a long way away. So I took her to the Uxbridge Arms, a dark pub in Uxbridge Street, full of young men in suits and pretty blondes with jobs rather than careers. Estate agents mostly, I always imagine. Nelly fitted in very well. Feeling I was the host, I bought the first round and was relieved to see she still drinks beer. We sat at a small round table wondering what to say. Good old Nelly managed to break the silence.

'So where do we begin? Cindy, it's criminal. To think what good friends we were, all the things we used to do together – and now we're groping around for something to say!'

Sometimes it helps to say the obvious. Nelly made me smile. 'It's been a long time.'

'Of course it has – seven years? Something like that. But I blame you. You totally disappeared. Turned your back on the lot of us.'

'I thought it better.'

'Better! Cindy, I was your *friend*. You don't do that to your friends.'

Do you know, it had never occurred to me to ask myself what they thought, whether they missed me. And when I saw that, even after all these years, Nelly actually looked hurt at my silence, I was amazed.

'Did you really mind? I mean, you all had your lives to get on with. And so did I, but it was so different. I didn't think you'd be interested.'

'So why did I ring you all those times? You never rang me back, never answered my letters. Of course I got on with my own life, we all did. So did you. But don't say I didn't try. And I know I wasn't the only one. We gave up after a while. You left us with no choice.'

I stared at her. The beer was becoming warm in my hand but I could not make myself put it on the table, or even drink it. I was frozen at the knowledge of my own selfishness.

'Sorry.' I said at last. 'I'm sorry, Nelly, I didn't think.'

She stopped looking anguished and laughed. 'We always had that in common, Cindy. Neither of us ever thinks. At least not about what we are doing. The difference is that I never think noisily, and you never think quietly. But it comes to the same thing in the end. Anyway, it doesn't matter now. Water under the bridge et cetera. I didn't meet you to give you a hard time about the past. You were under a lot of strain, pressure, whatever. I'm sure you did what you thought best.'

There was another silence. I was not doing my share. 'So what did you come for?' It did not come out as I had intended, but Nelly seemed to understand.

'I was organising the reunion, and I went down the list and you know I almost did not bother to send the letter to you. But, as I said, I have wondered about you a lot over the years and I thought no harm would be done. To be honest I knew that if I did not send it to you it would be out of pettiness, hurt feelings because you disappeared. You know, for ages after you left I still half-expected to get a call or a letter asking me to be godmother to the baby. Silly, really.'

I felt tears prick my eyes. How could I have been so foolish? Some sense of false pride or self-preservation had made me throw away my friends, good friends like Nelly, and left me what in exchange? The chilly bickering that passed for family life. And Tamsin. She was worth everything, but perhaps I could have had both after all. What a waste.

'She's never been christened.' I managed to smile. 'There didn't seem to be much point. So perhaps you could still be her godmother.' Maybe I have left it too late. This friendship, the christening . . .

'Oh.' Nelly was probably thinking the same. 'Anyway,' she went on, 'I was so pleased you rang, sorry you didn't make it to the reunion, but *so* pleased you rang. Your voice sounded exactly the same.'

'So did yours. Funny that, like a smell.'

'Thank you very much!'

'No, you know what I mean. You walk along a street and suddenly smell something – a shrub, or some food cooking, or a brand of tobacco, anything – and it takes you back in an instant to a whole different time and place. It's so strong you could be there. And sometimes it's to a memory of a place or incident that you did not even know you remembered. You must know what I mean, Nelly.'

She seemed doubtful. 'I'm not sure. I suppose I do – but with me it's music, not smells. I had it the other day. I was walking past some house and heard an old Cat Stevens song (well, it would have to be old, wouldn't it? The poor love's been blighted by a beard for aeons) – *Wild World*. I hadn't heard it for years. All at once I was driving in the dark down a winding road with an Italian boy I was expecting to be kissed by. It must have been ten, twelve years ago. Extraordinary. I couldn't breathe, I was so overcome. I had to stop and lean against a wall until the record stopped.'

'And did he?'

'What?'

'Kiss you.'

She laughed. 'And how! Gosh, he was good looking. Small, though. Still, you can't have everything. I have it with taste, too. I still can't eat Kentucky Chicken Sandwiches because I was eating one when my first ever boyfriend told me he was dumping me.'

'I was eating a prawn sandwich when I suddenly realised I was two weeks late and might be pregnant. I felt sick with fear, and they've made me feel sick ever since.'

'Let me get another drink. Same again?'

While she was at the bar being jostled by pin-striped oafs I realised that at last we had begun talking. Not making conversation, but talking. I felt a tremendous sense of relief. It was going to be all right.

She came back with two more beers and some crisps. 'I hope you're not planning to rush off. I'm hoping to make a night of it. I'm staying with some friends in Shepherd's Bush and they've given me a key so I can be like a naughty teenager and sneak in whenever I like. They've got a baby so they're always tired – honestly, it's never worth seeing them after about three in the afternoon – and they'll be in bed by ten. Let me tell you about the reunion.'

She did. An evening in Exeter, a meal, a nightclub, about half of our year turned up. It sounded quite fun, maybe if I had more confidence I might have enjoyed it. She ran through a list of half-forgotten names. Some were married, some living with partners, a couple had new babies. As I had guessed, all the ones who turned up had proper jobs (except for the two mothers who had husbands with proper jobs). On the other hand, none seemed roaringly successful. I had been too frightened. No one else was a Captain of Industry either.

From talk of those at the reunion, we turned to others from Reading and then I asked the question which I had been waiting to ask for hours. 'And Pete? Do you ever see him?'

She answered quickly. 'No.'

'But? You hear of him?'

'No, we were never particular friends,' she said after a while.

'No, I know.'

'After you left, we saw a lot more of each other.' She spoke in a rush now. She seemed more embarrassed though. 'You won't understand, and you mustn't think I'm getting at you – I've said my bit on that subject, but it was very odd, almost as though you had died.'

'He wanted Tamsin to die,' I said bitterly.

'Oh, come on now. He didn't want to bring her up, but he felt responsible for you. He didn't want you to have to give up university. He felt very guilty about that, that it was all his fault.'

'It wasn't.' I had been through this so many times, and I honestly knew that I did not blame him one bit for the conception, or even the unwillingness to become a father.

'You disappeared. We were the two people closest to you and although we had not been friends before, your leaving drew us together. We went through all the psycho-babble grieving stages – guilt, anger, grief – together.'

'I was not dead.' I was perhaps too fierce.

'But you could have been. You could have died in childbirth, the baby could have died for all we knew.'

'I didn't know you cared.'

'You didn't want to know. You could at the very least have sent one of us a postcard to tell us that you were all right, that the baby was a girl and was called Tamsin and weighed whatever.'

'Seven pounds one.' It is funny how the weight of a baby is forever engraved on a mother's memory.

'Oh, a good size for a first.'

And then we looked at each other and I laughed at Nelly sounding like a seasoned Auntie and she laughed with me and we had another whisky (we had long given up on the beer) and decided we had better eat or we would feel really ill the next morning.

We chose Indian and went to the one further down the road, the Malabar, which because Mr Nesbit knew of it I assumed was good. It was, but expensive, and frankly we had drunk enough to make us unappreciative of the finer arts of Indian cooking. Everything came in sizzling little cast iron pans which made us giggle – by then everything made us giggle

– and we were given disapproving looks by the middle-aged, middle-class, high-income couples who were there looking for marriage partners.

I told her about myself. About the years in between. By then I was bold enough not to care what she thought. Or maybe I did care, and realised that this friendship had no chance of being successfully resuscitated if I were not frank. Nelly was surprised, but she did not attempt to disguise that, which pleased me. She said she admired me and took an interest in the people whose houses I clean. I exaggerated a little, made them all sound more interesting, but she laughed at the right moments and made the right comments.

'Just think of the trouble you could cause,' she said. 'They all seem to know each other one way or another. You could tell old Mrs Whatsername all sorts of things about her niece and she'd probably believe you. In fact, play your cards right and you could probably make her leave everything to you.'

'I don't need to invent things about Amanda,' I said. I've only to tell Mrs Settrington a few truths about her brother and the fur would fly.' I laughed but I was feeling a little uncomfortable. After all, I had almost told Mrs Settrington about Mr Nesbit's crush on Seth; I had certainly dropped a hefty enough hint. That had not been very kind of me. 'Oh, they're all right really.' I said. 'My friend Liz says I'm too involved with them all, but some are almost friends. The teacher's nice, if shy. When I started I thought I was going to be some sort of old-fashioned upstairs-downstairs type. I practically thought I was going to have to say Miss Quince and wear a mob-cap.'

'Miss Quince? Not Amanda? Amanda Quince?' Nelly looked amazed.

'Yes. Amanda. Amanda Quince. Do you know her?'

'*Cindy*! Of course I do. So do you.'

'I know I do. What are you on about?' Maybe all the drink was finally getting to me. I did not know what she was talking about.

'No, I mean before. She was at university with us. Amanda Quince. Red-headed, quite pretty, a couple of years above us. She did languages, Spanish I think, maybe French. She was in her fourth year when we were in our first. You *must* remember her.'

I did not, of course I did not, but I did remember how familiar she had seemed when I first met her, and how that half-forgotten familiarity had blurred with time.

'How did you know her? I've no memory of her at university at all.'

'She acted a lot, she was one of the star players on the university drama scene. She was Cordelia in the *Lear* that Rich Helgut put on in our first year, and she was in *The Maids* – you remember, that dreary lesbian play – with me. She was one of the maids and I was Madame, much the least interesting part. Anyway you must remember because you did the props for it.'

'Of course.' And now I did. *The Maids*. I had only been involved on the periphery but I had been to some rehearsals and the first night of the show. The tall, laughing redhead who flapped her hands about and kept forgetting her lines . . . I had just started going out with Pete at the time so had not done much socialising with the cast. But I did remember now. 'You and her and some other girl . . .'

'Minny Shaker. That's right. Just the three of us. Something about mimosa. Well, never mind. Amanda was going to be an actress, everyone thought she would make it . . . but I never thought she was that good. Very pretty, but more actressy off the stage than a good actress on it, if you know what I mean.'

'She was quite good on the night, then got very drunk afterwards,' I remembered.

'That's right. And was so hungover the next day we thought she wouldn't make it that evening.'

'But she did.'

'Yes, and was much better and threw up in the wings. You *do*. You remember!'

I did not know what I was going to do now I knew. Did it matter? I did not want to talk about it any more. Suddenly I had to be on my own.

'Crikey, Nelly, look at the time. I must get back. I've got to get up in the morning. Besides which I'm slaughtered. I couldn't handle anything more.'

Silence fell as the bill came, and we sorted out the money. I was thinking about Amanda, and also wondering what would happen next with Nelly and me. I had had a wonderful evening

– the best for a very long time – but felt shy again. Maybe we should leave it there.

We walked round the corner to Notting Hill Gate and I waited with Nelly for a taxi. I suppose she assumed I would take the next one, but it was a fine night and I thought the walk home might clear my head. I wished the taxi would come soon, there was no longer anything to say.

When one arrived, Nelly hugged me warmly. 'It's been great. Really brilliant,' she said. 'Let's do it again. I'll ring you when I'm next coming to London. I come up quite often.'

'I don't have a telephone,' I said. She had not asked for the number, so I doubted she meant it anyway.

'Oh.' She paused, one foot in the cab, looking at me thoughtfully.

'I know! Come down to Torquay with Tamsin. I'd love it, go on . . .'

I was at a loss. She seemed to mean it but . . .

'Look, it's nearly Christmas now, so let's leave it until after. Say the last weekend in January. The sea's not so good for Tamsin at this time of year, but you can come again in the summer. Please.'

'Are you getting in, love?' a surly voice said from the front of the cab. 'Only I'd like to start running the meter if you're gonna keep me here all night.'

'Oh, sorry, sorry, yes,' and she hopped in and pulled down the window. 'Right then, the last weekend in January. You can ring me if there's any problem. It was a lovely evening. See you then. Frithville Gardens, please,' and she waved and shut the window and leant back in her seat and was gone.

There is still no invitation in Jane's flat for the Blakes' party. I thought that perhaps she does not keep them on the mantelpiece like the others, so had a bit of a nose around. It was not by her bed – I checked in the book on the bedside table, *Tales from Heroditus*, to see if it was being used as a bookmark, but there was only a postcard from someone called Mary having a wonderful time in Cornwall. Neither was it among the papers on her desk, nor in the toast rack on the kitchen shelf. I could not think of anywhere else where people might keep invitations. then I decided that maybe she just does not keep invitations at all, she is not after all one for much clutter, but there was nothing in any of the bins that I could see (of course I did not look too closely into the one in the kitchen, there are limits). I tried to find a diary on her desk, but there does not seem to be one. She must carry it about in her bag.

Or maybe she does so little that she does not need one. I do not. Everything in life is so regular – I clean for so-and-so on such-and-such a day, week in, week out, Tamsin has Brownies on Tuesday, if Liz and I go out it is usually on Friday. Tick-tock, tick-tock, on it goes.

Lynda has a massive desk diary which she keeps losing in the kitchen and which has nothing much in it anyway. Randal's diary is even bigger but is at least full of cryptic messages which I suppose mean something to him. Amanda is of course of the Filofax generation, as is Fergus. I think Mr Nesbit works blind, and Mrs Settrington has one of those tiny dainty ones which are fine until you actually need to write anything down.

So anyway it looked as though Lynda had not asked her childhood friend to her wretched party. Poor Jane needs a social life, and it would not hurt Lynda to ask her. I bet she would be a cheap guest: I know her type, one glass of wine and they go all giggly. There were a few like that at Reading. Lynda need only smile, say hello to her, introduce her to one person then ignore her for the rest of the evening. Randal need not even do that.

When I picked Tamsin up from school, it was Jane's turn for gate duty. She seems to be getting a little less shy with me now. She smiled and asked me how I was enjoying the Wilkie Collins.

'I'm sorry, I haven't quite finished it, and I took another book,' I said, on the defensive.

'That doesn't matter a bit – are you enjoying *The Woman in White*?' she persisted.

'Loving it. Too much. I can't believe it's doing me any good.' I said, and then felt myself blush at my words.

She looked at me closely. 'Is that why you are reading? To improve yourself?'

I waved my hands around feebly, and reminded myself of

Amanda. 'No. Well, I don't know. You don't want to hear the story of my life.'

She smiled. 'I don't know, it might be rather interesting. Anyway, I always think enjoying yourself is more important than improving yourself, don't you?'

It depends where you come from, I wanted to say. And don't patronise me, anyway. But I could see she did not want to talk down to me, that she was trying to make me feel at ease.

'What did you take today?' she asked.

I hope I did not sound as sulky as I felt. 'Another Collins. *The Moonstone.*'

'Oh, *yes*, well you'll love it. I expect you've noticed how many of his books I have. My tutor used to look down his nose and dismiss them, but I love him. They really involve you, don't they? And isn't that what it's all about? Who cares about all those clever people who are in some way *important* – you know, Martin Amis, Will Self – who are they talking to except themselves?'

Well, no, I had never heard of them, but her face was alight and excited and totally different and I could suddenly see why she is a good teacher. Her enthusiasm attracted me, but it also embarrassed me.

'Um – Lynda sent her love to you,' I lied. I was thinking of the party and whether or not Jane had been invited.

'Oh? I haven't seen her for ages,' Jane said sadly. 'I must give her a ring and make some sort of plan. Maybe a Sunday lunch.' I thought of Jane's dingy basement and Lynda's lovely airy house and knew it should be the other way around. I also realised that this confirmed my suspicions: Jane was not invited.

'Cindy. I wonder – if you'd like to, why don't you bring Tamsin round for Sunday lunch? This weekend? I would really like it . . .' She tailed off. Was she just being nice to me? I do not think so. I think in her way she is lonely. She is busy all day, but where are her friends? She cannot have many if she thinks inviting me will cheer her up.

'Oh Mum, yes please,' said Tamsin. I had not realised she was listening, but of course she was. She is at that age.

'I'm not sure. I thought we might go to Gran's,' I lied.

Jane backed off immediately. 'Oh well, in that case, maybe some other time.'

'*Mum*. We can go to Gran's any time. Please.' Tamsin begged.

I wavered. And then I saw that not only did Tamsin want to go, but Jane was feeling rebuffed. She had asked me in total friendship and I had turned her down. Who am I to turn away friendship when it is offered? Do I have so many friends that I can afford to ignore an outstretched hand?

'I would love to. Thank you.'

'Well, you know the way. See you at half-past twelve. Is that all right?'

It would have to be now. What am I letting myself into, I wondered. There's no fool like a lonely fool.

It was not my fault. I did it for all the right reasons, but I know I still should not have. It is one thing stirring things up between Mrs Settrington and her brother, but that is not actually interfering, not in the way I did today. I partly blame Nelly, although in my heart I know that is unfair.

I was at the Blakes'. Thank heavens there is only one week left till the blessed party. I think I would give in my notice if it were much further away, I am being driven to distraction by discussions of every detail. It is only a drinks party, after all. How much planning can a few glasses of wine and a half-dozen canapés take, I ask you? I think Randal might hand in his notice too, come to that. He is becoming more snide and vicious every time I see him. He is like Mrs Settrington when she is drunk – and that is him sober. I hope he does not drink too much at his party, I do not think I am brave enough to stand up to him. So far all the anger is directed at Lynda.

Lynda had a copy of a self-help book jammed into the drawer of her bedside table. The usual pristine copies of fat paperbacks were stacked up on top of the table, so I was curious to see which book she had made an attempt to hide. Pornography? The *Karma Sutra*? It was called *Infertility and How to Cope* by some man with a lot of letters after his name. *Infertility*? Why should she suspect she is infertile? She has not been married that long, only about two years, is not old . . . She is an hysteric, I decided, and knew I should have to watch my step with her that day.

I know now that the best way to deal with her is to flatter her about her house. 'It couldn't look nicer, now the building work is finished upstairs,' I said. 'I can't imagine a single thing which would make this house more perfect.'

'Oh, don't say perfect,' Lyndy said, handing me a cup of coffee. 'Perfection makes me nervous. I'd have to spoil something or I would feel I was tempting fate to do the spoiling for me.'

'I never had you down as the superstitious type,' I said.

'I think it's Muslim, the fear of perfection.'

'I never had you down as Muslim either.' She did not even smile.

We sat down together at the table. She crumbled a biscuit between her fingers and squished the pieces into the grain of the wood. It would be a bore to get out.

'Do you think I am a wimp?' she asked suddenly.

'A wimp? Why?' I do not think she is a wimp but I knew I would not be able to answer convincingly so I skirted the issue. I doubt she noticed.

'Sometimes, just occasionally, I do wonder at myself. You know, two years ago I was a mover and a shaker. Well, almost. At any rate I was independent, I had a job and a secretary and people knew who I was. I was never going to be Lew Grade, I don't pretend that, but I had a place in the scheme of things. In the scheme of the television world, anyway. And I know what happens when people leave. They are missed for a while, they are rung up and bothered with questions, then they are left alone. And forgotten. New faces come, office gossip moves on.'

'Are you thinking of going back to work?'

'Oh, no. Randal wouldn't like it. He's old-fashioned, you see, that was one of the things which first drew me to him. He wasn't ashamed to be gentlemanly.'

I thought of the rude, sneering man I had seen glimpses of behind the urbane charm and wondered how hard it had been for him to keep his courtly face on for long enough to woo and win Lynda.

'We had only been going out for four months when he asked me to marry him,' she said, almost answering my unspoken question. 'It was wonderful, like something in a book, truly romantic . . .' she brightened, and I could see her going back to their courtship in her mind's eye. Then she drooped again. 'I admire you Cindy, I really do.'

'Me? Why?'

'You get on with things. You have your child and you get out and earn what you can in the way that you can.' She did not realise how angry her words made me. *Earn what I can in the way that I can!* I have become accustomed to being patronised by Mrs Settrington, but not by Lynda. And the worst part of it was that she thought she was praising me. She went on, heedless of my silent rage. 'And I sit here and wait for Randal to come home so that I can cook him a good dinner and listen to his tales of woe about the day. At least his days are never boring.'

So now she was whining. Just because she has finished the decorating and does not know how to spend her days any more now that every wall is ragged and dragged and stippled and every picture hung.

'Did he tell you to give up work when you married?'

'Of course not! He didn't even ask me to, it was entirely my own decision. I knew he would prefer it that way, of course, he'd never made any secret of his views. No, I wanted to. And what with the new house, and making that nice . . .' And the hoped-for babies, I thought. I wondered if she was going to bring them up, but she did not.

'Do you regret giving up work? You enjoyed it, didn't you?'

'Yes I did, and I met so many interesting people through it – that's how I met Randal, you know. The thing I loved about it was all the different sorts of people I met, from all walks of life. I would do the background research on the guests for the chat shows, which often involved interviewing them before they appeared on the show. And now I only meet lawyers. Endless clever lawyers.' I had never seen her look so gloomy.

I searched around for a way to cheer her up. 'But I'm sure you're very good at it, talking to them I mean. Your job must have trained you to be interested in everything.'

'It trained me to look as though I was interested in everything. There's a big difference. Now I can't even manage that. I suppose it's because I think I've got boring myself. I still have just enough grip on reality to know that other people are not going to find the colour of my walls as interesting as I do. As I did.'

I was beginning to feel sorry for her. When I thought she loved the pointlessness of her life I could afford to despise her, but if she realises how empty it is I can pity her. Next she will notice what a pig her husband is to her.

'The thing is, Randal is so good to me,' she was going on. 'He provides everything for me, everything. I feel mean being discontented. Not that I am, of course. Just a little, well, empty sometimes. I know I'm so much better off than most people. There's Fergus with Lottie having left him in the lurch, and Jane Cox having to teach a crowd of working-class children how to read, which must be impossible, it's no wonder she's a little depressing, and Amanda still looking for Mr Right. I really mustn't complain.'

I thought I would hit her. Tamsin is a very good reader indeed. She could almost read before she went to school, I made sure of that. And Liz's children also read perfectly well. Jane Cox sends them home with their heads full of amazing new information, she surprises them and entertains them and keeps them asking questions. It is amazing how she does it, but she does. She may look prim and proper but she has something about her more important and worthwhile than any number of well-decorated kitchens.

I stood up abruptly and washed my coffee mug. I still had an hour to go before I could leave the Blakes' house. I had to keep my temper.

'Do Amanda and Fergus know each other?' I asked, to divert my own thoughts as much as anything.

'I don't know. Why?'

'Oh, nothing. Just your mentioning them like that, in the same breath, as two people unhappy in love, made me wonder.'

'What – you mean Fergus and Amanda? Oh, I don't think she's his type at all.' Women never think that other women are their ex-boyfriend's 'type', even after a gap of years. Funny, that. I can think of all sorts of people who would be Pete's 'type'. Or would have been then. I wonder what he is like now. What his type is. Whether we would even recognise each other.

'Maybe Jane is then. She has not mentioned a boyfriend.' I was hell bent on revenge for both Jane's and my sake.

'Jane? She's far too earnest for him.' I thought Fergus was

quite serious, but maybe he never got as far as talking to Lynda during their affair. I wonder how long it lasted, she has never told me. I am sure he was the one to finish it, though. I think she still carries a torch for him, and she has none of that guilt which women carry around years after they have broken, or even slightly wounded, a man's heart. 'She is also not nearly dashing enough. Like most men, Fergus likes to be seen with a pretty woman on his arm.'

'Lynda, if you don't mind, I would like to clean the kitchen floor, I need to get on.' I had had more than enough of Lynda's self-pity and half-witted opinions. She may have nothing to do other than sit around talking about herself, but I am hired to clean, not be the paid companion.

I did 'get on'. I cleaned with a viciousness which is always very effective. I cleaned the kitchen so thoroughly that when I finished I realised I was only going to have time for the most cursory Hoover and tidy in the sitting-room.

Lynda had left my money on the hall table and made herself scarce by the time I came to the sitting-room. I do not know if she realised how cross she had made me, somehow I doubt it. I suppose she was not to know that Jane Cox teaches Tamsin (or have I told her? I can't remember), and maybe I should anyway take her rudeness as a compliment. She is a nice woman, would not hurt me deliberately, would be horrified if she knew she had. She must have been implicitly excluding me and mine from her stupid analysis of state schools in London. But she is also quite stupid, and probably noticed nothing.

Either way I was finding it hard to think nice thoughts about her. I plumped up her settee and the silk scatter cushions, I dusted the coffee table and laid the magazines out in pretty rows, I dusted the mantelpiece, giving only the barest look at the invitations (she had put one of her own purple ones on her own mantelpiece – does she think she is going to forget to turn up?) Then I turned my attention to the little desk by the window. A few bills, one letter to Lynda and a half-finished thank-you letter from her. And the pile of purple and white invitations. Quite a thick pile, all crisp and stiff and somehow very inviting. With a pile of envelopes beside it. A couple of invitations were in addressed envelopes, obviously some afterthoughts, or maybe some people had said they were not coming and Lynda had decided to bolster up the numbers.

The thought occurred to me and I acted upon it almost without pausing. An invitation was off the pile and down the front of my sweater in a flash. One second later, and an envelope had followed it. They felt cold and hard against my chest. A corner of the invitation stuck into my skin, quite hard, hard enough to be uncomfortable. I only hesitated after the deed was done, but by then it was too late. After all I need not go through with it, did not have to post the card. It was just an idea . . .

My bag was in the kitchen. Lynda was still not home, so it was easy to transfer the card and envelope without being caught. I was back in the sitting-room by the time I heard the front door shut.

'That's it, I'm all done. I'll put the Hoover back and I'm off.' I could not look her in the eye. I could still feel the card against my skin, for a mad moment I wondered if she had X-ray eyes and could see through my bag. I put the Hoover and duster back into their cupboard as quickly as I could and shrugged my coat on.

'I'll see you next week,' I called into the sitting-room as I passed the door.

' 'Bye.' What was she doing there? Had I left some trace of what I had done? Was she counting the invitations, for heaven's sake?

She came after me to the front door, hand outstretched. She held a sheaf of envelopes and I felt my throat close in fear.

'Cindy, I've just been out and I forgot to post these. You wouldn't do it for me, would you? Only they're invitations for the party and I've left it a bit late as it is.'

I almost refused I was in such a panic, but of course did not. 'Of course, I'll do it on my way over to Fergus,' I said.

'Thanks. I don't even have the stamps, I know it's a bore, but if you don't mind.'

I practically snatched the envelopes and handful of change from her. 'Right, lovely, goodbye.'

'And next week is the party!' she smiled.

*   *   *

I had no choice then, did I? It was as though it were meant. She had handed me invitations and asked me to post them. I felt that the extra invitation, the one burning a hole in my bag, was included in that request. Lynda would not hurt anyone's feelings, she would not want to hurt Jane's.

I walked to the post office on Notting Hill. I took the invitations out of my bag and the blank one came sweetly with the others as though it knew its place. I looked at Lynda's writing, and knew I could not fake it with any authenticity. I wrote in neat block capitals, MISS JANE COX, 33 CHESTERTON ROAD, LONDON W10. I did wonder whether it looked like a mad piece of hate mail, but I reckoned that once Jane saw the invitation she would forget to wonder about the envelope. For the same reason I wrote nothing on the card, although usually Their invitations have names scrawled at the top. I thought that however I wrote the name 'Jane' it would look odd. The envelope would be forgotten, in the bin, the invitation would lie around, the mis-written name glaring out for at least a week.

My hand trembled as I stuck the stamp on, but only slightly. I was doing no harm, I was just cheering Jane up. Lynda would not mind. If I had been slightly braver I would have dared suggest Jane, Lynda would have exclaimed at her forgetfulness, the invitation would have been sent, the end result would have been the same.

I posted the five envelopes and continued my walk to Fergus's flat. For the first time since I had been working for him I was not consumed with thoughts of him as I approached his house. I no longer felt guilty. I felt proud, powerful, totally glorious. I understood what Lynda meant when she rambled on about 'planning people'. All I wanted now was Jane to meet her knight in shining armour at this party, and I would be God-like in my power.

I felt I was Their equal. And it was good.

9

I have never known Tamsin look forward to anything more than she did to having lunch with Jane. She was as good as gold all Saturday, scared stiff that I would change my mind and refuse to go. She was up on Sunday morning early, crept out of bed without waking me up and brought me breakfast in bed. A huge bowl of corn flakes which had sat in the milk too long, a cup of milk because she knew she should not make tea, and toast thickly spread with butter and Marmite. She looked so pleased and proud, standing by the bed with her offering, that I had no choice but to eat the whole lot. Only then did I notice quite how odd she was looking.

'Tamsin, what are you wearing?' I tried to ask mildly, but I could see there was going to be a tussle ahead to get her to look half-way decent.

'My leggings.' She, too, knew that there was a fight in the offing, and was determined to win it.

'Oh. I was hoping you'd wear your dress.' She has one smart dress, a Marks and Spencer smocked number in which she looks very pretty. I bought it for her to wear at Christmas at my parents', but I know she thinks it is too young for her. Perhaps she is right, but when she was little I could not afford to buy her a pretty dress that she would barely wear, and I do love her looking like a storybook child.

'Mum! I said I'd wear that dress for Gran, and I will, because that's different. But Gran's *old*.'

She is not, not particularly, but I let that ride. 'It's not to do with age, it's to do with being tidy.'

'Mum, I am perfectly tidy. Look, I did my hair and everything.'

She had, in two bunches perched asymmetrically in clashing scrunchies on the top of her head. She had put on her favourite leggings, pink ones covered in prancing Minnie Mouses, which have been too small for three months, but she will not let me throw them away. Underneath them she was wearing her favourite tights, thin multicoloured stripes, and on top an orange flowery belly-top Liz gave her which I have never liked. She looked like Spice Girls on LSD. Worse, she looked like every tabloid nightmare of an inner-city single-parented kid.

I was going to have to be tactful, and it was going to be difficult. 'Don't you think the belly-top might be a bit cold? It is December, after all.'

She looked doubtful. 'Maybe. I could put the lilac jumper on top and then if her flat is warm enough I could take it off.'

'That might mean too many colours. Possibly.'

'I like things being colourful.'

'Good. I hope you say the same when you're a teenager. You'll be the only one on the block not in head-to-toe black. Meanwhile do you think we could start again?'

'*Mum!* She sees me in school uniform every day, I want to look cheerful. I want her to see all my best clothes.'

'But not necessarily all at the same time. We're going out to Sunday lunch, not to a rave.'

'A rave?'

'Or a disco. She won't be dressed like that. Think of Miss Cox, think of how she dresses.'

If I hoped that the memory of her teacher's drab olive-greens and taupe ethnic knits would convince Tamsin to tone down her appearance, I was wrong. 'But that's just her uniform, you know, for school. I think she wears those clothes to be polite to us, because we can't wear what we want.' Has there ever been more proof of blind passion? 'I bet she's in normal clothes too.'

Tact was clearly getting me nowhere. I swung my legs out of bed and made my way to the shower. 'I'm sorry, Tammy, you can't go like that. Look at yourself. You've every colour of the rainbow on you. I'll do a deal. You don't have to wear the dress but you do have to change. Keep the tights on, put on your blue skirt and then you can wear any jumper you like, but not the belly top.'

She started to protest, but I went on regardless. 'You look very good fun in all those colours, but she knows that about you already. Do you want her to think that I'm a bad mother? Maybe, one day, if we get to know her better, I'll let you choose exactly what you want to wear. I'll tell you what. Double deal. If you change without complaining, you can wear what you've got on now to lunch with Gran the time we go after Christmas.' That would be a joke I would enjoy.

'But Gran wouldn't like it!' Exactly.

'Not a word more, Tamsin. If you're not changed by the time I'm out of the shower we won't be going. I mean it.'

I almost did. I was in two minds about whether I wanted to go, was not sure of how I should behave or where I stood. What would we talk about? The school? Tamsin? There was nothing else we had in common. Except our age.

When I came to dress I found myself in Tamsin's dilemma. Groovy or not groovy? Dowdy? Bright or dull? I settled for a plain skirt and a bright knitted jersey covered in daisies. It would have to do.

We did not know how to spend the rest of the morning, so after tidying up and pretending to read for a while we crossed the hall and knocked on Liz's door. She was still in her dressing gown, par for the course I suppose.

'Cindy, Tamsin. Come on in and have a cup of coffee. I've been wondering about you, haven't seen you for ages except passing through the hall. What have you been doing?'

Funny, isn't it. I had been feeling guilty about not seeing Liz – I had spent the evening with Nelly, and worked at Mrs Settrington's dinner party, and had sat at home with Wilkie Collins and not felt the need for other company. But as soon as I saw her I realised that Liz was feeling guilty too, and wondered why. What had she been up to?

The children went off to play schools and Liz and I settled down with a cup of coffee. And then did not know what to say to each other. Something was definitely up.

'So what have you been doing? Found yourself a boyfriend?'

Liz sounded as though she were teasing, but her laugh sounded more nervous than anything else.

'Oh no, you'd be the first person to know about that.' For some reason the thought of Fergus appeared in my head. It made me feel uneasy. 'No, not a boyfriend. But I did what you told me – remember you made me ring Nelly? The girl from university? Well, we met up last week. I couldn't find you so Mrs Perkins upstairs took the baby alarm.' Mrs Perkins is a widow, trying hard to make ends meet with dignity. I would not have dared to ask her to baby-sit so that I could go dancing, but I had seen that the magic words 'friend from college' put me up in her estimation.

'Cindy, I could have, you know that. You can't have tried that hard to find me, I'm always here.'

'Are you?'

It was a blind guess, more instinct than thought, but I saw her blush and knew I had hit some kind of mark. 'Liz?'

She ignored the implied question entirely. 'So what was she like? Are you still friends? Did you get wasted together? Go on, Cindy, tell me about it. I'm really glad you made the effort, you know.' She was, I could see that, and wondered why. I know, and it is not a good sign of my character, that if the tables had been turned, if she had found some long-ago friend and been reunited with her and felt there was a future for the friendship, that I would have felt at least a twinge of jealousy. But she was entirely happy, even, I thought, a little bit relieved.

I told her about the evening, and that Nelly had asked Tamsin and me down for a weekend after Christmas.

'Well, you should go! Tammy would love it. The seaside—'

'In January?'

'Yes, well. She's never seen the sea before, has she. It'll be amazing for her. Of course you should go.'

'We probably will, sometime. You sound keener than I do. You trying to get rid of me or something?'

Liz stood up and put the kettle back on. Both our cups were still three-quarters full so it was entirely unnecessary. She stood with her back to me and I knew she was about to say something awful. I almost put my fingers in my ears so I should not hear her next words, whatever they were. But then she spoke so quietly that I had to ask her to repeat herself anyway.

'What? Liz?'

She turned and faced me. 'It's me that's going. At least I think so.'

'Away for the weekend? Where to?' I pretended to myself that I was not grasping at straws. I already knew what she meant, almost knew the details, although they were irrelevant. I was about to lose my best, my only friend. I had to block that out.

'No, Cindy, not for the weekend. For good. But not that far away. Just a few miles north, it'll only be half an hour on the bus.'

'Why? I thought you liked it here.'

'I do. Cindy, Dave's asked me to move in with him. I think I'm going to do it.'

'Dave! But you said—'

'You knew I liked him.'

'Of course, but no more than any of the others.'

'Why don't you want me to go?'

Because I felt betrayed. Because I realised that I needed Liz almost as much as her children did. Because I knew how lonely I would be without her. Because I had just realised that I, too, would like to be offered a home by an honest man. Because with Liz around me there was someone worse off than me, someone who made me feel a little bit better about myself. Because I am a nasty, mean, jealous person who cannot be unreservedly happy for her friend but thinks only of herself.

'Why didn't you tell me?'

'I don't know. At first I didn't think anything of it. You know, we would all go out together, have a good time. I thought he fancied me, but I've got so used to being on my own I think I had forgotten how to play the game. I was honestly surprised when he first asked me out and I realised he might be serious. And I felt, sort of shy, about telling you. Because I had told you so often I had finished with men. I thought I believed it when I told you that, I really thought I didn't need them any more. But Dave . . . He's a good man, Cindy, you've seen that. The kids like him, he's good to them but he doesn't push it. That's worth a lot. And he's good fun, likes a night out, you know that.

And now we've spent some time in with him too and he's easy to be with. He's kind. I don't think I've ever known a really kind man before. Except my dad.'

'You've made up your mind.'

'I suppose I have.'

'That's why you wanted me to make friends with Nelly again.'

'I suppose. But not just because of me going. I would've encouraged you to anyway. I've said to you before, you know I have, I'm always going on at you to go out more, to let your hair down.'

'So who will I go out with now?'

'Don't be daft. I'll be going to Kilburn, not the other side of the world. Anyway you need something more.'

'More than what?'

'More than one friend who is your next-door neighbour.'

'I've more than one friend.' I felt hounded, on the defensive. This was not meant to be a conversation about my ineptitude with friendships. 'I'm as much friends with Neil and Keith and Sally as you are.'

'Are you? Have you ever had a real talk with any one of them? You laugh and joke, but you don't really talk. Only to me.'

'You can't confide in everyone you know. That would be ridiculous.'

'I don't mean that. I mean talk. Dave didn't even know you'd been to college until I told him. You don't tell anyone anything about yourself.'

'I'm a private person.'

Liz sighed. 'Oh Cindy, let's not argue. We're friends anyway. Aren't we?'

'Of course.'

We sipped our coffee in silence. I looked at my watch. Eleven o'clock. I could go home and sulk until lunch time or I could make an effort. I decided to make the effort. 'Okay Liz. If you promise to keep in touch with me I'll be glad for you. Of course I will. So now you've come clean, tell me all about it.'

She did, and as she spoke I realised that she loves Dave, that she will probably be happy with him. They are very well suited, really. Both good, honest people, straightforward, out for whatever fun their lives can offer them. 'I'm going to do it all properly this time,' she said.

'And you're not weeping on me now are you, girl?' she asked suddenly and I said no, not quite and that I was sorry I had been mean but (and for once I was totally honest) I could not help but feel a bit jealous of her.

Liz looked serious. 'Perhaps that's why I didn't tell you before. I said I was through with men, but you never did. You've steered pretty clear of them since I've known you, but I always thought you were scared more than anything else.'

'I've always told you how wise you are.'

'Then let me be the wise woman again. You go and see Nelly, and meet her friends and maybe you'll find yourself a nice Devon boy who'll take you away from all this and make an honest woman of you. Let you spend your days rearing babies and reading books instead of cleaning up after other people.'

'Maybe.'

'You know, this is a secret, but Dave says he wants to marry me.' Are people more self-obsessed and boring when they are happy in love or unhappy? It is a close-run thing, I often think.

'Aren't you married already?'

'I am not!'

'I thought you were, to Mo's father.'

'I did not marry that lazy bastard. Me mam tried to make me, but neither of us wanted it. I suppose we both knew it wasn't going to last.'

'Aren't Catholics meant to marry?'

'We're supposed to do all kinds of things we don't. But in the end we usually find we want to do those things. I suppose I'm still a Catholic girl at heart. I couldn't have got rid of any one of my babies – couldn't even stop myself conceiving them, come to that. The fact that Dave's never been married makes me very happy. We could get married in a Catholic church, with a proper Father, with no trouble. Until it was a possibility, I never realised how much I still wanted that. Oh, Cindy, I'm going to be such a good tidy Catholic wife!' It should have been comical, Liz with her chequered past suddenly reforming so completely, but for some reason it was not. Only touching.

Tamsin began pestering me to leave. Ayesha was looking at

her with admiration and envy – she is almost as much in thrall to Jane as is Tamsin.

'So you're going to lunch with Miss Cox! That won't be a barrel of laughs,' Liz said, and I smiled and shook my head and said Tamsin had been so keen that I had no choice, and then I felt disloyal.

Liz hugged me as we left. 'Now you're not to start fretting. I won't sneak off without telling you. It can't be for a month or so anyway.'

'Why don't we go out for a curry this week? You and me and Dave? I'd like it.' Liz looked unsure. 'Go on, Liz.'

'Well, maybe. Perhaps with some of the others.' I did not pursue it. I sensed I was getting the brush-off and I did want to behave properly after my selfish start.

Tamsin and I went home again and I heard her school reading for a quarter of an hour. We were both restless and finding it hard to concentrate, so we decided to take a little walk to kill the time until we could reasonably turn up at Jane's. We bought some flowers from the seller outside the Percy, strolled down Bassett Road past Amanda's flat and on down to the end of the road. The flowers dripped their water all down the front of my skirt. Tamsin skipped and chatted and I felt bad-tempered. It seemed unfair to me that Liz, rotten Catholic that she had been for so long, should suddenly find life falling so perfectly into place. Everything – the man, the house, the children and now the place in heaven as well. Without even bothering to go to Mass, say her prayers or even earn her own way (when it suits me I am very good at blanking out the Social Security money I still pocket every week). I knew I was being nasty again but I was almost luxuriating in my feelings. So what if I was being mean-spirited. No one would know.

We looped round and walked back up Chesterton Road towards Jane's flat. On an impulse I took a left and walked into St Charles's Square. Mass was just finishing, people pouring out of the little white gateway. A swarthy priest stood smiling at his congregation, greeting everyone, exchanging words with a few. Well, it is all easy enough for him, I thought.

I looked at the members of this club as they filled the street. They were nothing special. A mother was furiously dragging a small child, trailed by two others with sulky faces. I recognised some old men from the corner table in the Percy, their clothes slightly smarter than normal. There were quite a few families, a surprising number of young people and teenagers and some old ladies wearing black lace scarves on their heads. There were a few nuns.

And there was Amanda. She walked out on her own, her shiny, good-as-new missal in her hand. She looked serious, nodded briefly at the priest who smiled at her but did not appear to recognise her.

I turned sharply, dragging at Tamsin as I did so. 'Mum! What on earth are you doing?'

I slowed my step and walked round the corner, away from the church. I did not want Amanda to see me, I did not want her to see Tamsin. I wanted to keep my life private, did not want to make introductions and explanations. I suddenly realised that it might seem rather odd to Amanda that after all these years I had never told her I have a daughter. But I want to keep it that way. She can cry all over me if she wants, but I am not like that, I keep my own counsel. I am proud. Amanda thinks she is proud, thinks she is independent, but she is nothing. She cries to her daily woman. She relies on her father's money and influence, on her friends. She holds a plastic string of beads for comfort and sneaks out to church, hoping that the God she neglects when her life is going well will suddenly step in and help her out if she tips up once in a blue moon when she is in trouble and can get out of bed in time.

'Mum? Are you all right?'

I pulled myself together. Tamsin was looking at me with concern. My head was light, I felt a little dizzy. What was the matter with me? I slowed up, breathed deeply to calm myself down. 'I'm sorry, love. I thought we were late after being so early.'

Tamsin's frown was still firmly in place. 'Are you sure? You look funny. I thought you were going to faint.'

I managed a smile. 'Me? Faint? Oh, not me, I'm tougher than that.'

'Do you want to go home?'

I love that child. I knew what it cost her to say that, to offer to give up this lunch with her teacher and take me home. I felt ashamed of myself and stopped and gave her a hug. 'Of course not, poppet. Come on, we can turn up now, it's just down the road. I'm sorry if I frightened you. I did feel a little bit odd, but I'm all right now.'

The purple invitation was on the mantelpiece. It was the first thing I saw. I had almost forgotten about it and felt a lurch of guilt as I spotted it. I looked quickly away. Jane noticed nothing, she was exclaiming over the flowers and putting them in a vase. There was a little tick in the top right-hand corner of the card. Please God I don't get caught out. What on earth will I say?

Later, during lunch (roast chicken, two veg, a homemade cheesecake, a bottle of red wine) Jane mentioned the party. 'You didn't tell me that Lyndy was giving a party next week. I'm looking forward to it, although I doubt I shall know anyone there. Still, it's ages since I've been to a party of any sort.'

'You'll know me.'

'Oh? You'll be there? Good, well that will be someone to talk to.'

'I mean, I'll be working. I'm helping out.' I said quickly, terrified I had given the wrong impression.

'That doesn't mean I can't talk to you, does it? Unless you're busy, of course.'

That is the problem. We talk very easily on the whole, but there is still this barrier. She is frightened of offending me and I am nervous of sounding as though I am trying to set myself up as something I am not.

In fact my estimate of her was more or less spot-on, her background is very similar to mine. It sounds as cold and correct, with no brothers or sisters to sweeten the formality of her childhood. Her father worked for Lynda's father, but rose through the company (something to do with machinery parts) to become its managing director, and the boss's friend. Like me, she is the first person in her family to go to university, although unlike me she made the grade. We both read English, talked for hours about our courses, until I suddenly thought how pathetic it was that after so many years in both our cases university seemed to be the highlights of our lives.

There must be something more in the future: some dancing of our spirits.

Then Jane talked about teaching, and I could see why the children love her. She is obviously that rare thing, a teacher who loves teaching, who can imagine nothing more fulfilling than to be able to inspire one child to love learning. I wish I could be as motivated as she. She has the knack with children. She managed to include Tamsin in the conversation enough that she was not bored, but still we talked as adults. We played a couple of card games, still chatting all the while.

Maybe it was because of the wine, but I found myself confiding in Jane. I told her more about my feelings on leaving college, on beginning my cleaning work, on my home life, than I have with anyone other than Liz. I soon felt that with her I do not have to pretend. I even told her my secret dream, described the expensive pen that I have my eye on to reward myself when I finally finish a story. I told her how undisciplined I am, how I began writing as an exercise but how it has turned into this – a rambling journal more than any serious writing.

She asked me how long it was, and I told her (this is my third exercise book I am writing in now) and she looked at me amazed and said I should go straight away and buy myself the pen. Writing in itself was a discipline, she said. I deserved the pen. Briefly I wondered if she were treating me as she does the slow children at the bottom of the class, encouraging me because anything is better than nothing when you are barely capable of reading. I think that you have to write for someone, for an audience, but she disagreed. And then she asked me what I was really hoping to write, and I realised I do not actually know. Not poetry, not plays, nothing too experimental. Not a thriller, not sci-fi, not Wild West. Not children's either. 'See how negative I am,' I said feeling shamefaced.

'Looking at what you're reading, and hearing you talk, it is obvious to me. You want to write an old-fashioned novel with a beginning, a middle and an end,' she said.

'Well maybe, but what about?'

'There I can't help you. But it will come. In the meantime go and buy yourself that pen.'

We had finished lunch, drunk coffee, moved on to tea. It was half-past four and I was horrified. 'I am so sorry. I've stayed far too long. You must have been waiting for me to go for hours.'

'Not at all. I've really enjoyed it. Maybe you'll come again?' she seemed hesitant again. I cannot understand this relationship we are developing. Maybe it will make sense one day.

Tamsin and I walked down Chesterton Road and across Ladbroke Grove. I was reading the back of the paperback Jane had lent me – another Wilkie Collins, *No Name*, and Tamsin was subdued. 'You were right about her clothes,' she said. 'They weren't very jolly, were they?'

'Did you have a nice time?'

'All right. I can't wait to tell the others what her flat is like. Yes, it was a nice day, but it wasn't very exciting, was it?'

And I realised that although of course nothing exciting had happened, I was feeling warm with possibility. She had left me feeling that I could achieve something. The pen will not make me write well – that is up to me. But for some reason I now feel I can write well. I must look for a subject, and then begin to write. It will happen. I will show them all. I will be something.

10

Lynda is a born party-giver, I have to admit. Despite all those idiotic suggestions she made when the party was first being discussed, on the day it finally took place it was, I could see, a huge success. It was on Wednesday night, which meant I was there to help in the morning, but she had done the lion's share of the work before I had even arrived. There were mountains of dainty bits to eat on various plates – little stuffed pastry shells, rolls of smoked salmon wrapped around soft creamy cheese. We cut up raw cauliflower and carrot and whipped up huge bowls of different dips. It looked as good as Marks and Spencer. (Amanda is a great believer in M&S cooking, I have noticed.)

While I was in the house Lynda went to the florist and came back with armfuls of lilies and tulips and irises. They must have cost her a fortune. Then she arranged them in big bowls and jugs and vases so that the house seemed transformed into spring. She apologised to me for not letting me do the flowers, saying she loves them so much she cannot trust anyone else with that particular job. I did not mind at all, I like having flowers around, but I almost certainly spoil any bunch I try to organise into shape.

She seemed happier than she has for ages; more relaxed somehow, laughing and joking with me as we worked. 'This is fun, isn't it? I do love getting things ready for a party, there seems to be so much *potential* ahead. I know it's a bit silly, but I do like to wonder what will happen – whether any one will fall in love, or out of love, whether any important deals will be made, jobs changed, decisions arrived at.'

And then she sighed. 'Probably none of that, though. Too many people will be crammed into too small a space, they'll smoke so much that in five minutes the smell of the lilies will be overpowered by smoke, some husbands and wives will argue, some new flirtation will be struck up. And they'll all wake up with hangovers tomorrow and think they've had a nice time. Well, I can't hope for better than that.'

'Lynda! Don't be so gloomy. Look at the house, it looks wonderful. And all your friends will be here and they'll be laughing their heads off and you'll be right to be proud.'

'As long as no one tips the avocado dip onto the floor.'

'Well, that's what I'll be here for. So that you don't have to worry about that sort of thing. Of course it'll be fun. Come on, perhaps you will be the one doing the flirting.'

She laughed, then frowned. 'I don't think Randal would like that much. Although I must say he's a bit of a flirt himself. I think it helps relieve his stress.' Now there's an excuse I have not heard before. 'Still, I've done my best and you're right, I am sure it will be fun. Isn't it time we had a cup of coffee?'

I think I should start to charge people extra for the twenty minutes we spend having coffee in the middle of the morning. I used to think They had coffee with me to be polite, to show They realise that in this day and age we are, if not friends, then almost equal. Maybe that is how it started out. But now They use that twenty minutes as a kind of confessional. Each of them would be horrified if they realised it, but They tell me more about themselves as we sit at the kitchen table sipping coffee (Alta Rica at Lynda's, Nescafé with Amanda, real coffee with Mrs Settrington and Mr Nesbit, Gold Blend with Fergus) than I tell most of my friends. (Liz was right about that, but then I am more interested in hearing about other people than in letting them hear about me.)

That day with Lynda was a case in point. We sit down, chatting about where to put the dips and the ashtrays (far apart from one another – once she found a fag end in the hummus) and the next thing is she has jumped straight into a discussion of her marriage. Psychiatrists charge hundreds of pounds to listen to people boring on about their partners. With me it is all thrown in for six pounds an hour.

'If Randal has a fault,' she said, looking longingly at the biscuit tin, while I tried not to look astounded at the use of the word 'if' in that context, 'it is that he is just the tiniest bit low on patience with my friends. Not all of them, of course not, but if he takes against someone he just will not try. I mean, we all have friends that we sometimes wonder about, don't we? People who might not be our friends if we met them now, but who are part of our history. Well, those are the ones he just will not make an effort with, unless of course they are pretty.'

I made some noncommittal noise. What could I say? He is clearly a chauvinist pig and I could not think of any polite excuse for him quickly enough.

'Some of my old BBC friends are all right, we have them to dinner, but it's the ones from further back that he finds harder to – to be interested in, I suppose. That is one of the reasons I wanted to give a party. I knew I could slip them in and he would not really notice. I don't want to give my old friends offence, but neither do I want to upset Randal.'

I thought of Jane's invitation and felt sick. It was too late. Nothing I could do now would undo that mad moment.

'Perhaps he's jealous of them – because they've got a bit of your past he cannot share,' I suggested, going into full psycho-babble mode.

Lynda looked astounded, and then delighted. 'Do you think so? You know, you could be right. Oh, the poor darling, of course nothing before is as important as now.' And then she looked sad again. 'I just don't want to lose it, that's all. I don't know if you're right. He was never jealous of my ex-boyfriends, just doesn't particularly like any of them.' Her naïveté where Randal is concerned sometimes rivals Tamsin's.

'Do you mind my asking, did you say Fergus is an ex-boyfriend of yours?'

'Yes, he was. Perhaps the most important one. I'm still very fond of him.' She looked soppy, and I wondered just how fond of him she is now. 'I'll tell you something, though, and I bet this will make you laugh. Do you know one of the things that I really could not bear about him? You must have noticed it – his flat! He is one of the most untidy people I have ever met, and it drove me mad. He might as well live in an anthill!'

'I thought ants were very tidy.'

She looked uncertain. 'Yes, well, you know what I mean.

Anyway, tidiness isn't everything. Randal is very tidy.' This seemed more of a disappointment to her than a comfort, but I let it ride.

'I had better go, Lynda. And don't worry about tonight, I'm sure everyone will have a lovely time. They're all looking forward to it.'

'They are?'

'Yes, you know, Amanda, Fergus . . .' And Jane, God help me.

'Oh yes, of course. You had an idea about them, didn't you? I hope you haven't been matchmaking. Thank you, Cindy. I'll see you tonight. Six thirty all right? They're all invited for seven.'

Mr Blake let me in. He was dressed only in boxer shorts, which I thought odd for the time of day. He did not seem to find it remotely inappropriate, did not even look embarrassed. I bet he would not answer the front door to Amanda in his boxer shorts, but then I do not count.

Everything was laid out – tiny sandwiches, mini sausages, the dips, the ashtrays, piles of headless prawns waiting mutely on plates. The kitchen was to be my terrain, he explained, still in boxer shorts. Lucky their house is so hot. He showed me the champagne, asked me if I knew how to open it, showed me the white and red wine, the Aqua Libra, orange juice, fizzy water, Coke. They had thought of everything. A bucket in the corner was full of ice, Lynda had even laid out napkins and cloths in case of spillage. 'Although I'm sure you know where all that sort of thing is kept,' he said, over-jocular. 'Lynda's just changing. She said please would you keep an eye on the serving dishes and ashtrays. Make sure one stays full and the other empty, or something.'

'It's all right. She's run me through this already.'

'I'm sure she has.' He looked suddenly very tired. 'Well, I had better go upstairs and get ready myself. It would never do to be seen in my shorts, would it?'

Except by the staff.

The first half hour was pretty quiet. A few women turned up, their husbands would be coming from work, they said, oh dear were they early. They took champagne and gathered together, shoulders hunched, elbows tight to their sides, talking in low voices.

Then came the rush and I lost track of what was going on. Voices rose, laughs rang out, people trod on each other's feet and exchanged recent gossip with animation. I was amazed how much they drank, glass after glass, and apart from the noise-level rising they did not seem any different. I caught sight of Amanda, wearing slightly more make-up and fewer clothes than usual, laughing with a man I did not know. Next time I saw her Randal Blake was leaning over her, talking in a low voice. Their eyes both flicked towards a dyed blonde woman with old hands clutching her bag and they laughed. So Amanda is not one of the friends that he is not prepared to waste his charm upon, I noticed.

'Cindy, have you had a drink?' Lynda looked flushed and happy. Her evening was obviously going well.

'No.'

'Well, you must. Or you'll think we're all frightful,' and she burst into peels of laughter and moved on.

I decided to take her at her word. I did a quick tour of the party, filling glasses as I went, then poured myself a glass of champagne (well, why not, she had not specified Coke, had she?) and took a break. I leaned against the door frame into the kitchen and watched. Faces were flushed by now. One couple seemed to be having an argument, but they had arrived together so I did not think they were married. Another girl stood, swaying slightly, looking up at a tall young man with a bemused expression on her face. In one hand she had a sticky-looking glass, in the other a piece of cauliflower. She did not seem to know what to do with either, looked as though she were about to throw her arms around the man. Was she really having a nice time?

'Hello.' I jumped and turned. Fergus was standing beside me with an empty glass and a smile.

'Oh, sorry, do you need a drink?'

'I suppose I could do with one. I've only just arrived, how's it going?'

I gestured at the party. 'Seems to be all right. There's a lot of laughing and a lot of shouting. Most of it friendly.'

'Flirtation?'

So he remembered the conversation too. 'I don't know, what do you think?'

We stood shoulder to shoulder, looking at the people gesticulating, laughing, hands waving, red mouths opening and closing. 'Some of them must be. Or wanting to be. Don't you think?' he said.

'Not everyone sees a party as a happy hunting ground.'

'Oh yes they do.' He was totally serious. 'Either "networking" (ghastly word, don't you think?) or sex. That's all the English are interested in – ambition and sex. That's all any of it is about.'

'Romance?' I felt slightly sad.

'Not this lot, not romance.' Our eyes met and I looked down, suddenly awkward.

'Cindy – Fergus seems to have an empty glass.' It was Lynda, frowning at me in surprised irritation.

'Oh, I am sorry, I was going to get you one—'

'It doesn't matter at all.' He handed me his empty glass, and as I came back with the bottle I am sure I heard him mutter to me, very quietly, 'sex', with a wink at Lynda's back as she led him across the room to introduce him to someone more worthwhile.

The person she chose was Amanda. Obviously the idea of Fergus chatting her up was more palatable than the idea of him chatting up the hired help. Or maybe she was trying to break up Amanda and Randal's tête-à-tête. Either way I had been snubbed, and I returned to my task with slightly less willingness than I had before. It was silly of me, I know. I was there to help, and I could almost hear Lynda's thoughts, 'I'm paying her to serve people drinks, not to stand around talking to my friends.' Yet, for a moment, Fergus had been treating me as he might have any other woman in the room. For those minutes I had been able to step outside myself and feel accepted. It had been a mistake.

I found Jane standing on the edge of a conversation. The two women were paying no attention to her, their bodies barely inclined to include her. She was not trying very hard either, holding a warm-looking glass in her hand, a bright smile fixed on her face. I felt more sorry for her than I did for myself.

'Cindy, hello,' she said with a certain amount of relief as I filled her glass. 'Isn't this fun!' She spoke too brightly, and her eyes had the glassy look of repressed tears. Maybe I was putting my own feelings on to her, but she did seem very lost.

'Hello, Jane. Yes, everyone seems to be enjoying themselves.' I wanted to remind her of the distance between us. It worked, she seemed a little taken aback.

'How are you getting on with *No Name*?'

'I'm sorry, I have to keep moving around,' I said, and left her beside the two women who had taken the opportunity of Jane talking to me to turn their bodies the five degrees extra which ensured Jane could not even pretend to be part of their conversation any longer.

Maybe I was harsh to her, and if so I am sorry. But I could not risk being caught chatting to one of Lynda's guests again, especially not the one I had invited. And anyway, when it comes down to it, Jane is one of Them, and if I start to blur the edges which define us I will cause my own downfall.

The party began to thin out at about eight thirty. By half past nine almost everyone had gone. The last hangers-on were more or less swept out of the house at ten to ten, leaving only the Blakes, Amanda and Fergus, a prosperous-looking couple I had not seen before and another single woman I did not know.

'I booked a table at 192 for ten,' said Mr Blake. 'Shall we go?'

Lynda looked doubtful. 'I don't know, Randal, it's a nice idea, but—'

'Oh Randal, what a good idea. That would be fun,' Amanda interrupted.

'Come on, darling, Candy will take care of all of this, won't you?' Randal said, flashing his most perfect smile at me.

'Of course, do go, Lynda,' I said, Knowing My Place.

'The name's Cindy,' said Fergus. He sounded polite, but the look he gave Randal seemed remarkably hostile.

That seemed to decide Lynda. 'Well, Cindy, if you really don't mind doing it all on your own. Yes, I would love it. Shall we all go? I'll just go up to the loo and I will be ready.'

The others stood around waiting for her and I began collecting up glasses and ashtrays. Fergus followed me into the kitchen. 'I hope I didn't embarrass you,' he said.

'No, thank you. I doubt he'll remember, though.'

'Sometimes I wonder how someone with such piggish manners manages to succeed at his work. But he does.'

'Oh, he's all right, really.' I was wary, remembering my lesson of earlier in the evening, clearing up around Fergus as I spoke.

'I hope so, for Lynda's sake. Oh dear, I must be drunk. Forget I said anything.' Lynda's steps were coming down the stairs. 'I had better go.'

I thought, for a moment, that he almost kissed me.

But he did not.

I tidied up very quickly. I was bored with the whole evening, confused at the messages I was getting from Lynda, Jane, Fergus . . . I felt left out, Cinderella without a fairy godmother. I knew I was being irrational, I had been hired to clear up, it would never have occurred to me that there was any other reason for my being there. But yet. Fergus had treated me like a friend. He had even, unless I was flattering myself, practised his flirting technique on me – with due warning, of course. He had already made it plain that flirting was the reason for going to a party.

I tried to talk myself down from my feeling of desertion, but only succeeded in making myself more bad-tempered. I helped myself to another glass of champagne and swigged at it as I washed the serving dishes and last few glasses which would not fit into the dishwasher. When I left I slammed the door.

I walked down Cambridge Gardens to Ladbroke Grove. To go home from Lynda's I take a left up the Grove past the Percy and then home. For some reason I did not. Maybe I felt I needed some fresh air after the smoke-filled rooms at the Blakes'. Lynda was right, the lilies' scent was soon overpowered by Benson & Hedges. I took a right instead, told myself I felt like a stroll down Ladbroke Grove to Lancaster Road, up it, right. I found myself in Kensington Park Road, and just for the sake of it continued walking.

A group of boys – maybe not boys, maybe men, they certainly thought so, walked down the middle of the road, shouting and showing off to the one girl in the midst of them. For a moment I envied her. The restaurants were still lit, full of noise and smoke and sex. The door of L'Altro opened and a blast of heat and voices and smells forced its way out into the cold night air behind the couple which was leaving. The girl looked a little drunk, but only a little, and very happy.

I slowed my step.

I saw them at once, sitting towards the back of the restaurant. Amanda was sitting with her back to the wall between Randal and Fergus. Randal was lighting a cigarette for her, but her attention was on Fergus and she was laughing. As I watched, a waiter arrived with two plates of food. Lynda's back was to me, but I saw her gesture to her husband, looking after him as usual. The group looked relaxed and happy. No one saw me. I turned and walked back home.

I do not know why I did it. I just wanted to see the end of Their evening, I suppose. I did need some air . . . I did.

Liz is right. I must force some kind of change in my life. It will not be easy – how can it be? I cannot give up my work, I rely on the money now. Yet Liz says I am too involved with Them all. Perhaps I am – just a little bit. With some of Them.

Oh heavens, I must be drunk. I do not know what I am thinking of. Drunk or mad. I have only drunk champagne twice before in my life, let that be my excuse.

Soon it will be Christmas. I might break the rule of the last seven years and ask myself to stay with my parents, rather than just going down for the day. I need a break. I need to be reminded who I am, even if I do not like it.

And then, after Christmas, I will follow my sage's advice and take Tamsin down to Torquay. Perhaps I will find myself a nice Devon boy. They must exist.

I must sleep. My head is spinning. I am too full of viciousness tonight.

'It's absolutely extraordinary, but I really have no memory at all of inviting her.'

This was the conversation I had been dreading. I had hoped it would come up while I was cleaning, so that I could move about and keep my face away from Lynda, but she was busy all morning and only began to dissect the party with me when we sat down for our customary cup of coffee.

'Well, with so many coming, it's easy to forget one.'

'I suppose so. But the odd thing is, she was on my original list, but I decided to drop her as there were just too many people. I distinctly remember *not* inviting her, if you see what I mean, because I remember feeling slightly guilty about it. But then I thought that she wouldn't really know anyone else much so she wouldn't notice not being asked. She probably wouldn't even know we were giving a party. Unless you said something to her?' she said, giving me a sharp look.

'Of course not.' I managed to look affronted, although my heart was beating loud in my ears.

'Of course not, I'm sorry.' And I felt a little surge of triumph. Don't upset the Staff, even if they are giving your invitations out to all and sundry.

'Anyway,' Lynda went on, 'the odd thing was, there was an acceptance on the answer phone, but I assumed "Jane" was Jane North. She didn't show at all, now I think about it.' I felt retrospective panic – I had not even considered the danger of Jane answering the invitation. Lynda was still talking. 'I doubt she had much of a nice time, anyway. I saw her hanging around the edges of a few groups looking left out.' I did not like the bitchy tone of her voice. Furthermore I had always thought that part of the job of hostess was to make sure everyone was enjoying themselves. Silly me. 'But I still don't see how she got here.' Lynda was fretful today, and this puzzle obviously nagged at her. I had to put her mind at rest somehow.

'Well, maybe you wrote her an invitation before you decided not to send it, and it found its way into the pile waiting to be posted,' I suggested.

'I suppose so. Possibly. But I do think it's odd. I nearly had a heart attack when I opened the door and saw her standing there. Of course I was too well-mannered to close it in her face, I mean I couldn't, could I? And to give Jane her due I wouldn't imagine that she would be a gatecrasher. I doubt she has the gall, apart from anything else.'

'Maybe you mentioned it to her on the telephone or something and she took that as a serious invitation.' I was getting desperate.

'Oh no, I haven't talked to her for months. That's why it's all so odd . . .'

'The party seemed to go well.'

'It did, didn't it? You certainly looked like you were having a good time.' Why was Lynda so snide this morning? PMT probably. Serve her right. I had been talking to one of her guests for all of five minutes. Why should she mind so much? I decided not to rise.

'Good morning, good morning.' Mr Blake swanned into the kitchen, kissed the top of his wife's head, smiled sweetly at me and made himself (made himself, you notice) a cup of coffee. Lynda perked up a little. 'Thank you so much for your help on Wednesday, *Cindy*.' He shot an unpleasant look at his wife as he said my name, then turned on the smile again. 'It made all the difference to us, and you left the house wonderfully tidy. In fact I wanted to give you a little present to say thank you.' He dived into the little cupboard in the corner of the kitchen which Lynda grandly calls a larder, and came out with a bottle of champagne. 'Thank you,' he said again.

I was amazed, and Lynda looked equally so. 'Are you sure? Well, thank you, thank you very much.' (It did occur to me to wonder whether I was actually going to be paid for the hours I had put in, but that was a mean thought. Lynda is scrupulously fair.)

'A pleasure. I must say Lynda was right and I am sorry if I ever thought otherwise. The party was an inspired idea, I thoroughly enjoyed it, and I think everyone else did too.' He kissed her head again. 'Thank you, my love. And now I must go, I'm running late. Goodbye, darling, see you tonight. Goodbye Cindy.'

Lynda looked at the door which had shut behind him. 'He really did enjoy it,' she said sadly. 'I told you he would. Oh well, I had better get on.'

As I climbed the stairs to the top floor, dragging the Hoover with me, I could only think with amazement how I had got away with it, was not suspected, was still everybody's friend. If it was so easy, maybe I could help Jane out some more. That would be fun.

I went to Fergus's feeling invincible. Maybe I was not running BP, but I had changed something outside my orbit and survived. This could become a hobby, I thought. Now what could I change about Fergus's life?

My key in the latch, I paused and blushed. Fergus. I must be careful with him. Apart from a certain egocentricity (but not in Randal Blake's league, oh nothing as pernicious as that) I have no sense of his faults. His untidiness? Hardly a fault. His relaxed attitude to life? A positive virtue. I waltzed in to his sitting-room, dropped my bag on the sofa and greeted him cheerily. 'So how did the party go for you? I've just been at the Blakes' and he is looking very happy. Congratulated Lynda on its success and gave me a bottle of champagne. I have never seen him so friendly.'

Fergus was sitting at his desk, papers piled high all around him, tapping away at his laptop. 'Good morning Cindy. What? The party, well it was fine I suppose. We had a very noisy dinner afterwards. Pretty much of a late night. So I did not do much work yesterday.'

I not only did not take the hint. I genuinely did not notice it. 'And did you find the girl of your dreams?'

He looked up and frowned. I do not think he knew he was doing it. 'Cindy, do you mind? I'm in a panic for a deadline. If you could do this room last, I would be grateful.'

Even floating on my high I recognised that tone. Never mind the eye contact, the flirting, the standing up to Mr Blake on my behalf, it was back to Cindy the cleaner and Know Your Place. I felt slightly dizzy with a curious combination of shame and anger. I picked up my bag and took myself off to the kitchen without another word. He had left a pile of ironing on the kitchen table and I set to it at once. I hate ironing. It keeps you (literally rather than figuratively) in your place. No scope for amusement at all. He had probably planned it that way.

Part of my anger was directed at myself. It was the first time in years – probably since Amanda and the razor blade episode – that I had let myself down in that way. I had given away too much. That I was a human being. Why does Fergus do this to me? Make me let down my guard so incautiously? I have no handle on him as yet, and I think I need one. The Others are easy, I can manage Them with only the occasional hiccup, but Fergus – I am not yet totally at ease with him. He puts me on edge and I do not like that. I know why, of course I know why. It is because I am attracted to him. Not in the sense that I sometimes find myself liking Amanda or Lynda, or especially Jane. Not to put too fine a point upon it, I fancy him. The first man who attracts me for years, and it is one of Them. I must do something about it. One way or another. I feel very urgently that I must gain the upper hand.

Towards the end of the morning he came and found me in the bathroom. 'I'm sorry if I was a little brusque when you arrived,' he said. 'I was in a total panic about the piece I was working on. But it's all done now, for better or worse. To be honest I had such a terrible hangover yesterday I could not get round to doing anything. Do you fancy a cup of coffee?'

I said no, fairly stiffly.

'Oh, God, don't be offended, please. It really was not meant. In fact I had been rather looking forward to hearing your view of the whole thing.'

'I couldn't possibly have a view, I was just pouring drinks.'

He would not give up. 'Well, you seemed to have a pretty good take on what was going on when I talked to you. When I was allowed to talk to you,' he added with a grin.

I refused to be drawn. 'That was different.'

'Okay, Okay, I'm backing off,' he said, suiting actions to the words, but laughing at the same time.

'I'm sorry,' I said. 'I did not mean to be rude.' Well, of course I did, but we were like dogs meeting in the park, circling around each other, trying to establish our positions.

'Well, then we're quits. Come on, how about the coffee? Or no, look I've got a dreadful thirst on me after all that work, let's have a beer. Please?'

I relented. Do all women do as he asks? I suppose they do. He is like a very charming small child, totally relentless in his pursuit of what he wants and with as little awareness that his goal just possibly might not be achieved. I should think it usually is.

He opened the fridge door. 'Bugger, I'm out. I'm sorry, now you'll think I was tricking you. Let's go to the pub.'

I had been totally prepared to sit at the kitchen table and drink lager with him, but the idea of walking into a pub with him threw me completely. 'Oh, no, I couldn't possibly. I'll be late picking up – something.' And what was I doing even thinking of drinking beer in the middle of the afternoon? Just as I had been regaining my control I was losing it again.

He gave me a curious look, seemed about to ask me something, then changed his mind. 'Well, if you're sure. Here's your money, I'll see you next week. Lock up behind you, will you?'

He walked out, whistling, and as I heard the street door slam behind him I felt oddly bereft. He could have tried to persuade me, couldn't he?

We went for a little walk on Sunday, Tamsin and I. It was a fairly nice day for December, and we were feeling bored. Liz and her brood were staying the night at Dave's and I did not fancy Mrs Perkins's company much. Knowing Liz was not there made me miss her dreadfully: if she had been there I might well not have seen her, but she had taken the possibility away and made me feel the want. I almost hated her for it.

More than that, I am beginning to hate her for the effect of her words on me the other day. I suppose she is right, I do not have many friends other than Liz, but as I did not notice until she pointed it out, I cannot see that it is very important. I am self-sufficient. At least I have always thought that about myself. Maybe I am wrong.

Tamsin had been asked over to a school friend's house for the day, but I wanted her with me. I know that is selfish, but isn't it what all mothers do sometimes? Perhaps not. All I want for Tamsin is that she should be brave and independent, which she is. Nowadays it is me who clings to her for company, rather than the other way around.

We decided to walk up to the canal, to take a stroll down towards Maida Vale where we could look at the brightly painted barges, try to peer inside without the owners seeing us, fantasise about living on one ourselves. It had been one of our favourite pastimes when Tamsin was small, and we have not been there for a while.

We set off cheerfully holding hands, talking about school, Miss Cox, Christmas. But suddenly, I don't know why, Tamsin's mood changed. She dragged her feet, whined, said she wanted to go home, why couldn't she be dropped off at Marie's house, looking into people's barges was a babyish game and anyway rude.

I felt anger rise in me. Anger with Tamsin, for not under-standing that I wanted her companionship, and anger at the rat-hole of our lives. We are too close, too much to each other. There is nothing to dilute our relationship. She is always, always there. And I am always, always there for her. It is no wonder we sometimes snarl at each other, struggle for individuality under the weight of our love.

My understanding the problem does not help my anger, though. It is at moments like these that I long for someone else, a father-figure I suppose, someone who can do different things for her and with her. Someone to take some responsibility for her – and me.

We argued, I shouted, she stamped ahead. I wanted to smack her, hard, but managed to restrain myself. Back at home she sulked in the bedroom and I sulked in the kitchen. Winter lasts too long when you are lonely in a small space.

Christmas is almost with us. The decorations have been up in the streets for weeks, but now they are appearing in houses. There are three-foot trees in almost every front window in the street, some winking with electric lights, some decorated with old-fashioned wooden toys and candles that will never be lit, others covered in tinsel and plastic bells. I took *A Christmas Carol* out of the library in Ladbroke Grove and began reading it to Tamsin, but I think she is too young for it still. I am only working on Monday and Tuesday this week, then I will go down to Mum and Dad for four days. I have not spent so long under their roof since Tamsin was born, but I think I am looking forward to it. Mum seemed actually pleased when I asked if we could come, she managed to say yes without a single snide comment. Tamsin is delighted, and wants to spend one night with Steven and Joanne and Matt on her own. They have moved into their new house and are longing to show it off to us. Mum said they are going to give us Boxing Day lunch. I do not know if we can keep up this lark of a happy family at Christmas, but I do think that we are at least all entering into it with the right spirit. There will be no Ebeneezer Scrooge at the feast.

I make sure never to ask Them what they will be doing at Christmas. I have for years hated being asked myself so much that I respect Their privacy. It is bad enough being lonely, but no one wants to proclaim it from the rooftops.

Mrs Settrington did not have a Christmas tree up on Monday morning. I suppose there is no point when you are old and alone. I gave her a Christmas card and she gave me a card and a box of Roger & Gallet soap. She does every year, but I must admit I rather like it. I hoard it for special occasions and will not let Tamsin borrow it.

Then she surprised me by bringing up the subject of Christmas herself. 'I usually like to go to a hotel at Christmas,' she said, unpacking her shopping from the supermarket. 'It is such a relief to have someone else cooking the turkey.' As though she would bother to cook a turkey for herself. 'But this year I thought I should ask my godson, do you remember him, Mr Hardwicke, over for lunch. I thought he might be lonely here, far from his mother.'

'Is he not going back to America for Christmas?'

'No, he is given hardly any time off work so it would not be worth it. I thought I might have a little party, ask Amanda if she would like to come too and maybe Seth has some other friend in the same boat who would appreciate a good English Christmas lunch. I suppose I should ask Mr Nesbit as well, I'm sure he has no other plans. Cindy, there's no chance, is there, that you could help?'

'On Christmas lunch? No, I'm afraid not. I will be going to my parents' house.'

'Your parents? I did not know you had any.'

There is another example of cleaners living in a vacuum, with a vacuum. Of course I have parents and, given my age it would be fairly surprising if both were dead. But of course Mrs Settrington would never have thought about my home life – why should she? And now she does know that I do have parents, and that I go to see them, the knowledge will just be part of a fairly irritating memory. My parents are an inconvenience to Mrs Settrington. For the first time for years I felt rather proud of them. For existing, for having me to stay over Christmas like real parents.

'I'm sorry. I'll be leaving London on Wednesday morning, but I will be back with you again next week. I hope your party goes well. Happy Christmas.'

Then, that afternoon, Mr Nesbit did the same thing. He knew I occasionally helped his sister out when she was entertaining, and would I do the same for him. Yes, of course I would, when would he like me to come? Christmas lunch. I did not know whether to be amused or offended at their gall, and decided to be amused. Loudly and obviously, and maybe just the little bit rudely.

'Christmas lunch? No, Mr Nesbit, of course I cannot. I will be in Kent, where my family comes from.' (I thought that sounded grander than 'where they live'.)

And I received the same answer, 'Family? I did not know you had any.' Who do they all think I am, some modern-day Venus, rising from the sea on a shell, fully equipped with a duster and a tin of polish?

'Well, I do. Parents and a brother and sister-in-law and a nephew, with another on the way. Cousins, too, of course.' (I have not seen Sarah or her brother Jim for years, but they do exist. I wanted to make sure that my list of close relations was at least as long as his.)

'Of course. Well, I am sorry I asked you.' He looked hurt and huffy, and I relented. I find I have a bit of a soft spot for the old dear.

'Mr Nesbit, you can ask me any time. Except Christmas. How many people are you expecting?' Of course I meant, who are you expecting, but I know how to play the game.

'I am not sure. I do seem to have left it late, don't I? I have asked my sister's godson, Mr Hardwicke. I thought he might be lonely far from home at this time of year. He said would it be possible to bring a friend from work who is also on his own, and of course I said yes. Then I thought I should ask Mrs Settrington. She won't have any plans. Oh dear, this will be complicated. I am not sure I am up to it, maybe I should cancel Seth or just take them all out to a restaurant.'

I told him about the joys of ready-made Christmas pudding and stuffing, and pointed out that really Christmas lunch is not very different from your normal Sunday roast and of course he could manage it, and I laughed to myself at the thought of those two vicious old bodies planning exactly the same lunch, with the same guest list, the same staff, the same reluctance to ask the other. I was all for encouraging Mr Nesbit in his plan, and by the time he had finished his cup of coffee he was full of enthusiasm and energy for the project.

'I've found all the photographs of Seth's mother when we were young, and I thought I would buy an album and paste them all in together and give it to him for Christmas. Don't you think that is a good idea? He does love his mother, and I think he would be very interested to catch a glimpse of her past before she became an American.' I thought it was an imaginative and touching present, and told him so. When I went upstairs with my dusters and Hoover I left him sitting at the kitchen table making lists and singing to himself.

His bedroom was in dreadful disarray, which is very unlike him. The photographs were curling in little piles over everything – the chest of drawers, the night table, even little stacks on the floor where he had obviously been kneeling to look at them. Clothes were strewn on his bed, his bathroom was a mess, drawers were half open with various things hanging half out of them. He must have been very overexcited that morning.

I began moving methodically through the room, picking up the photographs, making neat little bundles of them. Of course I glanced at them as I did so, but to be honest they were not that interesting. Black and white pictures of strangers laughing together in straw hats, standing beside old cars or in front of grand buildings. One woman – little more than a girl, really –

appeared again and again, playing cards, standing with a horse, with a tennis racquet. She must have been very beautiful, even the poor quality of the photographs could not disguise that. Her eyes were huge and looked dark, her eyebrows were two perfect crescents above them. Her mouth was wide and full lipped, and seemed always to be smiling or laughing. This must be Seth's mother, a vibrant, dancing personality even in forty-year-old photographs. In one picture, one of the few in which she seemed still and almost solemn she stood staring up at a good-looking man who was smiling into the camera. He appeared not to notice that she was there, although one of her hands lay gently on his arm, but she looked totally absorbed in him. I realised with a shock that the man was a young, relaxed Mr Nesbit and, looking closely at the picture, was convinced that the woman was in love with him.

Poor girl. I suppose people were more innocent about homo-sexuality in those days, or maybe more secretive. I wonder how she discovered that it was no use being in love with Mr Nesbit, whether he had the guts to tell her or whether she found out some harsher way.

The only other photographs which interested me at all seemed, from the clothes, to be more recent. Mid-seventies, perhaps, taken at a table on a veranda. The scene looked foreign, although I could not place it, until I came across one in the same series which included a black man standing to attention, holding two enormous fish up by their tails and grinning proudly. I immediately decided that these pictures must be of Kenya, the holiday Mr Nesbit took with Mrs Settrington and her husband. And yes, the woman in the pictures could be Mrs Settrington, wearing light-coloured clothes with a vague air of safari about them. With her was a man, slightly older than she seemed, smiling broadly at the camera, a neckerchief tied rakishly around his neck. In one, they sat side by side at a table, holding glasses. On her face was that watchful, malicious expression I have seen occasionally cross her features. On the man's a solemn, soulful look as he gazed straight at the photographer.

I had spent too long poring over the pictures, and gathered up the remaining ones in a panic. It would never do to be caught prying. I hung up the clothes, tweaked the bedcovers back in line, straightened the rug. I pushed the drawers of the chest back in hurriedly, but one stuck. Something was jamming it open. I put my hand inside, felt the packet of papers towards the back, and pushed them down under some socks. Still the drawer jammed. Irritated, I pulled the drawer out to its furthest extension, but pulled too far. The whole thing fell out and I was left, holding feebly onto the handle and looking at a pile of socks, boxer shorts, and letters scattered all over the floor.

Letters.

Hidden in a sock drawer.

Well, everyone knows what that means. There is only one kind of letter which is hidden in a sock drawer, and it is certainly not anything to do with business or a bank manager.

Of course I knew I should not look at them, but that was not what made me hesitate. I was only nervous of being caught, not of doing wrong. I had spent long enough on the photographs . . . dare I have a quick look at the letters, too? Or should I save them for another time? But that was a week away, after Christmas. What if he noticed they had been moved and changed the hiding place? What if he had forgotten them and, seeing them again, threw them away. I could not take the risk. I had to see the letters, had to know who had written them. Seth's mother, perhaps. He must have been fond of her to have kept all the photographs, all the letters . . . what a shame he could not bring himself quite to be a woman's man. He would have been less lonely with a laughing beauty on his arm, would not have made china cows his heart's delight . . .

I went to the head of the stairs and listened. I heard a distant clanking in the kitchen. Good, he was busy.

Back in the bedroom I paused for only a minute. Perhaps my moral nature would prevail and I would slip the letters back into the drawer, unread. But I was only playing games with myself. Nothing could stop me now. Even now, writing this down, I cannot make myself feel guilty. I know that what I did was wrong, but remembering brings me no shame, only that entirely pleasurable rush of fear tinged with a feeling of power.

And then surprise. The letters were not from Gloria at all, nor from any woman. They were all signed 'Rory'.

It took a moment or two for me to remember why the name was familiar to me. Rory. Of course – Mrs Settrington's husband. Rory Settrington. Why had he written so many letters to Mr Nesbit? Even more interesting, why had Mr Nesbit kept them for so many years? Perhaps I was about to learn something interesting about my employer.

I was so absorbed that I forgot all about Mr Nesbit planning his Christmas lunch downstairs, forgot even to make the most cursory check for security. I sat on the floor where the letters had fallen, and quietly slipped the first one I picked up out of its envelope.

If I was hoping for juicy gossip about Mrs Settrington's drink problem or anything else I was disappointed. The letter was bland to the point of dullness. Just a friendly letter from one brother-in-law to another, a few friends (none I had heard of) mentioned in passing, an invitation issued for a weekend in the country. I looked at the envelope, and saw that the letter had been posted in Newbury. Maybe the Settringtons had lived there, there was no way of knowing.

I almost gave up then and there, but the pile of letters was too tantalising to ignore. The letter may have been boring, but there must have been some reason for keeping it.

I read five letters before I came to one which made my whiskers twitch with anticipation. The five were as unexciting as the first, but all the time I read I felt that there was something eluding me, some clue just around the corner. Then, in the sixth, was a postscript. 'Vince, old boy, be a pal and don't mention my writing to you to Patricia. She can be a little difficult sometimes, as of course you know, and I can see no reason to upset her needlessly. She asks for a lot of reassurance these days – I expect you know what about – and I'm just getting her on an even keel. Affectly yrs, RS.'

So there was a mystery, and it was something to do with Mrs Settrington. I still could not understand what it might be, why it could not be mentioned out in the open. Her brother and her husband were presumably the two most concerned with her welfare, and if they were writing to each other about the problem they should stop beating about the bush. If only for the sake of their readers. (How I could be having a sense of humour about my snooping when I could have been caught in the very act, I honestly do not know. But by now I was as engrossed as I would have been in a good novel. Nothing could have stopped me.)

I opened the next envelope, making an effort not to tear the flimsy paper. Trying to move fast was making me fumble. This one seemed warmer than the others had been, affectionate even. Rory said that his next posting was to be to Kenya, that he was looking forward to it but had enjoyed his three years in England. It had given him time to know Patricia's family better, particularly Vincent. It was a friendship he now treasured almost before any others, one which went beyond family duty. He very much hoped that Vincent would visit them in Kenya, as soon and as often as possible.

Kenya. I remembered the way Mrs Settrington had looked at her husband's painting of Mount Kilimanjaro on the first day I had met her. That fleeting, spiteful look. Also, perhaps, a little hurt? What had happened in Kenya? Then I thought back to the dreadful dinner party with Seth. He had been driven to mentioning Kenya then, challenging her – to what?

There was a crash from downstairs. I froze. Then I heard Mr Nesbit bleating up the stairs at me. 'Cindy? Cindy, could you pop down here a minute, dear? I've done something a little silly.'

I did not think. I honestly did not. I think if I had had time, even one second in which to weigh up what I was doing I would never have done it. But I did not have time, so I just scooped up the letters I had not read and jammed them into my back jeans pocket. There were only three, but as I pulled my jumper down over them I heard the crackle of paper and knew the bulge would show. Without even thinking clearly I remembered that my bag was on the chair in the hall, between me and Mr Nesbit. As long as he was not lurking there waiting for me I would be all right.

I put my head out of the bedroom door. 'Yes, Mr Nesbit?'

'Can you come down a minute, dear? I've dropped something and made a bit of a mess.'

'I'll be right down, Mr Nesbit.' I heard him go back into the kitchen, and quickly picked up the other letters and pushed everything back into the sock drawer. It did not occur to me that he would look for the letters before next week, not with Christmas and all his excitement about Seth. As long as the drawer looked the same as normal I would be safe. And in a week's time the letters would be back.

I put on a concerned face and ran down the stairs. Mr Nesbit was back in the kitchen, making little mewing noises of distress. I paused in the front corridor, jammed the letters in my bag, made sure the flap was covering everything, and ran down the rest of the stairs to the kitchen, where Mr Nesbit was looking in dismay at a broken sugar jar.

'Sugar all over the floor, dear, and I can't stand mice!' he moaned. I think he imagined invading hordes of rodents were on the point of streaming into the kitchen. I cleared up quickly, promised him he would be safe and put the kettle on.

'What you need, Mr Nesbit, is a strong cup of coffee,' I said, playing to the type he imagined me to be. It was not until we were sitting opposite each other eating biscuits and drinking coffee that I realised what I had done, the danger I had put myself into. I would lose my job, of course. Not just with Mr Nesbit, but word would get around in no time. They are all connected, after all. I do not suppose They would see it as borrowing, either. Although technically that is all it is. Why should it hurt him, anyway? Three old letters which he has probably forgotten.

I did not begin to shake until after I had left the house. But by then it was far too late.

Dad came to pick Tamsin and me up. It is the first time he has ever been across my threshold, and even so he would not let me give him a meal. He had insisted on coming, said that as it was Christmas and we were staying over we would have too much to manage on the bus. I asked if Mum would come up with him, perhaps we could do something in London together, go on some kind of outing. I don't know what is getting in to me, trying to make all these family plans, but anyway she would not come, said she would have too much to do, and it was far too expensive a time of year to think of extra treats. In February, perhaps, when there is nothing to look forward to. I felt put-down, and wished I had never suggested a treat. I wondered if Mum and Dad expected me to contribute towards my keep over the few days that we are there, but I do not see why we should. If they cannot have their own daughter and granddaughter to stay without counting the cost, they are worth nothing.

Still trying to arrive in Kent with the right festive attitude, I took some money out of my deposit account for Christmas shopping. I bought Mum a new dressing gown – quite slinky, a little bit 1940s glamorous – and the loveliest satin mule slippers with fluffy pom-poms. She is still pretty, Mum, although she doesn't make much effort, and I don't see why she should not have some entirely frivolous things. I was not quite so bold with Dad, and after a lot of thought came up with nothing more original than another jumper and a bow tie from Tamsin. I bought Joanne some lovely scatter cushions just like Amanda's for her new living-room, and Steven a power drill that Mum told me he wanted. For Matt there was a computer toy that Tamsin told me was all the rage.

I felt very pleased with myself as I wrapped the presents. Generosity leaves a wonderful, if self-satisfied, glow but apart from that I did think I had managed to please them all.

Tamsin and I were ready and waiting when Dad rung the bell. He hates lateness, apart from which I did want the flat to be tidy when he saw it.

'Ready, then?' he said as I opened the door. 'I've a parking spot straight outside.' He was wearing his maroon and green diamond-patterned jumper, last year's Christmas present from Mum. I wonder they have the shelf space for them all.

'Yes, we're all packed. Come in and have a drink.'

'I think we should set off at once, Mum will be expecting us.'

I felt as though he had hit me in the face. Why would he not come in? He looked jumpy, as though he were waiting for something unpleasant to happen.

'Dad, just a beer—'

'Cindy, love, you know what I think of drinking and driving.'

'Then a coffee.' I heard myself sounding pleading and hated myself for it, but I did want him to be able to report to Mum on how nicely I keep my home, how well I care for Tamsin.

He relented. He couldn't not. 'All right, just a quick one.' He followed me down the hall and into my flat. 'Oh yes, very nice,' he said as he walked in, but he was not really looking.

I have made my flat as nice as it can be in the last few years. Liz helped me paint it one weekend, a lovely clean pale yellow which makes it seem bigger. I borrowed a book from Lynda and we learned how to drag the paint. We laughed a lot that weekend. I bought some posters in the art shop and hung them in those plastic frames – I thought glass a bit extravagant for posters. They are all on the theme of water, which seemed to me a clever idea. There is one of Hockney's swimming pools, and another of Ophelia in the river. I bought a tapestry kit of a duck and sewed it up, but it took me a long time and I am not tempted to do another. Still, the living-room looks as different from my parents' as it does from Liz's.

I stood aside, pleased, to let Dad admire it. 'Very nice,' he repeated. Then added, 'but not very you, is it?'

Why did the remark send the blood to my head so that my face burned and I felt dizzy? It was not with anger, but with shame. He had hit some kind of mark, and it hurt like mad.

Tamsin did not help matters. 'It's lovely, isn't it, Grandad? Liz helped us, and Mum had to look ever so hard to find the right pictures. She said she wanted to plan them properly, like Mrs Blake does. That one,' pointing at Ophelia, 'reminds Mum of one of her ladies, she's got it on her wall, too. And she's got another one a bit like that swimming pool. Sometimes I just lie on the floor and look and look and look at it until I think I can jump in.'

Dad chuckled, but his eyes were uneasy. 'Don't want to do that, you'd end up like that lady there.'

'She went mad because her boyfriend went mad and didn't love her any more, so threw herself in the river and died. That's why she's got her clothes on.'

Tamsin sounded perfectly matter-of-fact, but Dad looked even more worried. 'Are you sure she should hear such tales, I know you've always been one for stories, but . . .' he asked.

'It's not mine, it's Shakespeare's,' I said wearily. 'Remember him?'

'Come on, Cindy, there's no call for giving me lip,' Dad said, and by his standards he was cross.

'Sorry. Shall we go?' It never works to plan things, to have expectations. You are always bound for disappointment. I did not realise until I saw his reaction quite how much I had been hoping that he would like my flat, my life. I had imagined us sitting on the settee, laughing together over a beer or two while he admired my handiwork and my taste. Or Their taste.

We were lugging the cases down the narrow corridor between my flat and Liz's when she came out of her door. 'Off, then? Happy Christmas,' she said giving Tamsin a kiss. I was surprised: she seemed to have come out deliberately, but we had said our farewells and exchanged presents the night before. Perhaps she just wanted to get a look at Dad. 'Is that everything? Can I help?'

'There's a couple more carrier bags, look like presents,' said Dad.

'Here, let me help you. Tamsin, go and get in the car with Mum. Grandad looks like he's in a hurry.'

Tamsin scuttled out of the door ahead of me and I, carrying a suitcase and Tamsin's backpack, could only follow. I put them in the boot, checked Tamsin had strapped herself into the back properly, and went back into the house for my bag and keys. Dad and Liz were standing together in the living-room, talking. Dad seemed to be finding it easier to chat to Liz, on whom he had never clapped an eye before, than he had to me, his own daughter. I was not even in Dad's car yet and already Christmas was going wrong, I was being overcome by Scrooge-like feelings.

Five minutes later we had set off. Dad drove in silence most of the way. He is never much of a talker in the car, but this time I felt he was brooding about something. Perhaps I was being over-sensitive.

Tamsin talked a lot for the first half-hour – how soon would we see Matt, could she spend one of the nights with him, what was the new house like, what was the new baby going to be called, was Gran excited, until Dad's indifference and my absorption finally wore her out and she fell asleep.

She had managed to lighten my mood a little, though, and Mum's welcome, which was genuine and warm for her, managed to put me back on form as a dutiful daughter. For Tamsin's sake if nothing else I was determined that Christmas should be a success.

'Not very practical,' Mum said as she shook her dressing gown free from its wrapping paper. 'Not very warm, I shouldn't think. But pretty. Thank you.' Her praise was grudging, her thanks formal. I wished I had bought her a terrylene wrap in beige and given the pink film-star gown to Joanne, who would at least have appreciated it.

'Wait 'till you see the slippers,' said Tamsin with a giggle. 'Mum said even if you didn't like them you'd be able to wow the (what was it?) jerry something, old people's ward in a few years' time.' Mum looked at me. There was a silence, broken at last by Joanne's high-pitched titter.

'I also said that it was a shame Mum never showed off her pretty feet,' I reminded Tamsin.

'Yes, let's see your feet, Gran. I didn't know feet could be pretty.' This time at least Tamsin had saved the situation a little, but things were not going well.

My mother and I were both veering between making a tremendous effort and either causing or taking enormous offence at trivialities. Maybe I was jumpy, maybe she was, I don't know. Dad skulked around the corners of rooms (hard in that house) looking hounded and Tamsin was on the whole oblivious to everything except the looming joys of Matt and Christmas Day.

I had brought Mr Nesbit's letters with me. I thought they were safest in my possession. I do not know what I imagined could possibly happen to them in my flat, but I did not want to let them go. I also felt that I needed to bring something of my own life with me to Kent. It was one matter to turn up and be the well-behaved daughter, quite another to leave everything of myself behind.

Was this odd? Perhaps, a little. They are not actually *my* letters, after all. But apart from Tamsin – always mine, my only possession that no one else can touch – and the old paperbacks in the bedroom cupboard, the letters were my only connection to the outside world.

Every now and again I remembered Dad's words about the flat. 'Very nice. But not very you, is it?' Each time the blood rushed into my cheeks and ears and I felt myself blush. How can he know what the real 'me' is? He knows nothing about my life. He never asks, shows no interest in Amanda or Lynda or Mr Nesbit. The only person he ever mentions is Liz, with whom he seems very taken. He asked how well I know her, looked very pleased when I said she is my best friend, wanted to know all about her life, spoke admiringly about how well she manages on her own until I thought I would go mad. Finally I answered back.

'I'm the one who managed to sort out a job,' I reminded him. 'She's the one who lives completely off the State.'

He frowned. 'You're not in a very pleasant mood, Cindy.'

'I'm just pointing out the truth. Mum wouldn't like her, anyway. She has enough trouble dealing with one illegitimate child – Liz has three.'

That gave Dad pause, all right. But he rallied and continued in support of his new heroine. 'Maybe her background was different, maybe they didn't hold with marriage.'

'Come on, Dad. She's a Roman Catholic, or was brought up one. And all the children have different fathers. At least they might do.'

I do not know why I was so disloyal about Liz. I think I was jealous: she was having more praise heaped on her in three days than I had received in six years. In some obscure way I felt threatened by Dad's admiration of her. For some reason I knew it was important to my safety to show Liz's feet of clay. I did not want Dad to trust her completely, instinct told me that he must not.

Every time I was cross with my parents, I thought of the letters. But I was enjoying the torment of waiting. I wanted to ration myself, to read one only when I could not bear the reality of Christmas with the Martin family for a moment longer. I tortured myself with the thought of them lying unread in my suitcase. I took them out at night and in the morning, put them in order of date by their postmarks, and waited.

I read the first one after Christmas lunch, when the rest of the family was digesting in front of the telly. I took the poodle for a walk, and while striding around the rec, for the third time, smiling inanely at other dog-owners braving the Christmas rain for the sake of their pooches (or to avoid helping wash the dishes) I decided to read a letter when I reached the house.

The first was tame enough: a farewell letter written to Mr Nesbit on the night before the Settringtons left for Kenya. But there were some tantalising references – one to Mrs Settrington's 'frail mental health', another to her unhappiness at their childlessness. Rory referred to the troubles in their marriage, admitted there was more than infertility at the root of it. He seemed very fond of his brother-in-law.

Reading the letter was almost as enjoyable as reading a Wilkie Collins: I almost knew the plot, *almost*, but was enjoying the struggle towards enlightenment.

* * *

No Name, my current Wilkie Collins, keeps my mind off the letters a little. It is yet another novel about illegitimacy – I wonder if Jane guided me towards it deliberately. It is not so obviously involving as *The Woman in White*, but I am loving it. Of course it is not really about illegitimacy any more than *Tess* is, but the whole trail of events in the novel begins when two sisters discover their respectable parents were not in fact married. I look at Tamsin and I wonder – will she be as horrified when she truly understands what it means to have no father? Even without the social and moral stigma faced by the Vanstone sisters, will she, at some deep dark level, feel disgusted by me? Will she love me or hate me for what I did? How can I explain it all to her without her despising me, yet without giving her any encouragement to do the same?

Perhaps Rory Settrington was illegitimate. Perhaps Seth is his illegitimate child.

Perhaps that is what my novel will be about.

Tamsin spent Boxing Day night with Steven in their new house. We had a happy lunch there – the easiest meal of the holiday, perhaps because it was not Mum and Dad's territory. Steven and Joanne are very proud of their house, with reason I suppose. It felt like a tidy box to me, everything in place, everything matching, but I suppose I have become used to the high ceilings of Notting Hill. Steve looks a little out of place in this flowery bower Joanne has created (even her kettle has flowers on it, even the swing bin in the kitchen), but he seems happy. Joanne is looking well pregnant now, although she is only about four and a half months gone. I felt a lurch of envious sickness when I looked at her stomach, proudly displayed in a clinging wool dress. I pushed the feeling down, though, my time will come.

In the evening I was bored, sitting alone with my parents. We ate a salad tea at six and the evening stretched ahead of me endlessly. Dad and Mum were prepared to settle down in front of the telly with non-stop cups of tea, but my throat felt tight with claustrophobia at the very thought.

I went upstairs and took another of Rory's letters. It was disappointingly shorter than the first. Rory Settrington spoke of bridge parties and painting, referred to their friendship with affection. But the meat of the letter was a cancellation of the open invitation to Kenya. Patricia's 'fragile health' was not up to it, and she would write and tell her brother so. Curiously, although Rory passed on the message, he added a rider: 'All I can suggest is that you change your plans, set off immediately before you receive her letter. I am sure that she will be happy to see you when you arrive: I most certainly will be.'

Fragile? Mrs Settrington? She is the least fragile person I have ever met. In fact I would say that Mr Nesbit is significantly more fragile than his sister. The way she rules over the Colonel, bosses Amanda about, virtually ignores her brother except when it suits her, these are not the signs of an emotionally fragile woman.

If her husband thought she was, though – and she certainly seemed to be playing that role successfully enough to fool him – what was he doing by going directly against her will, against what he must think of as her best interests – and asking Vincent to sneak over to Kenya in the hope that she would not mind?

I put the letter slowly back into its envelope and sat staring at the wall.

It was still only seven thirty and I could not reasonably go to bed. I wanted to ring Tamsin, but knew I should not. It was her first ever night away from me, and I hated letting her leave, but I knew it had to be done. I tried to read, but could not even concentrate on *No Name*. I wanted to read Rory's last letter, but had promised myself to save it for the next day, my last at my parents' house.

I missed work. Not work. I was missing Them. Their stories are so much more interesting than mine. I find myself bored when I am confined to my own life. Liz would be furious if she knew that.

Despite the cold, driving rain beating against the window I decided to go outside and take some air. I put my head into the living-room and told Mum and Dad I was taking the dog out. (Thank heavens for Blimp, he kept me sane over those few days.)

'Going to the pub, love? That's a good idea,' Dad said. 'Perhaps you will bump into some of your old friends.' I did not bother to answer. I have no friends in Kent.

A half an hour in the rain and wind shook me out of myself a little. On the way back I passed a pub, lights shining out an invitation. It made me a little homesick for Liz and the Percy. Perhaps I would go in, after all. I had my purse in my pocket and a Penguin 60s (Muriel Spark). Some strange, friendly faces and a half of Carlsberg might cheer me up.

When I let myself back into the house an hour later I was surprised by the silence. It was only nine o'clock but the telly was off. My parents could not have gone to bed yet. Then I heard something even more peculiar: they were talking to each other. Not would-you-like-a-cup-of-tea-dear talking, but a real conversation.

I was about to open the door of the living-room and join them when I heard my name and paused, hand on the flowery china knob.

'Cindy's not right, love, you must see that.' It was my father's voice. 'She never speaks except to Tamsin, doesn't seem to have any friends—'

'You said you met her friend Liz,' my mother interrupted.

'Yes, and she was a lovely girl. But she's worried, too. She told me.'

I was rooted to the spot, my blood beating thick in my throat, my head singing. The traitor. I should have suspected that she was up to something, sliding off with Dad like that.

'I don't understand you, Bill. Cindy looks perfectly healthy to me. She's eaten everything put in front of her.'

'I'm not talking about eating, Joan. She's silent, she's moody, she is only forthcoming on one subject and that is those people she works for.' I was amazed by this. Angry mostly, but also astounded that Dad had been paying so much attention to me.

'That's her job.'

'It's not her job, it's Them. It's like the rest of her life is make-believe; she's just their bloody cleaning woman, Joan.'

'Language, Bill.'

'Listen to me. Her friend – Liz – is moving out over Christmas. She's getting married. She says she's worried about leaving Cindy on her own.'

'She's got Tamsin.'

'Tamsin's a child. Liz says that if she didn't make her, Cindy would never leave the flat except to go to work and take Tamsin to school. It's not right.'

'So what are we supposed to do? She never comes near us.'

'She's our daughter. She's here now. Come on, Joan. Even Steven noticed, asked me what was up with Cindy. She's our bright one, Cindy, you know that. She needs more from life than this.'

'Is her flat tidy?' I almost laughed. It is so typical of my mother, that question. If you eat up and keep tidy you are all right.

'Yes, it's tidy. I am not worried about her in that way. But the flat – it's all wrong, Joan. It doesn't look like us, or Steven, or even her. I can't describe it, I'm no good with words, but it's not our Cindy. It made me feel odd about her.'

'She's always been odd. All that about books and writing and she throws it all in for a baby. She fought to get to college, you know she did, I don't suppose it was easy for her to be so unexpected. So after all that effort, why fall pregnant?'

'You wouldn't have liked it if she had got rid of it.'

'She needn't have told us. Or she could have married the lad. Plenty of children have divorced parents nowadays, there's nothing odd in that. But no, Cindy had to do things her way. She told me once she wanted to be better than a secretary. Well, if she thinks cleaning other people's toilets is better than typing their letters, good luck to her.'

There was a pause. I was frightened they would come out and catch me listening, but I felt too sick to move. Then my father spoke again, in a soft, sad voice I had never heard from him before. 'You're a hard woman, Joan. Isn't it time you forgot the past and helped Cindy find a future? She's just got us. She's got no friends.'

In an odd way I could cope with my mother's coldness. I expected little else from her. But to hear my father worrying, really caring, about me was more than I could stand. I ran up the stairs. I only just made it to the bathroom in time before being more sick than I have ever been in my life. On and on it went, stomach-wrenching retching until my eyes streamed and my throat felt as though it were bleeding.

Finally I lay in a heap on the bathroom floor, with not even enough energy to brush my teeth or make my way to bed. Then I felt someone in the room. I turned my head to see Dad standing in the doorway, his face white.

'Are you all right, Cindy? Was it something you ate?'

All I could say was, 'Did I tell you I'm going for a weekend in Torquay, Dad? I'm going to see Nelly, from university. A friend. From university. Nelly. In Torquay. A friend.'

Looking back on it, I don't think I reassured him very much.

I read the last letter on the bus on the way back home. My parents tried to make me stay longer, to recover from the 'stomach bug' as we all euphemistically called it, but I was firm. I would not even let Dad drive us back. I did not want him in my flat again. Mum offering to come too, 'for the ride' and 'to see your flat at last, Dad says it's ever so nice' made me even more determined to make my own way back.

I do not know if Dad was aware that I had been eavesdropping, but we never mentioned it. Mum put me to bed that night, brought me a cup of sweet tea – I swear if I were dying of uterine cancer she would bring me hot tea with the words 'this should do the trick'. She was business-like in her nursing of me: not cruel, not entirely without sympathy, but brisk. Dad came to see me in bed just before I fell asleep. As usual he did not say much, but I saw the concern in his eyes and in his clenching fists and almost felt sorry for him. Except I remembered his words, about my friendlessness, my work, my flat. I had felt his love for the first time since my childhood, and although it seemed to be unconditional, it also seemed to be short of the loving admiration of which I suppose I have always dreamed.

I took a few more books from the bedroom cupboard. I toyed with the thought of taking *Paradise Lost* and *The Faerie Queene*, but knew I will never read them now and if I do it will be through duty, not pleasure. Jane is right, there is no point in my reading to educate myself unless I am also enjoying myself. So I took *Jude the Obscure* and *The Warden*, and some of the American fiction I had been due to begin studying in October 1991. So long ago. *The Scarlet Letter* and Dreiser's *Sister Carrie*. Is all of literature peopled with fallen women? Are they always to be punished? Perhaps it really is a sin to fall, or at any rate to be caught out.

Dad waved us off with a worried face, Mum (who had actually come to the bus station) looked rather more cheerful. I do not think she was at all sorry to see us go.

Tamsin chatted a while, then turned to her book. I waited until I was sure she was absorbed and pulled the last of Rory's letters from my bag.

Nairobi
September 3rd

Vincent,

Those were the happiest weeks of my life. I suppose I had always known how I felt, but had attempted to suppress my emotions. I tried to do the honourable thing, tried very hard for all our sakes, but at last the truth is out. What swept away my reserves – apart from happiness at seeing you again after so long? I don't know, the heat perhaps, the very foreignness of Kenya. You were still my wife's brother, that evening in the camp, but somehow, so far from home, it did not seem to matter any more.

You asked me from when I can date my feelings for you. I evaded the question but now, in what I know must be my last letter to you, I think I owe you the truth. It was when you and Gloria were seeing each other. That whole affair made me very unhappy. Patricia was delighted, sincerely wished for you to marry, but I was convinced that Gloria was not right for you. I did not know why – or would not let myself know why – but I could not believe it would be a happy match. She was a lovely girl, Gloria, funny and attractive and clever and warm, but I knew she was not right. And then, when it was all over, when she left for America with her heart-break written all over her lovely face, I felt pity for her, but more than that I felt relief for you. And envy. You were man enough not to make the mistake I made out of pity and cowardice and even affection.

Yes, I have had other affairs over the years since my marriage. They were brief, urgent, secretive affairs. Nothing like ours. I am sorry that Patricia discovered us, sorry for her in her pain and misery, sorry because it means we will not see each other again.

But at the same time I am glad. Because it means the nastiness of secrecy has been taken from us. And I can be known as the man who loved Vincent Nesbit.

You, know, I was sorry when Patricia purloined my painting of Kilimanjaro at dawn – what a dawn that was, I will never forget it. I think I was as perfectly happy then as I will ever be, painting with you sitting in silence beside me, the smell of those French cigarettes hanging on the still air between us. (I used to loathe that smell, but now it will always make my heart beat a little faster.) Patricia was right, that was probably the best painting I have ever done. I wanted to give it to you, but I am glad I could not. Now I can look at it, and remember. Although Patricia must never know how much it means to me: if she did I am sure she would destroy it.

I will live the rest of my life in the shade, Vincent. But I will have a month of sunshine to remember.

You are of course right. I will not write to you again, or try to see you on my leave home. We have decided it must be this way and we must stick to that decision. If Patricia and I are to try to build a life we must make every effort. I must.

What I find so hard to live with is Patricia believing that she is the injured one in all of this. Of course she is in pain, a depth of pain I would have hoped never to have caused another human being. But her pain is nothing to mine. My heart has been torn from my body and only animal instinct keeps me alive.

For the first and last time, I can end this letter with my love. But, unspoken as it must now remain, it will always be with you,
Rory

I suppose I had known all along. I felt remarkably unsurprised, but still very excited at this letter. It explained the veiled references to Kenya, Mrs Settrington's distrust of homosexuals. Her brother and her husband. It is enough to turn anyone into a malicious old bat. I found the letter very moving: I have never received a letter like it. I wonder if the genuine emotion in it would soften Mrs Settrington's bitter old heart. Moving or not, that letter was very important. Its secret made it imperative that I return the letters without Mr Nesbit finding out that I had taken them. Neither he nor his sister must ever know that I know. Unless it suits me to tell them.

I was pleased to be back at work. Perhaps it is just people I need, perhaps I should think about an office job. Not that I could ever admit it to my mother. My CV would be a disaster, of course, but I am sure I could persuade most of Them to write me glowing references. I wanted to be a publisher once . . .

Amanda was more cheerful than I have seen her for a while. She has put an idea forward for a documentary and is hopeful that it might be taken up. She was in a very chatty mood, told me all about her Christmas with her family, said the behaviour of her sister's children had quite converted her to the idea of a childless future, but in the next breath added, 'and you were right, Cindy, even my love-life has taken a turn for the better. And the New Year has not even begun!'

'There, I told you it would not be long.' I was so pleased to be sitting back at her table that I did not even feel sour (but when will it be my turn? Where will I find Him?) 'Who is he?' I asked – she had brought the subject up, I thought the question was fair.

She laughed and blushed a little. I wonder why she seemed uneasy. Maybe she is not sure of him yet. 'Oh, it's too early for that,' she said. 'At this stage it's all in the mind – his as well as mine. At least I hope so. Oh, it's exciting. I'm as nervous as a teenager, keep jumping to the telephone. Not that you know him, anyway,' she added, a little late. I was not so sure.

'And does he? Ring?'

'Yes. But it's hard for him. He's very occupied. I wish I were a little more occupied.' She sighed.

'Well, you're looking very well on it,' I said. She was, really pretty, with a light in her eyes and a flush on her cheeks.

Just then the telephone rang and she leapt across the kitchen to answer it.

'Hello? Amanda Quince speaking.' Her voice was formal, her working voice, but I could hear the underlying tension. Then her whole body relaxed and she turned her back to me and held the telephone as tenderly as if it were a new-born baby and her voice dropped half an octave. He had rung.

'Hello? How are you? Fine, no it's all right, I'm on my own.' I had become invisible again. I quietly tidied the kitchen surfaces, looking preoccupied, my ears flapping.

'Tonight? I don't know, I was going to – yes, yes I do see. I'd love to. What time? No, of course, yes I understand. Do you mean that? Thank you. All right, then, see you at seven thirty. No, no I'm happy to eat early. I'll see you then. Yes, of course I am. I do. All right. Goodbye.'

She swung round, her hair flying, and said with a beam, 'Oh, it's wonderful, Cindy, I'm seeing him tonight,' (I mimed astonishment) 'I played it a bit cool,' (here I was genuinely astonished) 'after all, I don't want him to think I'm there for the taking, do I, especially as . . . Cindy, I do think this is going to work.'

I smiled a tight little smile, I could feel my cheeks were reluctant to be pushed apart by my treacherous mouth, but I had to try. In the abstract I suppose I am happy for her, but her luminous happiness after my dreadful Christmas, my certainty that with her expensive clothes and hair, her degree and her self-confidence, she had succeeded with Fergus where I had failed (without his even noticing that I had tried), all made me feel ill with misery.

I would have thought better of Fergus, would have credited him with more taste. Amanda is pretty, I suppose she is intelligent, but I would have thought that her thirty-something desperation shines out from her like a lighthouse beacon. She is all surface, Amanda. Sunday Mass or no Sunday Mass, I doubt she has a soul. You cannot chop and change with your soul, at least not as I understand it, but I bet the minute she has dirtied Fergus's sheets that missal will be gathering dust again. I am sure that Fergus, like everyone else, has faults, of course he does, but I never had him down as shallow. Perhaps all he is after is a roll in the hay. But if that is the case, he could have . . .

'Cindy, Cindy? Are you all right,' Amanda was shaking my arm, looking at me with huge worried eyes. Well at least I had stopped her thinking about herself for a minute.

'I'm sorry. I've been getting these funny turns. I'll be all right in a moment.'

'Here, sit down, you look awful. Are you sure you're not ill?'

She pushed me into a chair, gently forced my head down to my knees. I closed my eyes and let the blood run back down to my brain. When I sat upright again Amanda was holding out a tumbler with a small shot of drink in the bottom.

'Drink this. Whisky. I always take it for shock.'

I took the glass a little gingerly. 'I'm not sure I can hack whisky at this time of day. And I haven't had a shock . . .'

'Go on, it's medicinal.'

I tossed it back. The spirit hit the back of my throat, went up my nose, and its strength went straight to my head. I smiled at her, genuinely liking her concern. 'Thank you.'

'Are you eating properly? Do you want a sandwich? A pay rise?'

Sometimes her stream-of-consciousness daffiness is quite endearing. 'Of course I am. I have to take care of myself. There's Tamsin to look after.'

'Tamsin?'

'My cat.' I lied swiftly, instinctively. I still don't know why. Why do I not mind Lynda knowing about Tamsin, but am determined to keep her existence from Amanda? I suppose it is like my parents' reluctance to entertain their friends, a way of protecting my privacy. Since Nelly told me about Amanda, though, there has been another dimension to my secrecy. It is within the realms of possibility that I was faintly familiar to her when I began working at Bassett Road. I had been part of her theatrical production, we had exchanged pleasantries. If she knew I have a seven-year-old child it might just jog her memory. 'Weren't you the girl who left to have a baby? It was the talk of the campus. Everyone said you'd totally disappeared. Well, who'd have imagined it? I thought I knew your face. You did props, didn't you? Was it *Streetcar*? Oh, *The Maids*, yes, I remember. I got drunk, how awful. And here you are now. Well I never did.'

I cannot risk that. I will not. However much I sometimes like her she can never know that.

I was completely better by the time I saw the Blakes the next morning. I had spent the afternoon after cleaning Amanda's flat lying on my bed finishing *No Name*. It's a good title. I did not give Tamsin Pete's name, I did not think he deserved it or she would want it. I did not even put his name on the birth certificate. I was making myself a cup of tea and wondering whether that had been the right thing to do, when I suddenly had an awful thought. Pete's surname had gone right out of my head. I could not remember it at all. Something Scottish, that was all I knew. MacPherson? Less so than that. McBride? No, I'd have remembered the irony of that. I put down my tea and stared at the wall. How could it have happened that I could have forgotten Tamsin's father's name, making her in truth a child with No Name? Making her, like the Vanstone sisters, into Nobody's Child? One day she will ask, and then I will be beyond forgiveness. McKay? No, Peter McKay is a journalist my mother reads, not the father of my child.

I must remember, or find out. I will ask Nelly. She might know.

'Candy, happy New Year. Did you have a good Christmas?'

Mr Blake had walked into the kitchen, whistling, slapped his wife on the bottom, looked as though he were thinking about doing the same to me (I should like to see him try) and contented himself with a cheery greeting. Somehow he is more sinister when he is cheerful than not.

'Very nice, thank you. I went to my parents in Kent.'

'Oh, you have family?' (Why do they all look so surprised at that?) 'How nice. I hope you were looked after for a change, rather than always being the one looking after other people.'

That was kind of him, I could not help but realise. 'I suppose I was. Mum likes to do things properly.'

'Good, good.'

'And you?'

'Lovely, thank you. We went to Paris for three nights and pretended it wasn't Christmas at all. Much the best way to set about it, in my view.'

I glanced at Lynda. When she looks at her husband it is with more energy than I have ever seen anyone use for the simple act of looking. It is as though she is not watching him with just her eyes, but rather from somewhere behind her eyes, deep down beyond the brain. She uses her eyes, and her whole body, but, more than that, she is watching him with her soul.

Today I thought I saw the smallest shadow in her eyes as she looked at her handsome husband.

He left us together in the kitchen and Lynda asked me to help her prepare some food for a dinner party. I was surprised, as she prides herself on her cooking and never usually lets me do much in the kitchen. Perhaps she just wanted the company.

'It was Randal's idea to have people round,' she said as she flaked a salmon for fish cakes. 'I was very surprised, so soon after the party and Christmas, but of course I was pleased. I'm thinking of going on a cooking course, you know. Oh, I know I'm perfectly competent, but I'd like to extend my range. I really fancy one of those ones in Tuscany, you go for a fortnight to a beautiful house and cook and eat and laugh . . . but I don't suppose Randal would like me to go. Maybe next time he's away.'

'He seems very well.' I was peeling potatoes. I suppose it was obvious that I would be relegated to the kitchen-maid jobs.

Lynda brightened with pleasure. It is easy to make her happy – just say something mildly pleasant about her husband.

'Doesn't he? His case is nearly over. All his hardest work is done and now he can only wait and see. He is always very – energetic – at this stage in a court case.' She giggled and blushed and I was left in no doubt as to the form his energy took. She should be looking happy, then. Why the shadow in her eyes?

'Would you go on your own? To Tuscany?'

'I suppose so. Or maybe I could persuade a friend to go with me, that would be fun. Perhaps I could ask Amanda.'

'Amanda? Quince?' I laughed. 'It's not for me to say, but I don't think she's very interested in cooking.'

'I've always eaten well there.'

'Well, don't say I said anything but when I've tidied up after one of her dinners I've noticed a lot of boxes saying Marks and Spencer.'

'No!' Lynda looked absolutely horrified. I suppose she thinks ready-made food is for the likes of me. As if I could afford M&S fish pie. 'I must say, they're very good,' she added on reflection. 'Perhaps I shouldn't bother with all this—' she waved her fishy hands over her table.

'Of course you should. I bet Mr Blake likes your cooking. But maybe you could persuade him that M&S is the business while you go to Italy with Amanda.'

Lynda looked worried again. 'You might be right about Amanda. I just feel that I should see more of her. We were very good friends at one time, although I have to admit I sometimes noticed the age difference. It's a shame to lose touch. I don't want her to forget what friends we were.'

What an odd thing to say, when they live so near to each other, are part of the same world. I could understand Nelly saying it of our friendship, but Lynda and Amanda . . .

'She was at your party, wasn't she?' (as though I did not know).

'Yes, and in fact she is coming here tonight. There will be six of us only, us, Amanda, the Bedfords and Fergus.'

'Fergus?'

'Yes. Robert – Bedford – is in chambers with Randal. They'll talk law to each other all the evening. The wife's nice enough, works in publishing, but a bit baby-mad. I thought Fergus would lighten things up a bit.'

Fergus and Amanda. So it has all started. They saw each other last night, are meeting at Lynda's tonight. Soon she will come clean and tell me, with that gleaming smile, who her boyfriend is, and I will have to pretend I did not know, that I do not mind . . .

Lynda was still talking. I cut the potatoes into small pieces carefully. Very carefully, my hands were shaking and I did not want an accident. I tried to listen to what Lynda was saying. It could be important.

'You know, I think your instinct was right after all. I remember your saying that maybe Fergus and Amanda might suit each other. Well it looks as though you could be right. Do you remember that some of us went out together for dinner after the party? Amanda and Fergus were two who came with us.' (I know, I know, I saw them all.) 'Randal seems to think they took quite a shine to each other.'

I put the potatoes on to boil, looked at Lynda as she skilfully sliced onions. She smiled, but did not seem as happy as she was trying to sound. 'That's why he suggested we have them to supper. Says he wants all our friends to be as happy as we are. Isn't he wonderful? God, these onions are strong, look at me, my eyes are streaming.'

'Do you want me to do anything else here?' I heard my voice: it was very polite, almost cold, but I no longer felt like gossiping idly. She has everything, including the husband she loves so much. Why does she have to be so jealous of Fergus? I cannot believe she still holds a torch for him.

At any rate, I think Lynda felt the same as I did about our chat. 'No. Thank you. Do the sitting-room, why don't you. You won't have time to do everything before you go and I would like that to look nice.'

She wiped her eyes with her sleeve and watched me out of the room. I felt as though I had failed her in some way. Perhaps she did need to say more. For once I did not want to know.

The post-Christmas round is very exhausting. They all ask politely after my holiday, but are not really interested. Then They tell me about Theirs. Mrs Settrington was particularly quarrelsome that afternoon, or maybe the morning with Lynda had left me feeling less sympathetic.

She told me that Mr Nesbit had cooked a filthy Christmas lunch, apparently on my instructions, that Seth had saved the day with a delicious brandy butter he had brought with him from his flat, that Amanda had been as selfish as usual, put herself first, not given a thought to her aunt and uncle or even Seth, all alone in a strange country. She had turned down the invitation to Mr Nesbit's (probably because she did not want to eat reconstituted muck and who could blame her) in favour of going to stay with her sister. According to Mrs Settrington, it was highly unlikely that Amanda's sister wanted her at all, she had quite enough to do with the baby. What's more her parents had gone too, 'just like my niece, fantastically selfish, why on earth didn't she cook lunch for her own family, I'd like to know? It is absurd, having all those children and then expecting them to cook Christmas lunch. At least Vincent made the effort, realised that it is the duty of the older generation to provide for the younger at this time of the year.'

On and on she went, following me around the house in a

miasma of malice. She had been out to lunch with the Colonel, so I expect she had drunk a glass too many of sherry and was feeling liverish: I do not think even she would be quite so unpleasant without the help of some liquor.

'Seth brought a charming friend, I forget the surname, Evelyn something or other. Comes from a dreadful family, parents separated, one brother who lives abroad. I thought it very thoughtful of Seth to include Evelyn. They seem to be very close friends. It's nice to show people what close families are really like, give those without that advantage something to aspire to . . . Evelyn brought the Christmas pudding, very good, Fortnum and Mason, not the supermarket filth that Vincent had planned. Yes, it was a very enjoyable luncheon.'

I did not believe her, not for one minute. I almost pitied Seth for finding himself caught having Christmas lunch with those aging spiteful siblings. As for Mrs Settrington thinking she was setting an example of family unity just by being there . . . although of course she had overcome quite a lot of history to get to that stage at all, I supposed. Nevertheless I was sure that Evelyn had thanked her lucky stars that she was not on speaking terms with her family by the time the Settrington/Nesbit duo had finished its performance.

By now we were in the bedroom. I hate it when They follow me around, but none more so than Mrs Settrington. It is partly because I feel she is watching me to make sure that I clean properly – and I do not need to be checked up on – partly because I like the silence of my own thoughts, the chance to observe and analyse Their lives. When Mr Nesbit is pottering along behind me I can almost ignore him; when it is Mrs Settrington it is much harder. Her malice is like an acid wave washing up, retreating, rushing on, retreating, until I am left eroded by it, worn away.

Maybe that is just my excuse for what happened next. I was dusting the picture frames, Mrs Settrington hovering behind me spewing out her resentment of her brother. I felt sorry for him. At least he had tried to cook Christmas lunch and I was sure it was not as bad as she was pretending. Then I noticed which picture I was cleaning. It was the water-colour of Kilimanjaro, the one Mrs Settrington had pointed out to me the first time

I looked around her house, the one – I was sure – which her husband had mentioned in the letter to Mr Nesbit. I would like to say I spoke without thinking, but that would not be the truth. I had a second or two in which to consider and decide.

'Is this the picture your husband painted in Africa?' I asked, pausing and standing back as though to admire it.

She stopped in her flow of complaints and looked taken aback. 'Yes. He did a great many, but I always thought this was his best.'

'It's lovely. I wonder if . . .'

'What? It's Mount Kilimanjaro.'

'Oh, then it must be.'

'What?'

'Mr Nesbit was talking to me about it the other day – if it is the same one. He asked me if I had ever seen it, said he had noticed it was not in the sitting-room or dining-room and wondered if you still had it. He *will* be pleased.'

'Why should it matter to him?' She was sharp, on the attack, but she knew, or at least guessed. Her body was very still as she waited for the answer.

'Oh, he said he had visited you in Kenya, had the best time of his life. He said he went camping with your husband, and one morning they got up very early and your husband did this wonderful painting. It is lovely.'

'But I thought, this was before—' I was frightened by the change in her. She had gone quite white, her little old eyes suddenly seemed huge, her face looked more like a skull than anything living.

'Mrs Settrington? Are you all right? Sit down.'

She had already plumped down on to her small bed, her glittering eyes fixed on the picture. Remembering Amanda and the whisky I ran downstairs, poured Mrs Settrington a rather larger one than I had been given (her system is more used to strong alcohol than mine) and ran back up the stairs. Mrs Settrington took the glass and knocked the whisky back in one.

'Thank you, dear, you are very kind.'

Kind? When, with a malice to match her own, I had destroyed something she had treasured for years? I felt sick at myself, wished

I had poured myself some whisky at the same time as hers. But there was nothing I could do to change my words. She has heard them now and they will ring in her ears every time she looks at that picture.

Why did I do it? To punish her for ruining Mr Nesbit's Christmas lunch? What is that to do with me? To punish her for boring me, for disgusting me with her unpleasantness? I could have found a gentler way, not chosen to take the same path. Or did I do it because I am sick of my life, sick of Amanda and Fergus's young love, of my own sterile, lonely life? I do not like hurting people, I am not that cruel. But I do like – and I know this is not very praiseworthy – I do like having a secret power over Them. It gives me some sense that I matter in Their lives, even if They value me no higher than Their dishwashers.

This was unnecessary, though. It was one thing to arrange for Jane to be asked to Lynda's party. That hurt nobody and Jane liked it. Liked the idea of the party, at least.

But this . . . I was – I am – ashamed of myself.

From now on, I must only use my knowledge for Good.

After I had visited Mr Nesbit the next day I felt even more guilty about my behaviour towards Mrs Settrington. His version of Christmas was entirely different from hers. According to him, lunch was delicious, everyone enjoyed themselves, Seth in particular had been delighted with his first English Christmas for years, his friend Evelyn had been a bonus (so why did he look downcast at the mention of her?) and Mrs Settrington had been unusually relaxed and had persuaded them all to spend the afternoon playing pontoon.

A completely different story. Mrs Settrington's complaints the day before must have been fuelled by something the Colonel had said at lunch, or the colour of my shirt, or something else equally irrelevant.

So she did not spoil the Christmas lunch.

In a way, that makes her nastiness *about* it even more reprehensible. Doesn't it?

As it is the Christmas holidays still Jane was at home in the afternoon. Tamsin had begged to come too so I picked her up from Liz's in Kilburn at lunchtime. (I must organise a sitter for when term starts, Tamsin cannot go all the way up there after school when I'm late.) Tamsin was very excited but had promised not to get in my way or Jane's. In the event the three of us passed a very happy (paid – it is always comforting to realise that) half-hour around her little table drinking coffee (milk for Tamsin) and eating chocolate biscuits which I am sure Jane had bought especially.

It was Jane, not me, who brought up the subject of my writing. Had I started yet? Have I bought myself the pen?

'Not yet. I know what you said, but I felt it would be cheating if I bought it now.'

'So you haven't begun?'

'No. Still just, you know, my ramblings.'

She smiled. 'Maybe those would make a book in themselves.'

When I left the flat she handed me a copy of *Lady Anna*, a Trollope I had not heard of before. 'Here's another one for your collection,' she said with a smile. 'Good luck.'

I went home and started writing. That night, after Tamsin was asleep, I began to plan my story, make notes about characters and their relationships to each other and their backgrounds. I worked until midnight and was so excited that I woke at six thirty the next morning and did another hour's work before I woke Tamsin.

Lynda and Randal were out, so I whisked round their house in no time, not even paying much attention to the clues They always leave around as I was thinking so hard about my story. I let myself in to Fergus's flat just before twelve, slightly earlier than usual, and found him in the kitchen drinking coffee in his boxer shorts. He looked very embarrassed and disappeared into his bedroom to dress. How very unlike Randal, I thought, remembering how he had showed me ice cubes and discussed avocado dips in his underpants.

When he came out of his room I had tidied the kitchen up and was wondering whether to clean it or his study first.

'Study last, please, I've work to do this morning,' he said. 'I've finally pulled myself together and have started my novel. Last week I signed a contract to write a weekly column for the *Guardian*, which will pay the bills, and now at last I can concentrate on the thriller.'

'When did you begin?' I asked.

'Last night. Suddenly it all fell into place. I worked till midnight and was up at six. I didn't even bother to get dressed – as you saw. Sorry about that.' We laughed together, but I was thinking of the glorious coincidence of our beginning to write our novels at the same moment. A short distance across London from each other we sat down by the light of a bare bulb and began to write. It must be an omen. It must be.

'Cindy, you're a doll,' he said. 'You look almost as pleased as I feel.'

I was not sure how much I liked being called a doll; on another day I would probably have downright resented it, but today . . .

'Fergus, I—' I began, but lost my nerve.

'Yes?'

I changed tack. 'Am I the first to know?'

'Yes, I suppose you are. Why?'

'Then can I have the first copy?'

He laughed. 'I've only written a couple of thousand words. The finished copy – if there ever is one – is a long way off. But yes, all right. You shall have the very first copy, signed by the author's own hand.'

I had not had the nerve to tell him about my own writing. I was frightened he would laugh. But I made a promise to myself that I would return the compliment, that he should have the first copy of my book, too. I wonder whose will be in the bookshops first.

It was only when I was washing the kitchen floor, humming to myself (under my breath so as not to disturb him) that I realised that I had been told his news not only just before his mother and brother and best friend, but also before Amanda. The thought made me unreasonably happy.

I thought of the sexy twinkle in his eye as we laughed together, I thought of the sight of his body in the boxer short: a good body, not a journalist's body. There was no sign of the legendary long boozy lunches on him. He looked fit without being gym-bound, neither paunchy nor weedy and skinny. I had liked the sight.

I moved to his bedroom. It was as messy as usual. I waded my way through discarded clothes, old cups of coffee, overflowing ashtrays. I would have thought Amanda would have imposed some order on this mess, but there were no signs of her.

No signs at all.

I looked through the bins in the bedroom and bathroom. Nothing feminine. There was a glass of water on only one side of the bed. Beside it was *Holidays in Hell* and *High Fidelity*. No books on the other side. Not that I would expect any necessarily. Not from Amanda anyway, and certainly not with the purpose of her visit in mind.

There was only one toothbrush in the bathroom, no trace of make-up or scent. Coal tar soap, the same as usual.

I thought back to the kitchen. I knew he had gone to dinner with Amanda at the Blakes' on Wednesday, last night was Thursday. There had been one plate in the sink, smeared with egg and baked beans. A real bachelor's supper. Well, he had been working, he did not need to see her every night.

But would it be likely that he would begin a new love affair and a few weeks later start to write a book? Could he have the emotional energy for both? Possibly. Perhaps the two are tied in, the one form of energy feeding the other.

I do not know. But I doubt it.

Perhaps I have been wrong. Perhaps Fergus is not Amanda's new boyfriend. I am not at all sure how to find out, but I will. Oh, yes, I will. And in the interim I am very cheered by the possibility that I have been wrong.

On Monday morning at Mrs Settrington's house I noticed that the Kenya picture is no longer hanging on the wall. Neither of us said a word about it. I wonder where it has gone.

Whoever it is has hit home-base with Amanda. She is obviously totally besotted, is walking on air, making no attempt to do any work, moons out of the window as though hoping the mystery He might walk past her door. Sickening, really. You would think she was nineteen, not twenty-nine.

Gentle probing brought me no closer to discovering who he is. She says he is wonderful, but it is all very complicated, she must not be too hopeful. I asked if she had introduced him to any of her friends yet and she looked horrified and said of course not, then looked confused. I wonder what is going on . . .

I know this much about him – he is another boxer wearer. I found a pair, red and green striped, in the bed. (I suddenly had a memory of Pete's powder-blue Y-fronts. How odd it is how forgotten memories can reassert themselves. I wish that particular one had stayed buried.) I made the bed, folded the underpants, and left them tidily on the end of the bed, chuckling to myself as I did so. This was better than the razor blade.

It was not, though. Amanda has lost her senses so completely that she just laughed when she saw the stripes at the foot of her bed. 'How embarrassing, Cindy, what must you think? Where were they?'

'Inside the bed, tucked down one side.'

'We thought we'd looked everywhere. It was a complete mystery. But he had to get back, we couldn't waste any more time. Thank you. He *will* laugh.'

Mr Nesbit is not nearly as cheerful as either Fergus or Amanda. It is as though the success of Christmas lunch left him on a high which has now receded, leaving him feeling let-down and gloomy.

He spent most of Thursday morning in his sitting-room with his embroidery, but he did not seem to be making great progress. He blamed his old eyes, and the poor light, and the closeness to each other of the different shades of green which he was using. I think the problem was really with his attention span. He was thinking of something entirely different from his canvas: Seth Hardwicke.

'He's a very good boy, came to see me yesterday with a bottle of very good claret. I shall ask him to supper to help me drink it. I don't think I shall ask Evelyn this time, three would be too many for the one bottle. And I'm not sure how well they are getting on any more, Seth says Evelyn is being difficult. They share a flat, you see, and Seth says Evelyn is quibbling about the telephone bill. Of course it is true that Seth's family is in America, but Evelyn has the bigger bedroom . . . Evelyn found the flat, but still . . .'

I was not particularly interested in Seth's flat-sharing arrangements, but I could see my duty today lay in making conversation, so as I dusted a rather stunted-looking bull, I said, 'Oh, what a shame, Mrs Settrington said what close friends they seemed. You know what a match-maker she is, I wondered if she was hoping for a marriage.'

It was just a passing comment, a joke, but Mr Nesbit gave up all pretence of doing his tatting and looked at me in deep surprise. 'Marriage? I really don't think that Patricia of all people is that liberal. Not even I – I mean the Church of England must hold on to some vestige of self-respect. Although I wonder what would have happened if Henry VIII had been homosexual.' He chuckled at the idea, but I was completely baffled.

'I'm sorry, I . . .'

'I should think Patricia was pleased at how close their friendship seemed because I—' He stopped, looking sad and very confused.

'I shouldn't have said anything. I'm sorry. She just seemed so pleased with Seth's friendship, told me all about Evelyn and her Fortnum and Mason pudding, I just—'

'*Her* pudding?' Now the old man was laughing. '*Her* pudding?' he repeated with glee. 'I see it all! My dear girl, Evelyn is a *he*. You've grabbed hold of completely the wrong end of the stick. Didn't you know that Evelyn is a male name as well as female?'

Of course I knew, and saw at once how ridiculous it had been of me to assume that Seth's friend was a woman anyway. I could not help but join in the laughter against myself.

Then I remembered there was something else I must do. I had thought my approach out before arriving, but Mr Nesbit had been too preoccupied for me to bring the matter up until now.

'Do you mind my asking you something? My parents are thinking of going to Kenya for a holiday and I remembered you mentioning that you have been there. Where do you think they should go?'

With a little guiding, I made sure Mr Nesbit told me about Kenya, Kilimanjaro, the picture. And with that conversation I was covered.

Liz brought Ayesha down from Kilburn to spend the day with us, and after a coffee and a gossip with Liz, Tamsin, Ayesha and I took a bus up to the gate and ate hamburgers in Tootsie's. It was afterwards, as we were walking home through the drizzle past an Indian corner shop where the owner was grumpily packing up his street display of vegetables and flowers that I had the brain wave. I suddenly realised how I could find out the name of Amanda's new lover. It was not sure to work, but was certainly worth the try. I would order some flowers to be delivered to Bassett Road while I was there. I would write some nondescript loving message and sign it – how? With just an initial. They were obviously playing their love affair fairly secretively, so it would tie in. I would sign the message *F* and watch her closely when they arrived.

Of course the success of my plan would depend on Amanda's being there, and also on the element of surprise involved. I might have to be very quick indeed, but it would certainly be worth the risk. If nothing else, I would be making Amanda happy. All women like being given flowers.

Pete gave me some flowers once. Blue irises. It was one of our happier moments, and I still feel uplifted when I see the flower. I nearly called Tamsin Iris. Silly, really.

I was lucky. Amanda was there when the flowers were delivered. I heard the doorbell ring, watched Amanda rush to the intercom, heard her excited answer. 'Flowers? Are you sure? Yes, Miss Quince, how lovely.' She buzzed the door and ran downstairs to take them. Blue irises. I am an old romantic really. I positioned myself so that I could hear her coming up the stairs and see her as soon as she walked through the door.

The flowers were hooked into the crook of her elbow and she was tearing open the envelope. 'Aren't they pretty?' She asked. Isn't it funny how women always look self-conscious when they are sent flowers, no matter how pleased they are?

Her eyes were scanning the card. She frowned. 'This is odd.' She read the message again. 'They're all illiterate. Look, they've gone and put an *F* there. It's nowhere near the same. Although, I suppose . . . Anyway, they're lovely. Oh, I told you it was going well. Aren't I lucky?'

I sat down that evening with a pen and paper and wrote out the letter *F* in all the scripts I could imagine. I could make it look like a slightly wonky *I* or an affected *E*. But the more often I wrote it the more one letter glared out at me. *P*. A capital *F* could easily slip into looking like a capital *P*.

So who on earth begins with P?
Whoever he is, he is not Fergus.

I had from Tuesday to Friday in which to brood. Oh, I had work, and Tamsin and *The Scarlet Letter*, but they were not enough. I have my story too, which is not going anywhere. I spend a lot of time re-casting the plot and have not brought myself to write the opening sentence yet. Having been obsessed with Magdalen Vanstone I can now think of nobody but Hester Prynne. Perhaps writers should not read after all.

In between thinking of Hester and Tamsin and Vincent Nesbit's love life, I have been thinking about Fergus. Jane told me I should be bold, have the courage of my convictions, set pen to paper. Should the same not apply to Fergus? Should I – dare I – encourage him to look at me? I am sure he likes me. I know he is an incorrigible flirt, but I think he looks at me with more than a flirt's eye. He treats me as an equal. Most of the time. We are both writers. He is not involved with Amanda. I am sure Lynda's soft spot for him is not reciprocated. Not beyond nostalgic affection for a married ex-girlfriend who is still around.

I have said before that I am pretty enough, and I do not think that is boasting. I should say that I am prettier than Lynda, eyelash for eyelash. Given the right kit I could be as attractive as Amanda. Maybe never so flash.

On Thursday afternoon I had my hair cut at a different (and more expensive) hairdresser. I asked for the 'Rachel' cut and could tell by his barely concealed sneer that I was already out of date, but I knew it would suit me and I was right. I went to French Connection and bought myself a long slinky skirt and a short electric-blue jumper. It is time I showed off my figure.

When I opened the door to Fergus's flat on Friday I felt suddenly nervous. What if he noticed my new clothes and realised why I had bought them? I felt a fool, but it was too late for me to go back.

He barely looked up as I went into the study. 'Hi, Cindy. All right?'

I nodded and made my way through to the kitchen. After a minute or two he followed me.

'I need a beer. Would you like one?'

I nodded again, all at once too shy to speak, and he opened two bottles of Beck's and handed me one.

'Well, aren't you going to ask me how it's going?'

Of course I knew what he meant and wished he would ask me the same question. How could he, he does not know.

'How's it going?'

He smiled and leaned back against the fridge, taking a swig from the bottle. His hair was all standing on end and he looked tired, but I think he is wonderful looking, big nose and all. (I am getting as soft as Amanda now.)

'It's wonderful. I've never enjoyed anything more in my life. Well, hardly anything,' and he grinned at me and I swear I could hardly stand up.

'It's a thriller, you said?'

'Yes, the plot just came upon me – almost a year ago now – and I've been turning it over in my head and wondering if it would work, whether I would ever organise myself into writing it and suddenly wham! it's got off the ground. I'm writing about a thousand words a day at the moment, so I feel I'm getting somewhere.'

'You are lucky.' I was immediately worried about giving myself away, but Fergus was too wrapped up in his own thoughts to notice.

He looked surprised. 'I suppose I am. But it's come about through bad luck in a way. First the *Mail* didn't renew my contract, but then that freed me from office life and I talked the *Guardian* into taking me. Then Lottie doing a runner. I don't suppose I would ever have got going if I'd still had a girlfriend cluttering up the flat.'

I had to laugh. The idea that anyone or anything could make his flat more untidy was idiotic.

He caught my look – he is a great one for eye contact, Fergus – and laughed too. 'All right, you don't have to say anything.' He took another swig of his beer and looked at me over the top of the bottle. 'You look different today – have you done something?' he waved the bottle at me and I felt embarrassed. I knew I would overdo it, now he will think me a fool.

'Oh, just a bit of a hair-cut,' I mumbled.

He looked at me more closely. 'Well, it suits you, and

you're looking very smart. Are you going somewhere later?'

I know I am a fool. I know it. Now, writing this down, I am almost too embarrassed to say what happened next. I can only hope that the embarrassment will fade and the incident will be useful as experience. I have had so little of that – experience – with men in the last few years that I suppose it is no wonder that I made an idiot of myself.

You see, I misunderstood Fergus. When he asked me if I was doing anything later I thought he was asking me out. I know it was mad, all he was thinking about was his book, he was just passing the time of day with me, being friendly, clearing his head of the silence so that he could begin work again.

He was taking a mild interest in another real human being so that he could begin to concentrate again on his pretend ones.

If it were not so humiliating, it would be funny to remember the look of shock (not just Fergus-like surprise this time, real shock) on his face when I said, 'Oh, well, I was thinking – no, I'm not doing anything, thank you.'

He is very well-mannered, Fergus, I will give him that. He put his face back in order as quickly as he could and said gravely, 'Good, well maybe we'll have another drink when you've finished here.'

I realised then, of course, that he had just been paying me a compliment, that it would never occur to him to ask me out, but that because he is a gentleman he will buy me a quick drink to spare my feelings. I tried to smile, but I could not see him, my eyes were so full of tears.

'I'll get started then,' I said, and pushed past him.

I cleaned energetically and thoroughly for three hours. Then I put my head around the door of the study. He looked up, distracted, then remembered the predicament he had got himself into and stood. 'Ready?' he asked.

'It's all right, sorry to let you down but I've just remembered I told my neighbour I'd meet her child from school today – she's going to the dentist.'

He sat down again. His body looked relieved but his face looked politely disappointed. 'Oh, what a shame. Of course I understand. Maybe some other time.'

He is a gentleman, Fergus. Which does not make my shame any the less.

When I finished writing that last passage – the evening on which it had happened – it was still only eight o'clock.

Friday night, eight o'clock, all togged up in my new clothes, my nerves jangling at reliving my embarrassment on paper. Tamsin was asleep. I looked at my story line and it suddenly seemed soulless. I picked up *The Scarlet Letter* but could not concentrate. On impulse, I ran upstairs with the alarm and asked Mrs Perkins if she would listen for Tamsin while I made a telephone call.

Liz answered on the first ring, and I almost lost my nerve.

'I felt like going on the town tonight and wondered if you were doing anything,' I muttered.

Liz sounded delighted. 'I should think that's the first time in all the years I've known you that it's you suggesting we go out. We were going to spend the night in, but there's nothing on telly. Give me half an hour to put me slap on and catch a bus and I'll meet you in the Percy.'

'Are you sure?' I asked and then, before she could change her mind, added, 'Brilliant. Mrs Perkins is in and she can baby-sit.'

'Dave, you don't mind if I go out, do you?' I heard her saying, and heard him answer, 'No, but don't go off with any strange blokes. Remember you're spoken for now. Tell Cindy to keep an eye on you for me.'

'Hear that?' she laughed. 'I'm not my own woman any more.' But she sounded proud of her enthralment. 'I'll see you in a while.'

I walked slowly back home, buttered up Mrs Perkins, redid my face and made my way to the Percy. All the time I was thinking of Liz and our friendship.

Perhaps this was to be the last time that Liz and I would go out together on our own. She would sink into Kilburn domesticity and then there would be babies. We would see each other less and less often until we lost touch entirely.

I went out to have a good time. What I asked for, I was given.

Sally and Jim were already in the Percy when I arrived and

they said Ed and Paddy would be coming soon, where was Dave? Liz was teased for having reduced him to baby-sitting before she even had the ring on her finger and she flushed and laughed and looked pleased.

We had a few more drinks when Ed and Paddy turned up, then decided to go dancing, and moved off in a group. Liz made a few noises about going home but we all shouted her down and, looking at me, she agreed to stay with us.

I am putting off writing down what happened next, but I cannot do it much longer.

Someone asked me to dance. I had felt him watching me from the edge of the dance floor. I felt good with my new clothes, my hair, a little bit of drink inside me. I know that I dance well and I suppose I was showing off a bit. I had pushed Fergus out of my mind, at least I thought I had.

So when he asked me to dance I said yes. He was quite nice-looking, dark, big brown eyes. He could be half-Moroccan or Portuguese or something, that kind of look and not very tall. He danced brilliantly. At last I had found a partner who really knew what he was doing. He danced with me, not at me or with himself.

We stopped, had a drink, talked a little, danced some more.

Liz came over and said she really did want to go home now, was I coming? And I said no, I was having a good time. She said she would stay, I told her not to, I could look after myself, I would not be much longer.

She looked doubtful, smiled, said, 'I'm always encouraging you to go out and let your hair down, I can hardly drag you home now. Be careful.' She kissed me – which is unusual – waved, and disappeared.

My partner, John (at least I know his name) was waiting and when I turned back to him I saw in his big brown eyes the glad assumption that if I was not going home with Liz I would be going back with him. I had no intention of doing anything more than dancing until the club closed and staggering back home to Tamsin.

Two hours later I was on a mattress on the floor in a squat in Queen's Park, my seven year celibacy finally over. I turned away from John and thought of Fergus and tears rolled silently down my cheeks into my ears and nose.

John is a better dancer than he is a lover. But that was not why I cried.

After a slightly more satisfactory experience the next morning (well, I was there, why not?) I arrived home to find Tamsin luckily still asleep. I had just finished showering when Liz appeared with Dave and the children. She thought we should all go out for breakfast at the caff, she said, but I knew she had been worried that I might not have made it home. As soon as we were alone she wanted the details. She was crowing, delighted congratulating me. I just felt sick. I was not going to see John again. No, he had not been using me, if anything it had been the other way around. Well, I had to prove I could do it, didn't I? It was all right, he was a nice enough man, I'd enjoyed dancing with him. It was all, including the cross-questioning by a girlfriend, a little like losing your virginity. And if she wanted to ring up Dad and tell him at last I had been laid, here was the number and she had my full permission.

The last brought her up short. She muttered something, then stopped and looked confused.

'I know, you only did it because you were worried. But you don't need to be. I'll tell you a secret. I've started writing a book. And I'll tell you something else. Next weekend I'm going to Torquay to stay with Nelly, the girl from college. And a third thing. I'm thinking of giving up cleaning and finding some office work.' This last was not really true, it was much closer to being a vague thought than a serious intention, but I don't want Liz worrying about me any more.

It worked. She looked delighted. 'There! I told you seeing a man would put it all into perspective. You're looking better than you have for ages.' I doubted it. Exhausted, in any old clothes pulled from the drawer, confused by myself, I needed nothing more than a long bath and a longer sleep.

She read my thoughts. 'Or you will do when you've got your head down for a while. I'll keep Tamsin. Go on, see you at dinnertime. We could take the kids to McDonald's for a treat.'

A true friend.

*   *   *

I thought I could keep out of trouble for that week. I had my past weekend's experiences to muse upon, and the trip to Nelly to look forward to (or dread). Then Mrs Settrington caused trouble on Wednesday. She had been fine on Monday morning, but by Wednesday afternoon she was back on form. Maybe she has bad bio-rhythms or something in the afternoon. (Whatever happened to bio-rhythms? People used to run their lives by them and you never hear of them any more.) On Monday I had worked smoothly through Mrs Settrington's and Mr Nesbit's houses. On Tuesday I had seen Amanda, full of the joys of young love, trying to concentrate on writing her proposal. 'Isn't it odd about those flowers?' she said over our coffee. 'Paddy said he didn't send them. But I can't think of anyone else who could possibly have sent them. Especially with that message.' (I had referred to 'eating early' on the card.)

'Paddy?'

'Oh, that's his name. Sort of,' she laughed, leaving me very baffled. 'Perhaps he's just guarding his back, I don't know . . . Anyway it's all going swimmingly. Aren't I glad Mal was off the scene in time! Of course Paddy claims he was waiting for that to happen, but I think that's just retrospective romanticism.'

So she was cheerful, her boyfriend is 'sort of' called Paddy and I cannot possibly know him (unless he is my friend from the Percy? Unlikely.)

She asked me about her aunt, said she had not seen her for a while, had rung her one evening and been given the brush-off. She asked which days I work for Mrs Settrington, and said she might call in while I was there as it would be 'more fun'.

When I heard the doorbell ring the next afternoon, I half expected it to be Amanda. And there indeed she was, holding a bunch of flowers and wearing a grey jersey dress and a hesitant smile.

'Amanda. Well, as you're here you'd better come in. I suppose those flowers are for me? Would you, Cindy dear?' Mrs Settrington barely looked at the flowers and pushed them rudely at me. 'I expect you want a drink, but you're either too early or too late. Tea?'

Amanda followed her aunt to the kitchen, while I finished

Hoovering the living-room. By the time I joined them Mrs Settrington seemed much more mellow, and the two women were talking together comfortably.

'Have some tea with us, Cindy,' said Mrs Settrington, and Amanda smiled with relief. 'I was just telling Amanda about our Christmas lunch, what a shame she didn't come.'

'I gather Uncle Vincent cooked up a storm and Seth brought a wonderful friend,' Amanda said, with a glint in her eye which was not lost on me.

'And Evelyn sent a wonderful Christmas pudding from Fortnum's,' said Mrs Settrington. (When will I ever hear the end of that wretched Christmas pudding?)

'Mummy made ours,' said Amanda. 'Delicious as usual.'

'I'm glad she contributed in some way to poor Fiona's burden.' Mrs Settrington's vicious mask was back in place. 'As I was saying, it's a shame you don't see more of Seth, Amanda. Evelyn seems to have taken him over entirely.'

'Is she pretty?' Amanda asked.

Mrs Settrington hesitated. Her little eyes flicked at me. She took a gamble. 'I don't know about pretty, but – Evelyn – is very attractive.'

'Well, lucky old Seth.'

'Yes. You had better watch out, Amanda, soon you'll be on the shelf.'

'Better be on the shelf than marry the wrong man,' I said quietly. I should have kept my mouth shut but I felt sorry for Amanda. It is not as though she is not desperate to get married herself.

She rallied. 'True enough. And I think it very unlikely that Seth would ever be the right man. Certainly not for me, and I'd be surprised . . .'

Amanda did not know quite what she was saying. But I did. Unintentional as her words were, they certainly had a strong effect on Mrs Settrington. 'You shouldn't judge too swiftly,' she hissed. 'You can't know anything at your age. You're spoilt rotten, always have been. You've not managed to find yourself a husband, so don't presume to pretend to know anything at all about marriage.' She had jumped up, was standing with fists clenched, bending over Amanda, who just looked stunned. I knew I had to divert Mrs Settrington's attention from Amanda. I am trying to do good with my knowledge, now.

'Seth's not getting on so well with that Evelyn now, according to Mr Nesbit,' I said. It worked. Mrs Settrington turned towards me, but before she could speak I continued, 'Apparently he's not being reasonable about the tenancy agreement.'

'Seth?' Amanda was obviously grateful for the diversion.

'No. Evelyn. He keeps arguing about the telephone bill.'

'*He!*'

I laughed. 'I know. I made the same mistake. When Mrs Settrington first told me about her Christmas lunch I assumed Mr Hardwicke's friend was a young lady.' I was overdoing it with the 'Mr's and the 'young lady's. Mrs Settrington was breathing heavily and I wondered if I should be frightened.

'You seem to know a lot about your employers, young lady.'

'Only what they tell me,' I lied, holding her gaze.

'Aunt Patricia, you seem tired. Do you want me to go?' A feeble attempt from Amanda to make her escape.

Mrs Settrington drew a deep breath. 'No, Amanda, I'm sorry. Yes I am tired. I feel a little fragile. Finish your tea. And you, Cindy. I may lie down in a moment, after you've gone. I can't think how I misled you both about Evelyn. No he's far from female, he's a very attractive young man. Perhaps you should meet him, Amanda. I am sorry to hear he and Seth are not getting on so well.'

We were all sitting around the table again, playing at being civilised adults. Mrs Settrington's face wore a bland, tired little-old-lady smile, but her eyes were cunning.

'Mr Hardwicke is thinking of moving out of their flat,' I said. 'Mr Nesbit has offered him a bed. In the spare room.'

Complete fabrication, of course. Whatever made me do it?

We arrived at Torquay at a quarter to eight. It was dark and drizzling and cold and I wondered whether the trip was a good idea. Tamsin was cross and tired when we arrived, so I hoped that Nelly had nothing planned for us that night.

She was there at the station, wet and laughing to see Tamsin. 'I can't believe it! Now I know she's real and it wasn't an elaborate excuse to avoid handing in an essay. Tamsin, I knew your mother before you were born. Isn't it odd we haven't met before? Come on, the car's over there. Let's run – it's pouring.'

Nelly swept us up in her enthusiasm and warmth. We ran behind her to the navy-blue BMW parked in the tiny car-park. I made sure I did not show how impressed I was with the car: Tamsin on the other hand had no such compunction. Most of her friends' parents do not even have cars.

'Now, I thought Tamsin might be tired, so we ought to have supper straight away. Is that right? I don't really know about children.'

We were driving along a wide road beside the sea. Coloured bulbs hung in loops between lamp posts. The twinkling lights enchanted Tamsin, more than made up for the rain.

'So I thought fish and chips tonight, after all we are by the sea – and I sometimes think there are more fish and chip shops in this town than in the rest of England put together. Is that all right?'

Tamsin agreed enthusiastically. Suddenly this visit, about which she had been in two minds, seemed like fun.

Nelly stopped the car, took our orders, and jumped out through the rain into a chip shop. She came back with the warm packages.

The smell of fish filled the car and, despite the sandwiches and crisps we had eaten in the train, I suddenly felt very hungry. Nelly chattered on, leaving Tamsin and me to overcome the tiredness that travelling brings. We barely listened, just looked out of the windows wishing we could see more.

Nelly's flat is in a block called Shirley Towers. I thought it sounded awful, but I could not have been more wrong. She is on the fifth floor, has two bedrooms and a lovely big living-room. There is so much space, I could not get over the amount of space for one person. I don't know why I felt it so much – after all Amanda's flat is quite big – but I was very aware of the difference between my home and Nelly's. Oh, my flat has tall windows and high ceilings, but the rooms are small, carved out of a dignified Victorian house by a greedy developer keen to squish as many people together as he could. Nelly has no cornices, but mine are interrupted by flimsy partition walls. These people with rich parents are lucky.

'Drink?' she said as we were taking in our surroundings. 'Gin and tonic all right?' and she poured us both one. We unwrapped the fishy parcels and ate immediately – imagine, gin and tonic with fish and chips. It was delicious and soon we were all talking happily. Nelly was brilliant with Tamsin, never talked down to her, chatted away as though she had known her all her life. She should have been her godmother, I suppose. Then she showed us our room. Her room. She had moved out so that we could share her king-size double bed, told us she would be sleeping in the small spare room

It was wonderful. All pale and clean and pure. A huge, impressionistic painting of the sea hung on the wall opposite her bed. All angry blues and greys, I looked at it and felt its storm wash over me. A huge window on another wall would probably show the real sea in the morning. The carpet was the colour of dry sand and the walls were the palest, June summer sky blue. If you looked closely you could see clouds scudding across the room. The effect was so subtle I had to look twice to make sure I had not imagined them.

'Mum, this is the best room I have ever been in,' said Tamsin. 'Isn't it nice of Nelly to lend it to us. Oh, can we come again in the summer, *please*.'

Nelly and I laughed and I sat on the bed and watched Tamsin as she put on her pyjamas. She brushed her teeth in the shell-decorated bathroom and slipped happily between the sheets. There would be no difficulty in her sleeping well tonight.

After Tamsin was tucked in, we went back into the sitting room. There was a moment or two of hesitation, but the ice had been broken. Nelly told me the plans she had made for the weekend – she wanted to take Tamsin to a model village just outside Torquay, she had to spend a couple of hours in the hotel, then she had booked a baby-sitter and a table at a fish restaurant and she planned a night on the town for us. Was that all right?

I asked her about her job. She is Functions Manager in one of the biggest hotels in the town, loves the job, enjoys coming up with wacky ideas to tempt the tourists and loves living in the west country.

'I love my job, honestly I do. I began working in hotels as a stopgap, something to do until I was "discovered", but now I'm hooked. There's something very nice in working in an industry which is just there to help people have fun. And I would never have been able to buy this flat without the job. I love it, even if I move to another hotel I reckon I'll keep the flat on.'

I was surprised. 'Didn't your father buy it for you?'

'My father? God, no. He wouldn't part with a penny even if he had one. He says they stinted themselves for all those years so that they could send Penny and me to boarding school, and now they want some treats for themselves. Fair enough, I suppose. Apart from anything else the business went belly up in '92 and they've not really been able to afford the fun they had planned. No, this is all mine. Or the building society's. I saved for the deposit and I pay the mortgage.'

I suppose it was the wine, but I suddenly felt dizzy. So Nelly had been given no handouts. She had finished her degree, got herself a job and earned herself this piece of heaven. This privacy, this self-respect. This seaside flat. I looked at her but did not see her. I was seeing the inside of all of Their flats and houses, and added on to the catalogue was this one. I could have been like her. She is no more clever than I am, no more hardworking.

'I must just check Tamsin.'

'Oh, she's all right, we'd hear her.'

I went anyway. I opened the bedroom door softly and looked at my sleeping child. Her hair was over her face, she was spread-eagled across the bed. She had taken over my side of the bed as she had taken over my life. Without her I could have had a career, a nice flat, friends like me.

I asked myself if I could hate her, but felt a wave of repugnance at the very thought, a lap of tenderness for her that overcame the very possibility of such iniquity. No, I love her unconditionally. She has brought me more than any career or smart house could have given me. She is my reason for being. I remembered that first night of her life, the warmth of her, the sweet smell of her breath and gentle rise and fall of her chest. I wanted to lie on the bed beside her and hold her as I had then but I restrained myself. Nelly was waiting.

I went back in to the sitting-room. Nelly had poured us both more wine. 'She all right?' she asked, clearly knowing the answer.

I looked at her and nodded. 'I'm sorry, Nelly, I'm shattered. Do you mind if I go to bed? I know it's early, but if we're on the town tomorrow night . . .'

'Oh.' She looked disappointed. 'Oh, okay. I was hoping for a natter, but never mind. We have tomorrow. Go on, get your head down. I'll see you in the morning.'

The next day was easy. Every now and again I sensed Nelly looking at me, seeming to be on the point of saying something, but each time I caught her eye she looked away, talked fast about something – anything, and the moment passed. We took Tamsin to the model village and she was delighted, entranced by what she called the mini-magic. While Nelly went to the hotel – a gift fair was about to begin in Torquay and she had to make arrangements – we strolled around the town, admired the boats in the marina, the green ironwork railings of the shopping centre, the red rock cliff falling into the sea, the stunted palm trees bravely aiming for the sky.

'It's like abroad,' said Tamsin in wonder, looking at the steep hills rising behind the town, studded with grand villas. 'Like those pictures. I want to live here one day.'

'We'd never be able to afford one of those.'

'Maybe we could live in a hotel. That one – look, The Grand, look at its towers, all pointy. It's like a palace, like Disneyland. Or we could live in one of those little coloured houses on the beach.'

'Those are bathing huts, you couldn't live in them.'

'Oh, Mum, I could.'

We strolled up the hill to meet Nelly, who gave us a magnificent cream tea in the huge lounge of her hotel. The view of the town below and the sea beyond stretched for miles. I was beginning to be of Tamsin's opinion. Life would be good here. Nelly introduced Tamsin to the chambermaid who was baby-sitting in the evening, and she took Tamsin off on a tour of the hotel while we moved seamlessly from cream tea to gin and tonic. I could become used to this life.

In the evening Tamsin was left behind, perfectly happy in Nelly's flat discussing a career in hotels with her new best friend the chambermaid. We set off for our evening of self-indulgence.

Nelly took me to a restaurant that was something outside my experience. At first I did not think it would be up to much – just called Number Seven which does not seem to me to be making much effort (but then They always go to 192, which is the same idea), and the menus were written up on blackboards. To my mind it seemed more like a pub than a proper restaurant, but it did not take me long to see that it was more like the kind of place They go than a pub. There were black plates shaped like shells (scallop shells, Nelly told me), pictures of lettuces against black backgrounds on the walls (lettuces! I ask you), wooden floors, and huge heavy fans that looked as though they were going to fall on our heads hung from the ceiling. I was unsure about the food, I am never that relaxed around fish unless it is wrapped in batter, but it was delicious.

Nelly told me more about her job, said the only thing she lacked in Torquay was a real best friend, a soulmate with whom to spend her free time.

'I wish you could come here, Cindy,' she said and I laughed.

'You'd have to promise Tamsin a job in the hotel. She's in love with your life.'

We went dancing, to a club called the Valbonne which was filled with people like us – or like Nelly is and I could have been. Estate agents, hoteliers, solicitors in articles, young people determined to have a good time. They greeted Nelly enthusiastically, accepted me as her friend, bought us drinks, danced with us, joked with us. They were a good crowd. I enjoyed myself unreservedly, danced exuberantly and did not go off with some other John.

It was not until I lay in bed, head slightly spinning from the thumping of the music and the cigarette smoke, that I felt angry. Not with Tamsin, never with her, but with myself. I lay in that large bed with my daughter asleep beside me and hated myself for my failure to achieve. I resolved to go back to London, hand in my notice to the whole lot of Them and start again. Whatever it takes, I will do it. I will finish the novel, but I will not rely on that. Fergus told me that no one earns enough money to live on novel-writing – except for a lucky few, Jeffrey Archer, Barbara Cartland, Dick Francis presumably. I hated myself, but I hated Amanda too. Swanning through university, turning up drunk at her play, drifting into a job at the BBC, drifting out of it again, and surviving. I survive too, have prided myself on that for years (perhaps too long), but her level of survival is so much higher than mine. She still has her flat and her rugs and her bottles of white wine. She can still find herself hope in some new man. I wonder if she has ever been reduced to a John.

I thought the cleaning would bring about changes in my life, and it did, some, but I have not made the big leap yet, away from the Housing Trust and the Social Security. I want to be like Nelly. I want to be like Amanda. I would even like to be like Jane.

Plans made at two in the morning with a spinning head are very rarely carried through. On Monday I went to Mrs Settrington as normal and then, after a sandwich at the Uxbridge, moved on to Mr Nesbit. Mrs Settrington had said nothing to me about my announcement that Seth was to move in with her brother, and I hoped she had said nothing to him either. She would at some stage, though, and almost as soon as I was on the train home from Torquay I had been trying to work out a way to make my lie true.

In the event it was easy. Mr Nesbit brought up the subject. He talks about Seth all the time. I don't think he is in love with him – I did originally, but his feelings are more complicated than I supposed at first. I think he sees Seth as a younger version of himself, with the added attraction of being the son of Gloria. He is always comparing Seth to his own, younger self, then adding with a wistful little sigh, 'but of course he is so much braver than ever I was, so much more sure of himself'. I suppose that is to do with Seth's admitting to being gay.

So there I was on Monday, worrying about my lie, dusting the endless shepherdesses, half-listening to Mr Nesbit rambling on, when the answer popped into my head. It was easy, of course.

'When did you say Mr Hardwicke might move in?' I asked, as soon as Mr Nesbit had drawn breath.

The question had a bad effect: Mr Nesbit looked shocked, clung on to his wrist, cleared his throat but said nothing.

I was not worried, I could now see my way around the problem.

'Only I should like to give the spare room a spring clean before he arrives,' I added innocently.

'Move in?' he croaked.

'Yes, isn't that what you said? I am sorry, I misunderstood you. When you were talking the other day about Mr Hardwicke's problems with his flat I thought you said he might move in here for a while. Where could I have got that idea?'

His eyes filled with understanding and he looked so happy I felt quite proud of myself. 'I thought you were suggesting – well never mind,' he said. 'Yes of course, I had quite forgotten that thought, and to be honest I have not yet suggested it to Mr Hardwicke. Don't worry about it today, I'll tell you on Thursday. Now, then, coffee or tea?'

Isn't he a duck? I could never have managed any of the others so easily, but he fell into the trap as neatly as could be. He thinks it is his own idea, I have absolved him from any guilt, and he is truly happy. Even if nothing comes of it I am in the clear with Mrs Settrington.

She, of course, will be miserable. But then she is not as nice as Mr Nesbit, so I honestly do not mind.

Another weekend came, with its inevitable dreariness. Weekends were when we missed Liz and her children most. We were always aware of her absence from the moment we woke on Saturday morning. There is a deadness behind her wall. I hope some new tenants move in soon.

We kicked around the flat for a while, and then I suggested going down to the supermarket and buying a treat for supper. Tamsin could choose anything she wanted and I would buy myself a bottle of wine. We would have real, grown-up supper like They do, with Tamsin and me as the only guests. Tamsin entered into the spirit of the idea. We dug out a tablecloth Mum gave me one Christmas, found some candles kept against power cuts and laid the table perfectly. Then we walked together down the Grove towards the supermarket. Tamsin chose steak and chips and a frozen apple and toffee Danish pastry. She chose some carnations to put on the table, and seemed to have forgotten all about her gloom of an hour before.

On the way back up the Grove we met Jane. Tamsin is too grown-up to hug with the abandonment of the very young child, but I could see she was hugging Jane with her eyes. Jane looked drawn and tired, but she stopped and talked to us. She always makes time. I felt sorry for her, all alone, buying her supper for one, not so much as a cat to keep her company. On an impulse, I asked, 'Why don't you come and eat with us? If you'd like to?' Then, so that she did not feel that she was intruding, I added, 'We need cheering up. Our neighbours – Ayesha Stone, you know her from school – have moved out and we miss them.'

If there had been any hesitation before, that made up Jane's mind. 'I would love to, if you have enough. Thank you. I was just feeling a little gloomy myself, and somehow the thought of an evening in had no charm for me.'

I sent Tamsin ahead with the keys and ran back for another steak. Thank heavens we had tidied up before we left for the shop.

The three of us passed a very happy evening. Jane admired my flat, said she loved the colours, how had I made it so light, hers was always in the dark. We ate and drank and were at ease. Later, after Tamsin had slipped next door to bed, we drank a last cup of coffee before she left. I felt quite like one of Them.

Writing or no writing, there is no way out of the cleaning until I find another job. So on Friday morning I was up at Lynda's as usual, preparing to clean and dust and polish and gossip as usual. For the first time for ages I was thinking only about the mechanics of cleaning, with no thought at all for Lynda and Randal Blake's lives.

I was no sooner across the threshold, though, than I was drawn back into their story. I met Mr Blake on the doorstep – or at any rate I saw him. He barged past me without a word of greeting, letting the front door slam behind him in my face. Things must be bad if he was forgetting his oily charm.

I found Lynda upstairs in her dressing gown, lying on the unmade bed and weeping. I hovered uncertainly in the doorway. 'Is there anything I can do? Are you ill?'

She shook her head and waved me away, then, changing her mind, called me back.

'Do you mind if I ask you something?'

'Of course not.'

'It's a bit embarrassing, but I don't know what to do. Cindy, you have a child, tell me, those pregnancy test things, can they ever be wrong?'

So that was the trouble. The old baby business again. 'I don't know. I have heard people say that they are never wrong if they say you are pregnant, but they can be wrong when they say you are not. If you see what I mean.'

She nodded, her face suddenly transformed into smiles behind the watery eyes. 'That's wonderful. I want a baby so much, you don't know how lucky you are, so I could be after all.'

I did not want to raise her hopes. 'Well, it's obviously better if the thing tells you yes.'

'I know, of course I do, but I'm two days late and it tells me no and I must be, this can't go on for ever.'

'Poor Lynda. But you haven't been married that long have you, you don't have to worry.' My reply sounded as flat as I felt – but what could I do other than try to comfort her with platitudes?

'And I won't be married that much longer, I sometimes think. I shouldn't say this to you, but things aren't good for us. Randal works so hard, and it makes him impatient, and then he shouts at me, and I'm so worried about this baby thing and that just makes him more cross . . . oh, I don't know. He's been working late so often recently, not coming back until ten or eleven and then refusing to eat, says he's not hungry. And this morning, for instance, all I said was how I'd love a baby, and wouldn't he like a son, a darling little Patrick—'

'Patrick?'

'Oh yes, we agreed before we even married that our first son should be called Patrick. It is my father's name, and it's Randal's middle name, you see. His mother always calls him Paddy, says she wishes she hadn't given in to his father, who insisted on Randal. Anyway, he stormed out of the room, slammed the door behind him, shouted at me that I'd be bloody lucky to get any child from him the way I was going on and I was never to say the name Patrick again. I mean, what a stupid thing to say. Then I heard the front door going. When I heard your steps I was hoping he might have come back to say sorry.'

She was sobbing again, but my mind was not with her. Paddy. Paddy of the early suppers, the complicated life. Randal Blake is sleeping with Amanda and letting her call him his mother's pet name. He is every bit as much a stupid bastard as I had thought, but I did not think Amanda would sleep with her friend's husband. She must be desperate, the sad bitch. I wonder if Lynda suspects – all that talk of Amanda needing to remember what good friends they used to be, what was all that about? Perhaps she does not even know that she suspects, but just feels uneasy. The idea of going on a cooking holiday with Amanda was founded on something more than friendship. I wonder . . .

Meanwhile I had to deal with the weeping heap that was my employer. I made soothing noises, ran her a bath, went downstairs and made her a strong cup of real coffee. When I reached her room again she had not moved, was still lying face down on her rumpled bed, still talking. I don't know if she had even noticed that I had left the room. I turned the bath off and suggested she dry her eyes and drink her coffee.

'It's like heroin, I'm addicted,' she said.

I had lost all track of what she was saying. 'What?'

'These blessed pregnancy tests. I do one on day twenty-eight, twenty-nine, every day until my period starts and I have to go through the whole month again. I just know if I had a baby everything would be all right again. What is the point of it all, this house, this effort, without a baby? If we had one we would be a family, Randal would have to be home more, spend more time with us. It would all be all right again.' Not with Miss Fancy-Pants tossing her hair at your husband, I thought grimly.

'Lynda, don't get so upset. They always say if you're tense you don't get pregnant.'

My words had no effect so I gave up the soothing approach and tried something more brusque. 'Come on, Lynda, lying in bed feeling sorry for yourself won't get you pregnant. And if you are, all this tension is bad for the baby. Look, drink the coffee, I've run you a bath, get dressed and come downstairs. This is just another day. We all have to get through them.'

She dragged her feet on to the floor. 'You're right of course. But if only Randal weren't so cruel to me . . . I try so hard.'

'Perhaps you try too hard. Too hard to please him, too hard to be perfect, too hard to be pregnant.' I can speak more freely when They are upset. They are so relieved to be listened to that They forget to be high-handed.

'I can't help it, that's how I am.'

'You can't help it but you can try to control it. Go on, give Mr Blake a hard time in return. Don't cry and look pitiful, but buy him ready-made food and go out on the town with a girlfriend. Play it cool, he'll come back to heel. Isn't that meant to work?'

'I couldn't. Not to Randal. I love him, I don't want to hurt him.' She did not seem totally convinced by her words. Even if she was, I was not.

'So be brave for his sake. Come on, I'm going downstairs to clean the kitchen. I want you bathed and dressed when I've finished.'

She smiled. 'You must be a wonderful mother. You remind me of Daddy's nanny.'

Cleaner, housekeeper, cook, butler and now nanny. Is there no end to my talents?

Lynda came downstairs before I had finished the kitchen. She looked brushed and made up and much more in possession of herself. 'Thank you, Cindy. You knew just when to bully me. You're right, up to a point. I'm going to try harder to stand up to Randal. A bit. And for a start I'm not going to do another pregnancy test for four days. I won't even buy one so I won't be tempted.' She gave me a brave smile and went off to read the paper.

Poor old thing. It is hard luck, when so many people have babies they do not want (and I don't mean me and Tamsin, I mean those others out there, the beaters and abusers and cold care parents), that she cannot manage to fix herself a perfect baby to put into her perfect house. I wish I could do something to help her.

Think as hard as I could, I could come up with no answer to Lynda's problem. I suppose the affair between Randall and Amanda will run its course – I would have thought it unlikely that he will leave Lynda's comfortable domesticity for Amanda's shambolic existence. I am sure she would never put her man first in the way Lynda does.

I was so preoccupied with thoughts of Lynda's dilemma that I forgot to be embarrassed about Fergus when I let myself into his flat. I wondered why he was looking sheepish but it was not until I was halfway through the ironing that I realised that I had not seen him since my embarrassment, and by then I could blush away the memory in private. He stopped work halfway through the afternoon and wandered into the kitchen. I told him about the weekend in Torquay to divert attention from thoughts of my folly, and within ten minutes he seemed more relaxed. It felt good to be able to put him at his ease.

'I'm glad you enjoyed yourself,' he said. 'I don't suppose you get many chances to get away.' (Why did he suppose that – an impertinent presumption if ever there was one, no matter how much truth there may be in it.)

'I have a good enough time up here,' I lied. 'I'd miss London if I went away too often. Fergus, do you mind if I ask you something?'

He looked a little alarmed, but as usual his good manners came to the rescue. 'Not at all, what is it?'

'It's nothing to do with me, but I know you're an old friend of hers, and I don't know what to do. It's Lynda. I'm worried about her.'

'The bastard.' The words burst out of him, and he looked even more surprised than normal.

'I'm sorry?'

'Nothing, ignore me. Why?'

'She's not herself. She wasn't dressed this morning when I turned up. That sounds silly, but—'

'I know,' he said quietly. 'I used to know her very well remember. Do you know what the matter is?'

I hesitated.

'Come on, Cindy. I'm fond of Lynda, for old time's sake. To be honest I didn't treat her that well myself. I suppose I feel a little guilty about that. There's something about Lynda . . . well, that's another story. *Do* you know what the matter is?'

'She is hoping for a baby.'

He laughed. 'I can't help her there. Or at any rate I don't think Randal would appreciate it if I did.'

'To be honest, that's only part of it. She's – oh, she's not happy. I think she just feels a bit cut off, you know, not working and all.'

At least I do that. At least I work, get out and see other people. Who knows what sort of a state I would be in otherwise?

'Randal,' he said. But it was not a question, he was not even talking to me. I realised I should ignore him. He looked directly at me, I think for the first time that day. 'Thanks, Cindy,' he said. 'You're a good girl.'

'I like Lynda,' I said. 'That's all.'

There was a moment of silence as we stood, looking at each other across his cramped kitchen. Then, at the same moment, we both said, 'I'm sorry about—' and laughed awkwardly and I am sure I blushed.

Fergus opened the fridge door and pulled out two beers. 'Let's drink to that.'

I think perhaps I should stop working for him. It is not getting any easier.

On Monday Mr Nesbit told me that Seth will be moving in next week. I spring-cleaned the spare room. He spent a lot of time choosing which pair of shepherdesses to put on the mantelpiece. I could see he was torn between wanting to put some of his most precious objects in with Seth and worrying that they would be broken. I could also see that the dithering was making him painfully happy.

On Tuesday Amanda was out so I gave her flat a thorough going-over. I am not pleased with the girl, and bad temper always makes me more efficacious. Her flat was cleaned much better than she deserved as a result. I wondered as I scrubbed the bath (wincing at the thought of Randal sloughing off his adulterous body in the shiny white enamel) whether I might not stop working for her, operate my own personal morality clause. But I decided I would be cutting off my nose to spite my face. It would be much harder to keep in touch with what is going on if I am only cleaning one of their houses.

When I found the diary by her bed I knew I could never leave her. An appointments diary, not a what-I-did-today diary, but then you cannot have everything. (Funny, isn't it, until recently she has been a committed Filofax girl. She has taken up those dainty little clutch bags, which must mean she has to slim down her possessions.) I sat on her bed, ear cocked for the sound of the flat door slamming, and skimmed through the thin pages. Nothing is more boring than someone else's diary. They are always full of cryptic messages, initials and squiggles that can mean nothing to anyone except the writer and are often confusing even for their creator.

This one was no exception. If I had not been looking for

something particular I would have not wasted the time on it. I began my search in the week of the Blakes' Christmas party. The first date was easy to pick out. Only two days after the party, 'Randal 7.30 192'. A little close to home, but obviously still innocent. Three days later 'Randal 7.00 Windsor Castle'. Probably the pub on the other side of Notting Hill. A little further away from home, but still pretty dangerous territory.

There was a break over Christmas, when Amanda had been staying with her sister. A rash of dates written in handwriting too large for the space confused me for a moment. 'John Ashley C4, 12.00; P. T. 4.00' (Could that be 'Paddy'? No, Beeb was squished in beside the initials. She must have made a New Year's Resolution to try harder to find work.) Then, 'R. 6.30 El Vino's, Fleet Street'. Right into his working territory, far from home, using only an initial. Whether the affair had started or not by then, romance was obviously in the air. And the next day: 'P! El V 6.30'. So the switch had been made to Paddy, with how many girlish giggles and sly looks it made me sick to the stomach to imagine.

Then came the famous 'early supper'. 'P. Langan's 7.00' and the affair was on. P was scrawled down, in an increasingly confident hand, almost every other day. No wonder Lynda is looking drawn. I turned the pages faster. Now my suspicions were confirmed, the detail did not interest me. I needed to look into the future now, see if by any chance there was another date planned. Yes – two days ahead. On Thursday, another 'P: Puces, 7.00' Puces? what did that mean. I stared at the word, which seemed familiar. I *must* find out what it meant. I did not know what I would do with the information, but I had to have it. After staring blankly at the page for what felt like five minutes I heard the door slam, and jumped up, pushing the diary into the pile of paperbacks on the bedside table. I quickly picked up the bin from underneath Amanda's make-up table and walked innocently out of the bedroom door into the living-room.

'Good morning, Amanda. I didn't hear you come in, you made me jump.'

'Morning. Sorry. Have you seen my diary? A little black one, I set off without it and can't remember where I agreed to meet someone at lunch . . . Oh God, I can't ring and ask, I'll look such a fool.'

'No, I'm sorry. Have you tried down the back of the sofa?'

'Bugger, bugger, where can it be? I remember, I was on the telephone in my room last time I remember having it . . .' She disappeared into her bedroom and came back a second later waving it above her head. 'By my bed, what an idiot I am. Now let's see, oh good it's not until half one, I've plenty of time. Good, see you next week then, Cindy.'

'Seeing as you're here Amanda, I don't want to be difficult, but do you think you could give me some money? You haven't paid me for three weeks, today makes four, and it does add up.'

'Of course it does, oh God I'm sorry. Let me get my purse.' She pulled her wallet from her dainty bag and I could easily see there was no chance of it holding seventy-two pounds or anything near it. Still, she put on a good show of looking and pulling a face and appearing rueful. 'Oh Cindy, I am awful, I haven't managed to get to the bank. Can I give you a tenner now to keep you going and the rest next week? I don't suppose a cheque is any good to you?'

I was livid. Why should a cheque be no good to me? Does she assume that people like me cannot handle bank accounts? If she had not been so obviously acting surprise and apology I might have been less angry, but I did not see why I should cover up her lies and bankroll her at the same time. I looked at her standing in front of me in her expensive clothes with her wide open dark-blue eyes and confidential grin and I hated her. I really hated her.

'No, a cheque would be fine. Only I have to pay my rent, I don't like getting behind.' I smiled a smile as false (but I am sure a great deal less charming) than hers. 'If you don't mind.'

She had the nerve to look cross. 'Oh, All right then. Now I'm going to be late. Where's a pen?'

'I have one in my bag.' I was not going to be shaken off. I was within my rights, she owed me. Furthermore she had just told me that she had plenty of time. I will not be bullied by her.

She wrote the cheque out grumpily, made a great play of checking that I had added up properly, then left the flat without saying goodbye.

I helped myself to a beer from her fridge and drank it at the kitchen table, reading yesterday's *Independent*. A pathetic revenge maybe, but it cheered me up. Remembering to take the empty beer bottle with me, I left the flat without taking out the rubbish and walked straight to the nearest NatWest and paid the cheque in.

I have Tuesday afternoons off and I had promised Mrs Perkins upstairs that I would walk her horrible dachshund, Fritz. She has had flu for a week, and her little flat stinks of bad tempered dog. I think it is cruel keeping even Fritz in such a small space (maybe he would be more even tempered if he were not always cooped up), but she will not get rid of him. Her husband gave him to her for their forty-fifth wedding anniversary, the last he lived to see, and she loves the little dog. I do not mind helping her out with him sometimes, Tamsin is very fond of him and Mrs Perkins is kind to me.

I decided to take him up to the canal. There is a little park at the foot of Trellick Towers which Fritz likes, and afterwards we would stroll down Portobello, sneering at what passes for art in the modern galleries.

I am glad I did. I had stopped wondering about Amanda's meeting place, thinking I would just have to manage to look at her diary again next week, until I saw the sign painted over a yellow restaurant. 'Le Brasserie du Marché des Puces.' *Puces*. A French word meaning Lord knew what. Who cared. This was where they were meeting. Right on their own doorsteps, the fools. I suppose nice and handy for Bassett Road. But they are mad, they are bound to get caught . . .

And I stopped in my tracks, looking up at the sign. Yes, they would get caught. Of course they would . . .

It did not take me long to work out how they would be caught out. I thought of telephoning Lynda and alerting her to her foul husband's tricks. But then I decided that was too cruel, and there was another, better way, which with any luck would mean that the affair would stop without her ever knowing about it.

Fergus was the key, I realised that. The question was how much to tell him. I had to put him on the right track, but I did not want him to realise quite how much I knew – or how I knew it. I was sure that he did not like Randal, and that he was fond enough of Lynda to make some effort to help her. And then the answer came to me.

I rang Fergus from a telephone box, and left a message on his answerphone. 'Fergus, it is Cindy here. I am sorry but I took a message for you on Friday, wrote it down and I've just found the piece of paper in my bag. Sorry. A girl rang on Friday and said she needed to talk to you. Could you please meet her at the Brasserie du Marché des Puces in Portobello Road on Thursday at half past seven. Thank heavens I found the message before Thursday! The other awful thing is that the paper got wet and I can't read the name properly. Lottie, I think, or Libby or Liddy. Something like that. I really am sorry. See you Friday. 'Bye.'

There. It was done. Now I just have to wait and see what happens next.

I could not keep away. I should have, I was asking for trouble, but I could not resist it. I borrowed Fritz in exchange for Tamsin, and took him for a stroll. No one must see me or they would be frightened off.

At ten past seven Amanda was sitting alone at a table at the back of the restaurant with a large glass of white wine. The least he could do is turn up on time. The plan would not work if Fergus turned up before Randal.

Randal breezed in at a quarter past. I watched Amanda stand to meet him, saw him turning on the charm to apologise for keeping her waiting. They sat down together. Good. I left and took a turn around the block.

At twenty-five to eight I was walking past the restaurant again, on the other side of the road. I had borrowed Mrs Perkins's coat, pretending that I had left mine downstairs and did not want to disturb Tamsin, and had a scarf over my hair. I did not think They would recognise me unless they were really looking at me.

I had arrived just in time. I saw Fergus walking briskly down the road, looking at his watch. He paused before going in, obviously casing the joint to see who the mystery woman was who needed to talk to him so urgently. Good. He had fallen for the trap. I saw him start, look more closely, look at his watch again. So what would he do? Would he politely leave them to it, or would he presume innocence and join them for a glass of wine? Then he braced his shoulders and pushed the door open.

I could not see what happened next. I did not dare step too close. Then I heard shouting. Another couple arrived, looking at their watches. 'We're a bit early', the woman said. 'I told Jenny quarter to, but never mind, we'll have a drink while we wait.' I followed in their wake, sneaking a quick look in through the door as I walked on by. Amanda was sitting, shrinking back, looking panic-stricken. I heard Randal say, 'You're making a terrible fuss, Fergus, we bumped into each other in the street and thought a drink would be nice,' and then I heard Fergus shouting again, 'I saw you holding her hand, you bastard!' and a feeble 'Messieurs, please,' from a small waiter. I walked quickly across the road and darted into the small park opposite, by the council estate. I was suddenly feeling nervous. Fritz might be a liability – a lot of people notice dogs more than people and I did not want anyone wondering why a dachshund kept strolling past the wine bar.

Then I heard a crash, and peeping round the corner, saw Fergus and Randal Blake tumbling out of the door, Amanda close behind them, bleating, 'Paddy – Randal – Fergus, please! Stop it!' and punches were flying and the waiter was threatening to call the police and I knew I had seen enough.

I handed Fritz back to Mrs Perkins, brushing aside her thanks. Tamsin was asleep when I let myself back in through the door. I turned my radio on to Classic FM and made myself a cup of tea. I felt wonderful. At last I had done something useful for one of Them. Jane's party invitation was nothing, a mere bagatelle, but I was sure that Fergus's intervention would scotch Amanda's and Randal's romance. Unless of course the passion was such that he would leave Lynda for the redhead. That possibility worried me, but only slightly. Amanda might be all misty-eyed about him, but I was sure he was a pragmatist. Amanda was an amusement on the side, he would not want to risk the status quo for her. The affair had only been going on for a month or so, after all, it could hardly be a grand passion – could it? Amanda is letting her desperation to find Mr Right cloud her judgement, I am sure of it, while he is taking advantage of that desperation for a bit of fun.

Good old Fergus, what a hero he is. It would be wonderful to be defended like that, a knight in shining armour riding to the rescue . . . I wonder if it will ever happen to me. I dreamed for a while over my cup of tea. I was delighted with Fergus, even more pleased with myself. Between us we had saved Lynda's marriage. (Why she wants to keep her marriage going is beyond me, but that is her business.) Maybe in his relief at not being found out by his wife, Randal will return to her arms with renewed vigour and she will fall pregnant at last. Maybe she will sense that the danger is over and will relax into pregnancy. Fergus can be godfather. Randal will not dare object . . .

I went to bed in a very good humour.

The next morning Mr Blake was at home with a black eye and a blacker temper. Lynda told me he had been mugged on the way back from chambers. He tried to be civil to her and jumped each time the telephone rang. She looked very happy to have him home.

Fergus was waiting for me when I arrived at his flat in the afternoon. He stood and pulled two beers out of the fridge without even asking. I took mine mutely. His lip was split and swollen, he used his right hand gingerly.

'Thank you for the message,' he said coolly, sitting at the bar stool by the fridge. I nodded. 'You don't remember the name, do you?' I shook my head. I had not planned what I would say if he brought up the mystery girl. I suppose I had hoped that he would forget all about his original reason for going to the Brasserie. 'Only I was stood up,' he went on.

'Oh, dear. I am sorry,' I managed to say. 'I am sure I wrote down the place properly.'

'I'm sure you did,' he said calmly. 'But I think you knew that no Liddy or Libby would show up, didn't you?'

I looked up from my beer bottle for the first time. To my surprise the look that met mine was warm and humorous. I smiled back, tentatively. 'Well, yes, I suppose so.'

'I think you knew what I would find there.' I nodded. 'Do you want to tell me about it?'

'Need I?'

He thought. 'I suppose not. I suppose it makes no difference. How did you find out?'

'I overheard something I shouldn't have. I told you I was worried about Lyndy, and then it all fell into place.'

'I see. Do you want to know what happened?'

So he had not seen me. I smiled broadly in relief. 'I think I can guess. I was at the Blakes' this morning. It's a question of "you should see the other bloke".'

'Does Lyndy know?'

'I don't think so.'

'I don't think she needs to, do you?'

'No. No, that's why I rang you. I'm sorry. I shouldn't have. I just did not know what to do.'

'Don't think that's the end of it. Randal's not like that. But maybe he's been warned off.'

'And Amanda—'

He curled his lip. 'A silly girl. Maybe she's more frightened than him. We could hope for that.' (How wonderful it was to be included in a 'we' with Fergus.)

'Maybe you should know . . . Lynda's got it into her head that you are going out with Amanda.'

'That dinner . . . I see. I suppose Randal gave her the idea? Never mind, I doubt I'll be getting any more invitations to the Blakes' in the near future, don't you?' He swigged back the beer and tossed the bottle into the bin. 'I'll leave you to it, Cindy. And, although to be honest you were out of line, thanks.'

'Fergus, do you mind my asking you something?'

He turned back to me with a laugh. 'I wondered if you would. No, of course I won't tell Lyndy, or Randal or Amanda. I'm not entirely sure either of us come out of the story very well. I think we had better both keep quiet.'

Tamsin and I went up to lunch with Liz on Sunday. The house is small and very full with them all, but they seem very happy. She is turning out to be as good as her word, keeping everything much tidier and cleaner than she ever managed before. She even cooked us a proper roast lunch and Dave had made an apple crumble.

It hurt me. It is all very well playing these games, locking myself away with my novel and my dreams. But when will it be my turn? Dad used to sing a Seekers song – years ago, when singing was a possibility. 'When will the good apples fall on my side of the wall, when will I taste the first fruits of love?'

I suppose I have had the first fruit. But it is time for more.

Maybe Fergus will notice me soon.

I did not say anything to Mr Nesbit about his sister. I nearly did, but I felt I had done enough interfering for one week. And besides, she is engineering her own downfall, what can I, or Mr Nesbit, or anyone else do to stop her?

Mrs Settrington was up in her bedroom when I arrived on Monday morning. It was unlike her, she is usually very neat and correct. I wondered if she was ill, but although she was lying on her bed she was dressed and sent me away fairly rudely. She was reading and sipping at a glass of water.

Except it was not water, was it? Later in the morning she came downstairs and I went up to straighten her room. I picked up the almost empty glass and carried it through to the bathroom to wash. On an impulse, just before I tipped the end down the drain, I sniffed the liquid. Sweet and strong. Gin. In the morning. No wonder she was in bed.

Of course I said nothing. It was not until I emptied her bedroom bin that I became really worried. It was full of pieces of glass, not wrapped up in paper or anything, just lying there. (I always said she was selfish.) I lifted them out very carefully, tipping them into my dustbin liner. And I saw that mixed in with the glass were pieces of paper. They had been torn up into small pieces, but as I laid them out haphazardly on the carpet it was soon plain to see that it was the Kenya picture, smashed and torn and utterly beyond mending.

I took the bin bag downstairs. The clock in the hall struck twelve and I saw Mrs Settrington pull herself up from the armchair in the sitting-room. 'Twelve o'clock,' I heard her announce cheerily to no one. 'Sun over the yard arm, as Father used to say. I think it's time for a little drink.'

Oh God, what have I done?

17

Each time I wonder whether my interference has not done more harm than good, I remind myself of Mr Nesbit. Seth moved in over the weekend and Mr Nesbit is in seventh heaven. I did not see Seth – I doubt I ever will as he works in the City and, so Mr Nesbit tells me, rarely comes back before nine – so I have no way of knowing if he is as delirious with pleasure as his landlord. I do not actually mind. If nothing else he has himself a comfortable berth thanks to me, with a housemate who will certainly not argue about the telephone bill.

'It's wonderful having another human being in the house,' Mr Nesbit said as he gathered his wallet and little basket together to go shopping. 'I don't know why I did not think of having a lodger years ago. Of course I don't see much of him, but I know he's there. I don't want to be in his way, I am sure he must want to go out and about with his own friends but I like to feel I am useful to him. I'm off to the fishmonger, Cindy, I'll be back in half an hour.' I watched him from the window as he tripped down Farmer Street towards the Gate. He did not even glance towards his sister's house as he passed it. I remembered how I had left her that morning and wondered whether I should check on her on my way home. She is so difficult though, she would only treat my concern as an impudence.

While Mr Nesbit was out I cleaned Seth's room. You would hardly know he was there, he is so tidy. Everything hung neatly in the small cupboard, the jumpers in the drawer arranged by colour. Although he is English, he has been abroad so long you would think by his possessions that he is American. The wool is so soft, his tweed jacket so fine, the shoes so polished. His bathroom equipment is pretty American, too. Mouthwashes and toothpicks and dental flosses, bottles of eau de cologne, even moisturising cream. Well, well, so the magazines do not lie.

Mr Nesbit came back and began organising dinner, laying the table in the small kitchen, trimming and chopping, mixing oil and balsamic vinegar and parsley.

He is not lonely any more. I think I have done him a good turn. I left his house satisfied with myself, and felt only a flicker of guilt as I walked by Mrs Settrington's house without stopping.

I think I have done the stupidest thing yet. I wanted to make Lynda happy, to give her what should rightfully be hers, I wanted her to be happy, and knew that believing herself pregnant was the only happiness she sought. I think I even hoped that by doing what I did I could make the baby happen. I was confusing myself with God or something. I vaguely imagined that if she believed she was pregnant she might suddenly become pregnant. That my lie would become truth. I have managed that before, after all, turning an invention into reality. If the edges are a little blurred sometimes, does it matter? Mr Nesbit believes that having Seth to lodge with him was all his own idea when in fact it came about because I had to unstitch a lie that I had told on the spur of the moment. And that is all right, isn't it? Only Mrs Settrington, and possibly Evelyn, mind about Seth's move to Farmer Street. I caused no damage.

But this . . . I can only hope that by some fluke I am not discovered.

The disaster began on Tuesday, with my visit to Amanda. I arrived to find the flat empty and a note on the kitchen table. 'Gone out. Sorry, no money. Drop in this afternoon if you need it badly.'

I was glad not to see her. I do not feel that I behaved wrongly last Thursday, but on the other hand I did not want to face her. Her flat was quite tidy, although all the bins were full. It looked as though she had been turning out drawers. I looked briefly at the papers she had thrown away, but they were mostly old postcards, invitations, banal letters from girls who signed themselves 'Fi' and 'Binky'.

It is mere chance that I saw the Clearblue pen in the bathroom bin. I was bored with Amanda, bored with her bins, tipped the contents into my black bag haphazardly. The dustbin bag was full by the time I reached the bathroom, so when I tipped the bathroom bin into it so carelessly some of the contents fell on to the floor. Including the Clearblue pen.

I felt sick. I really did not want to know what it told me. But of course I looked, the pen was there as a message to me.

And Amanda is pregnant.

How could she be so stupid? She is nearly thirty, I was nineteen. She has had millions of affairs, I had three. She has a career (of sorts), I was a student.

Maybe Randal Blake told her he was sterile. Maybe Amanda is so busy being a Catholic that she uses no contraception (but then why did she not fall pregnant by Mal or Rollo or Jim or any of the others whose names have figured on invitations on the mantelpiece over the years?)

I should have put the pen back into the bin bag and thrown the whole lot away and forgotten it, but I did not, did I? I suddenly saw a picture of Lynda in my mind's eye, smiling bravely and saying, 'I'm not going to do a test for four days, won't even buy one, so I'm not tempted.' Four days ago she had made herself that promise. I wish I had not remembered that scene, wish I could just have hoped that she was lucky. But instead, overcome with my success for Mr Nesbit, I just could not let well alone. I had the idea and acted on it immediately. I picked up the plastic pen and shoved it into my pocket. I could still change my mind, after all.

I usually spend Tuesday afternoons writing, or reading, or walking Fritz. Private, happy ways of filling up the few precious hours when I am neither working nor with Tamsin. This afternoon I could not concentrate on anything. I took Fritz all the way down to Wormwood Scrubs and back, almost killing him with the distance. I turned over the possibilities again and again. Three times I took the pen out of my pocket, checked its result, found it still confirmed pregnancy, and nearly threw it into a bush. Each time something held me back. That baby should be Lynda's, not Amanda's. My occasional impatience with Lynda was lost in the sense of unfairness at what had happened to her.

Where had Amanda gone that morning? To the doctor? To find her lover at work? To find Lynda? God forbid.

I turned back for home, my feet almost as sore as Fritz's, the pen still in my pocket. There was nothing I could do, they all had to survive their own stories and leave me to live mine. That is what I had decided in those hours of pacing the Scrubs. I must go and see Liz, must ring Nelly again, must come to terms with my own life. This was all a temporary madness, I told myself.

Until I reached home and found, in the second post, a letter from the bank saying that Amanda's cheque to me had bounced. There were 'insufficient funds' to cover the seventy-two pounds.

All my hard-won equanimity fled from me. Perhaps I over-reacted, but I felt deeply insulted. Whether Amanda knew the cheque would bounce or not, she should not have let it happen. It would have been better by far had she come clean, admitted that she could not pay, given me that tenner with a true apology, maybe even laid me off. But lying to me with those wide-open eyes, refusing to take a job because it would compromise her dignity, sleeping with her friend's husband . . . it just did not add up.

I had three-quarters of an hour before school finished. Plenty of time. I slammed my flat door behind me and walked briskly to Lynda's. I have her keys, but thought I should not use them when she was not expecting me. Of course this might not work, it all depended on whether Lynda had used another pregnancy test that morning, on whether she was pregnant or not, on whether she had been as sloppy as usual with the tester, whether she had changed brands . . . but I was so angry with Amanda that none of that seemed to matter.

I marched up to the door and rang the bell. Nothing. I rang again. Nothing. Did I dare use the key? What if she came back while I was there? I did not think about it for long. I know Lynda trusts me implicitly. I opened the door, and ran up the stairs to Lynda's bathroom. The house was as impeccable as ever, cut flowers not a day beyond their prime in the hall and on the landing. It was funny how I noticed them as I passed. Quickly, on my knees by the bin in the bathroom. Yes! There it was. She was as nutty as ever, still testing, still hopeful, still with Clearblue . . . and still not pregnant.

I took Amanda's tester from my pocket, and dropped it on the floor beside the bin, plastic windows pointing up. The two blue lines were thick and clear. An unmistakable declaration of pregnancy. Jamming Lynda's in my pocket, I skipped down the stairs and was in the hall just in time to hear the front door open.

'Lynda? It's Cindy.' I spoke before she could see me, determined not to seem furtive. 'I'm really sorry to let myself in. I rang at the door but there was no answer and I was in a panic. I lost my purse over the weekend and I've been looking for it everywhere. I suddenly thought it might be here from Friday, I couldn't remember using it after I left here.'

'That's all right. Did you find it?'

'Yes it had fallen down behind the coats.'

'Oh, good.' Lynda was clearly distracted but that was fine by me. I wanted to get out of the house as quickly as I could.

'Well, thank you. Sorry to bother you. See you tomorrow.'

''Bye. See you then.'

Perhaps I should have stayed on for a spot of counselling but I thought I had done enough for one day, and there was Tamsin to be met from school.

Well, it worked. I rolled in the next morning to find Lynda almost hysterical with joy.

'I've been longing to tell you, oh it's so wonderful, Cindy I'm pregnant. D'you remember I said I'd been doing the tests every day and I was going to make myself wait? I did one yesterday and it was negative again and I was so depressed I just did not know what to do. Randal's been better recently, the pressure must be off, but you know what I really wanted. Anyway, I went out for lunch with a friend – bored her rigid I should think, oh God, I must ring and apologise – and when I came back – it was like a miracle! I can't have waited long enough – the wretched thing said I *was* pregnant! And if I hadn't been sloppy I would never have seen it! I must have missed the bin when I threw it away, and I saw it lying there and went to pick it up and it had changed.'

I felt very confused, listening to her delight, watching her almost dancing around the room as I took off my coat and hung it up. I was as pleased for her as if she were pregnant, and of course I know she is not. But after the hard time she has had recently (even if she has not known the extent of it) she deserves some happiness. On the other hand – what will happen tomorrow, or the next day, when she discovers she is not pregnant at all? Will the two days of pleasure be worth the agony of disappointment?

'I'm really glad,' I said. And I was. 'But it's very early days, I shouldn't tell too many people.'

'Don't think like that,' she cried. 'Oh it will be all right, I know it will.'

Most of me doubted it but a little part of me, crazy I know, hoped that she would be right.

'Have you told Mr Blake?'

For the first time she stopped smiling. 'Yes,' she said cautiously. 'He is a little shell-shocked, I think. But pleased. Basically delighted. He says he'll have to get used to the idea. So will I, in a way. It's something I've been hoping for for so long, and now it has happened I feel almost numb.'

'You don't look numb,' I laughed. 'You look full of energy.'

'Oh dear, do you think that's bad? Perhaps I should be feeling iller? Perhaps I should be sitting down, resting?'

'It doesn't work like that, Lynda. Take it as you find it. Your body will tell you whether to dance or rest soon enough.'

Why was I playing along with it? It was as though I believed in the pregnancy as much as she did. The odd thing was, I did.

I took myself to the job centre between cleaning the Blakes' and Fergus on Friday. Bizarrely enough, Lynda was still 'pregnant'. I could not work out how late that must make her – at least a week I should think, almost two. Perhaps she is, I found myself hoping, perhaps she really is.

I woke in the middle of the night on Friday. Suddenly, completely and for no apparent reason. Lying looking into the darkness, waiting for the first bird to begin its warble, I thought about the past few months and was frightened. What have I been doing? Playing God, moving these people around a chessboard of my own imagining. I cannot go on doing this, I realised. I am blurring reality and imagination. These impulses should be directed towards my writing, not my life. Or Their lives.

The first thing I noticed when I opened the door of Mrs Settrington's house on Monday morning was the smell, which hit me in the face with the unpleasant impact of a mildewed wet flannel. Then I heard a moan, and pushing open the door saw her. She was in a heap at the bottom of the stairs. She was in her clothes, but had been sick all over her powder-blue jumper and messed herself. For a moment I was too shocked to move. How long had she been there? There was no way of knowing, but I was sure the accident had not happened that morning.

I rang for an ambulance straight away and then tried to see what I could do. She was floating in and out of consciousness, did not seem to know me. She kept calling for Rory, then contradicting herself. 'No, no keep him away, don't let me see him like this. I am not filthy like him, I am always clean.'

Her skin smelt of old alcohol, that smell that drunks have in the pub on the morning after the night before. Not to mention the morning before the night after. I held some water to her mouth and she gulped eagerly. For a moment or two rational light returned to her eyes.

'Thank you, dear. I fell, hurt my shoulder. I'll be all right.' She did not seem to be aware of quite the mess she was in, and I said nothing. 'I'll get up now, I think I'd like a cup of tea and a bath.' She tried to pull herself up, but fell back, moaning. 'It hurts, it hurts, Cindy.'

'I know. Stay still, the ambulance is coming.'

Then she was wandering again, calling me Gloria, Rory, other names which meant nothing to me.

'Shall I call Mr Nesbit?'

'No, not Father, he's not well, he wouldn't like it, no, don't call Father, not now, not until later.'

'Mr Vincent Nesbit?'

'I have no brother, not any more. No brother.'

I gave up, she was in and out of the decades like Doctor Who.

It seemed a long time before the ambulance came but when

it did the two men with it were brisk and efficient and not at all disgusted. They parcelled her up and took her off. I wondered whether I should go with her, but decided I would do better by staying in Farmer Street and tidying up. I did not know whether to ring Mr Nesbit or not: he was the obvious person, but she might turn against him.

I rang Amanda, told her the hospital where her aunt was going, asked her to ring her mother. Then I began tidying. The house was in as good order as ever, but the bed was neatly made which made me think that she must have fallen at least the night before, if not earlier. She always leaves the bed unmade on Monday mornings for me to change the sheets.

There was an empty gin bottle in the bin in the kitchen. I found three half-empty glasses in the house, two holding gin and one whisky. It was as though she had put them down, forgotten where they were and just poured another. In the cupboard of her bedside table was a half-bottle of whisky, mostly drunk. The cupboard was not tall enough for a whole bottle. Her drinking was worse than I had imagined. It was much worse than too much sherry with the Colonel, or one more unnecessary whisky before bed.

I looked at the patch on the bedroom wall where the Kenya picture had hung. She had put something else on the same hook, but the new picture – an oval water-colour of two small girls at the beginning of the century – was smaller than the older one and the darker patch of wallpaper framed it by two inches all around.

Mrs Settrington has always drunk quite a lot. When I was very first working for her I noticed how quickly the gin went down between one visit and the next. She is usually a little tipsy at the end of her dinners – the time with Seth was the worst, but by no means exceptional. She comes back from her lunches out very ratty, and then sleeps heavily for an hour and wakes up bad-tempered. The Kenya picture – the true story behind the Kenya picture – cannot be blamed for her drinking. I cannot be blamed for her fall. A little bit of me felt as bad as though I had pushed her. I had not shoved her down the stairs, but I almost had. That little bit of knowledge I had given her, together with her godson moving in with her brother and reopening the old wounds might – just might – have pushed her over the edge. Made the drinking seriously dangerous, rather than just a lonely woman's crutch.

Amanda was in on Tuesday morning. I was expecting not to see her, I thought her sense of shame about the cheque must be enough to make her hide. Far from it, there she was, looking very penitent, and holding a large wad of cash.

'I'm mortified, I really am,' she began. Why can she not just be embarrassed, or ashamed like everyone else? 'It was the most appalling thing to do to you. That was why I was cross when you said you would take a cheque, I just crossed my fingers that it would go through.'

'You should have told me. I would have understood.'

'I know, I know, but I was ashamed.'

'A false shame, Amanda Quince. What you did was much worse.' I liked the sound of my words, did not care about her suppressed smirk. She was truly in my hands now. Anger made me speak out. I no longer care if I lose that job, or any of them. I have had enough. I thought she might sack me (I wished I had taken hold of the money before I let my tongue get the better of me) but instead she burst into tears.

'You don't understand. Please don't be cross with me. I know it was an awful thing to do to you, and I'm sorry and here's all the money and a month in advance.' Of course, her mother's up in town, she probably handed out some cash.

'I thought you had a documentary lined up.'

'I did, but I've only been paid a tiny bit in advance, and my overdraft's enormous and I know that's not the point, I should have been honest with you and I'm sorry and I'm *pregnant*.' The last word came out on a huge howl.

'Pregnant?' I needed time to think.

'Yes, I'm pregnant and it really is the last straw. What am I to do?'

Suddenly the cheque seemed unimportant. It is not that which has made me grow to dislike her so much. I looked at her and saw all that I might have been, and knew how differently I would have used my good luck. I remembered the first time I ever met her in Bassett Road and how she had offered me coffee and waited to drink her wine until I was out of the house, remembered how lightly she had spoken of lodgers and how for one mad second I had imagined myself in that position. I thought of her, drunk on the university stage, confident as always that her charm would carry her through this crisis, any crisis, and she had been right. I thought of the succession of floppy-haired boyfriends whose names and photographs had appeared on the living-room mantelpiece through the last five years. I thought of Lynda, affectionate, sweet, irritating Lynda, her longing for a baby and her misplaced trust in her husband. I remembered Randal Blake looking into Amanda's eyes at his party, saw him leaning over her in 192 while his own wife sat by oblivious.

'What does the father say?' I managed to ask.

Renewed sobs. 'He doesn't want to know. It's complicated. Oh, I might as well tell you, he's married. He says it was all my fault, says he never said he'd leave her, which is true, he didn't, but I thought . . . I thought we were in love! I can't have it, my father will kill me. But it would be worse if I didn't, if they found out.'

'Why?'

'Because we're Catholic, I can't have an abortion. I'll have to keep it, what will I do?'

I thought of Liz and her atavistic desire to marry in church. I thought of Mr Nesbit and his words about Catholicism, and suddenly understood. Here she was, modern, uninhibited Amanda, going her own sweet way through life but still, when it mattered, having her rope jerked by her upbringing. *I'll have to keep it, what will I do*?

For a mad moment I thought of suggesting, in my most ingenious manner, that she give the baby to Lynda to adopt. She needs one, it would salve Amanda's Catholic conscience, Randal would have his son . . . But why should Randal be rewarded?

'I suppose a child would be quite nice.' Amanda was calming down. 'I've always wanted one, in theory. This is not the best time, but when is? Oh, I don't know.'

My head spun. For a moment I thought I was about to have one of my funny turns. A child is not a commodity, not something you buy at one moment and then change in the sale. Why, with that attitude, should she be allowed a child? When I was pregnant it never occurred to me to abort the baby. I considered adoption for a while, but abortion, never. And thank God. Tamsin has held me together all these years. Without her . . .

Without her I could have been an Amanda, or a Nelly, or a Jane. I could have had a job, earned proper money, been respected by men like Fergus.

I suddenly saw my way forward. Amanda has everything I would like. The only thing she does not have is a child. I could not bear her having that, too. Not in this way. Not sanctioned by her Church and family, with the career under her belt, with the friends for life who will not now desert her. No, she had to be stopped.

'Have you thought it through?' I smiled, I spoke softly, I patted her shoulder.

'Of course not, I've only just found out.'

'Will you be able to go on with your work? With a baby? Who would look after it?'

'Don't be difficult, Cindy, a nanny I suppose.' (She could not quite help herself talking down to me, even in the depths of self-absorption. Every time I falter she makes it easier for me.) 'While I'm working. And me when I'm not. And my mother would help, and it could go and stay with Fiona.' Her eyes brightened, she was talking herself into having the child.

'Do you mind if we have a cup of coffee?'

'No, good idea.'

I made the coffee and she sat at the table and waited for it, talking to herself about how she would organise her life with the baby. I was thinking hard, wondering how much to tell her. I turned, holding the two cups of coffee and she looked at me expectantly.

'You don't remember me, do you?'

'Remember you? What do you mean?'

I stood still: I wanted her really to look at me, at my face, to see *me* rather than good old Cindy, the perfect treasure.

'I can't blame you, I didn't recognise you at first, either, although I thought you seemed familiar. And then of course you get used to someone, only see them in their present incarnation. The moment passes.'

'What are you on about?'

Amanda was looking faintly alarmed.

'I was not in the play, I worked on props.'

'Which play? Which props?'

'In the play you were a maid, a dreary soul. And my friend Nelly wafted around the stage as Madame. Funny, if you think about it.'

'*The Maids*. Genet. What do you know about that? At university . . .'

'And I did the props. I was never very interested in acting but I quite enjoyed backstage work. We did the whole play in black and white, the clothes, the props, everything. But we made one mistake – the inside of the white leather jewellery box was red velvet. Do you remember? I never noticed until the first night we did the play, it glared out in the middle of all that black and white. I felt such a fool, it was my responsibility. But then you—'

'I turned up blind drunk. I'd just broken up with – I don't even remember his name now. Why did you never tell me?'

'I didn't recognise you either. Then I met up with Nelly again, I hadn't seen her for years, and I mentioned your name and she reminded me.'

'Why didn't you tell me?'

'It was just before Christmas, it seemed too late. Too much water under the bridge, all that sort of thing. What good would it have done? It would only have embarrassed us both.'

'So why are you telling me now?'

I handed her the coffee, sat down opposite her, never taking my eyes from her face. Her eyes were wide and dark. She looked almost frightened.

'I have a daughter. I've never told you that, either. She's seven, she's called Tamsin.'

'You have a daughter? You are extraordinary, Cindy, I mean I know it's nothing to do with me but we've known each other for years now, you might have mentioned it.' She was trying to sound light-hearted but she was watching me warily. Then suddenly a shutter clicked in her memory. 'Seven? I remember . . . it was you? You left at the end of your first year because you were pregnant?' I nodded. 'Everyone was talking about it. I remember I did another play with Nelly in the autumn term after that, what was it, *Streetcar*, she was the sister and I was Blanche, I asked her what had happened to you, nobody seemed to know. She did not either. But you were a sort of object lesson to new undergraduates for a while.'

'The girl who kept her baby.'

'Yes, I mean others got pregnant, but I don't remember anyone else having the baby. So what happened to you?' I did not dignify the question with an answer and she blushed. 'Sorry, yes I see.'

'I don't think you do, Amanda. I don't think you see at all. Of course you are luckier than I was, you already have a career and your own flat, but it still won't be easy.' (I must not become angry, I must stay calm.) 'A new baby ties you down more than you can imagine. You cannot leave it in the day, or in the night. You have no sleep, your brain concentrates so hard on reminding you how to survive physically that it packs up mentally. You wouldn't be able to go off in your smart clothes raising money for your documentaries for months. When you do you will have baby sick on one shoulder and a spare nappy in your handbag instead of your presentation. Mothers are not as good as they are cracked up to be, either. I had Tamsin from my mother's house and we left six weeks later. And after all, why not. She had her own life, her job, my father. There was no reason she should start again. And my brother – he and his wife have a child slightly older than Tamsin, they would help if they could, but how often can they be asked? They have their own work, their family.

'I had my baby at a bad time, but as you say, which time is good? Don't let me influence you, Amanda, but if you go into this saying that it will be easy, believe me, it won't.'

'I wasn't saying it would be *easy*,' she protested, looking appalled.

'If I had finished university and taken my degree, think how different my life would have been,' I went on, ignoring her interruption. 'I've been catching up with contemporaries recently and it probably won't surprise you to hear that I am the only one I have heard about who cleans other people's houses for a living. Oh, I'm not saying I would be running Channel 4 or editing the *Guardian* if I had stayed on, but I am quite sure I would not be doing this.'

'I wouldn't have to do it, either.'

'Of course you wouldn't, I'm not suggesting you would, I'm just saying that you have no idea how wide the ripples spread. It won't be a year out of your life, or two, it will be sixteen or eighteen.'

'I'm sure Daddy would help me send it to boarding school,' she said.

'Oh, all right then, nine years if it's a boy, eleven if it's a girl – isn't that how it works?'

She took her first sip of coffee and I saw her hand was shaking. 'Would you help me, Cindy?'

'Help you?'

'With the baby?'

I looked deliberately blank. 'You mean, be your nanny? What about Mrs Settrington, Mr Nesbit?'

'I'm sure we can find them someone else. Oh Cindy, would you, would you help me?'

'And then leave at three to pick up Tamsin from school? What would you do then? I couldn't be your nanny, Amanda. There are precious few jobs I can do, that's why I clean. Tamsin ties me, I have to fit in around her.' I paused and then could not resist adding, 'Besides which, without causing any offence, could you afford me?'

I saw her dark blue eyes flinch and suddenly felt sorry for her. When I spoke again I could hear my voice had softened. 'Amanda, I'm sorry. I remember what it was like. It is the most frightening thing that can possibly happen to someone, I do understand.' For a moment I did. I forgot about my envy and her high-handed treatment of me over the years. I forgot everything except the memory of looking at that pregnancy test and knowing I had no choice but to carry the baby.

She roused herself. 'What about her – Tamsin's – father? Didn't he want to know either?'

'He took responsibility, offered to pay for the abortion.'

'Are you Catholic?'

'No.'

'Why did you keep her?'

There it was again, that mindless adherence to a tradition which only occasionally means anything to her. The rosary when the boyfriend dumps her, the attendance at Mass when she is temporarily and unavoidably celibate . . . I cannot decide whether I admire or despise it. I think I feel more admiration than not, after all strength is always admirable. And one thing I have learned is the strength of her Church. But yet it seems to imply a lack of individual will, a shirking of responsibility for one's own actions. It is as though it is one thing to be forced into keeping a child because your faith tells you to, another – and sheer madness – to do it because you feel you should. Her incapacity to recognise her pregnancy as a future child goaded me on.

'I've often asked myself that over the years. I don't know. I still don't.' Of course I do not regret it, but I wanted to avoid telling her that.

'I'm frightened, Cindy.'

'I know.'

'So what do I do?'

'Can you go to the father?'

'I told you, he's married.'

'Has he children already?'

'No.'

'Perhaps he'll be grateful to you. Perhaps he can adopt the baby. What's the wife like? Understanding? Kind?' What was happening? I could hear my voice, soft, persuasive, concerned. I could feel the poison running through my veins like the first hit of gin after a long hard day. I was suddenly appalled at myself, knew I had to stop.

With the realisation I felt a wave of exhaustion wash over me. I pulled back, took a breath.

'Oh Amanda, I can't tell you what to do. All I can say is think very carefully. Don't make a mistake over this one. Either way it will change your life. But don't go into it imagining other people will help. They will rally round for a month or two and then you will be on your own. Do you have a mortgage on the flat?'

'Yes.'

'Maybe the social services will help you with that.'

To a girl who had dismissed waitressing as beneath her, I

knew she would not like the thought of the social services – although I would like to ask her the difference between taking money from your rich relations and taking it from the state.

'Cindy, can I ask you something?'

'What?'

'Do you mind?'

Mind? Of course I mind. Mind that now she will indeed have everything, deserving nothing. Mind that she thinks that she can lean on me just a tiny bit and I will look after her baby as well as mine. Mind that a year ago she probably could have done just that. But then I saw I had misunderstood her.

'Mind? Mind what?'

'Being alone with your baby. Missing out, you know.'

It was the first time anyone had ever asked me that. Not Mum or Dad, not Steven or Joanne, not Nelly or even Liz had ever asked me that. Perhaps that was why I answered so honestly, more honestly than I had even been with myself. 'Yes, I mind. I mind desperately, more rather than less as the years go past.' I spoke with no hidden agenda: I had forgotten my resentment, my determination that Amanda should not have her child. 'But of course I love her,' I added.

'Of course.' She answered absently, dismissively. She was not crying any longer, but was thinking hard about what she should do. I drained my cup of coffee and began the tour of the flat. We did not speak again until I was leaving, when she came up to me and put her hand on my shoulder and said, 'Thank you'.

'What for? I should be thanking you, for the money.'

'Thank you for telling me – about Tamsin, and *The Maids* and everything.' She laughed, but there was more sorrow than mirth in her laugh. 'Who'd have thought it?' she said, as I had always known she would. And then she hesitated, and then she kissed my cheek. 'I mean it, thank you,' she said again. And I left.

Why did I feel so bad? She had kissed me, but it was I who felt like a Judas. And yet I had done nothing but tell her the truth.

18

Lynda is not pregnant. Why do I write that as though I am surprised? My head is spinning with all that has happened recently. Lynda is not pregnant. Of course she is not, she never was. I know that. She does not, but I do. She thinks she has had an early miscarriage, that is what the doctor has told her, he is not even going to put her into hospital, give her a D&C. Just as well, really. Yet she seems to wish that she could be hospitalised, as though that would confer some sort of status of pregnancy upon her.

'He says it is very common,' she wept to me. 'Says that if it had not been for the wonders of modern technology I would not even have known that I was pregnant, would have assumed it was a late period. I suppose he's right. But at least I know I can be pregnant, that there is hope. He says that – oh I don't remember what bloody percentage he put on it – but that thousands, millions of women miscarry their first child without even realising it, said a lot of things about the womb warming up. Warming up! I'm getting on, I need to do more than warm up.'

She needed to warm up literally, too, though. Her teeth were chattering and her whole body was shaking uncontrollably. This was a different Lynda from the elegant party-giver, the loving wife, the home-maker. But it was also different from the self-pitying, spoilt Lynda that I had occasionally seen. For the first time I was frightened, and it was nothing like the fear I felt when I had stolen the invitation or the letters. Then I had been frightened for myself. Now I was terrified at what I had done to Lynda. I was unsure that she would survive this blow intact, and there was nothing I could do to help.

I gave her aspirin and hot lemon and told her maybe she should go to bed and try to sleep. 'Yes, maybe you're right. I'm not up to much else. But it's so good to have you here to talk to. Randal—'

'Yes?'

'Oh Cindy, I'm sure he does not mean to be cruel, he just does not understand. He said "bloody hell, why did you bother to tell me you were pregnant in the first place if you couldn't hold on to it?" How could he talk to me like that? I know it's not the same for men, but . . . And then he said, "it would be that one, wouldn't it?" and I asked what he meant and he said well it would have been better after I'd had one because then I might be more sane. He may be right, but he didn't need to say it, did he?'

'He must be in shock, too,' I said calmly. 'It's his baby too, you know. He probably minds more than he thought he would.'

'Do you think so? Oh, I doubt it. He's said nothing positive to me about this baby, nothing at all, and now it isn't even a baby any more and I just don't know what to do.'

I can only hope that in time Lynda will be comforted by the memory of her 'pregnancy'.

It is all I can do.

Mrs Settrington is out of hospital. I went to see her but she had been discharged in the morning. Then Mr Nesbit told me that she has gone to stay with Amanda's mother in the country until she has her strength back. She broke her collarbone and is incapable of managing by herself. Poor Mrs Quince.

'I think they will hire someone to live in for a while after this unpleasantness,' said Mr Nesbit. 'Of course we all keep thinking of Father . . . funny how history repeats itself. Now, I must pop out and buy a piece of beef. We're having a little dinner party tonight. I am cooking the main course and Seth is preparing the hors d'oeuvres. And maybe some flowers, too. I'll see you later, dear.'

Yes, I did good there. He hardly ever talks about his porcelain any more. He has a spring in his step. He no longer follows me around the house talking about nothing. Mr Nesbit's life has improved for the better under my care.

This letter arrived this morning:

Shirley Heights
Torquay

5th March
Dear Cindy,

I wish you had a telephone! I've been meaning to write to you for ages, but am too lazy to put pen to paper! Thanks for your letter, I loved having you and it was great to meet Tamsin after so long. She does you credit.

I was going to write and ask you to come and stay again, but I've had a brilliant idea. You said you wanted a change, that you felt stuck in your cleaning. Well, it's done you brilliantly while Tamsin was little, but now she's at school all the time you must have more time. There are a couple of vacancies in the hotel coming up – when the season begins to hot up. I haven't said anything to anyone here, but would you be interested? It could be just the change of scene you need. One of the jobs is in the personnel office, one is in the kitchens. Neither are that grand, but both could lead on to greater things. After all, we are part of a huge chain which does leave a lot of room for manoeuvre. I don't know if you can type at all – you would need basic word-processing skills for the personnel job. Anyway, think about it. You (and Tamsin of course) could stay with me in the flat until something was sorted in the town.

I don't want to push you Cindy, but it would be fun for me. I have a lot of friends down here, but no one who makes me laugh as much as you used to – and did again when you didn't have that tortured look on your face!

Think about it. Meanwhile I think I'm coming up to London in a fortnight or so. I'll send you a postcard when I know the date for sure, and then maybe you could ring me.

See you soon.

Big kiss to Tamsin, love

Nelly

I cannot think straight, do not know what to do. In a way it is very tempting but – a hotel? I really do not know. Is she patronising me, has she pulled strings? She had mentioned the idea while we were there but I thought she was joking.

I could leave London easily enough, I think. And it would be lovely for Tamsin to live by the sea. But could I leave all of Them? What would They do without me?

'Penniless divorcée sells children's story for £100,000.' Jane left the newspaper cutting on her work table for me with a note. 'See – there's hope for us all! J.' The woman had written the book in cafés while her baby slept in the pram beside her. She was living on benefits, alone in a strange city. And her book has sold to America for all that money. I sat on one of Jane's hard kitchen chairs and read the cutting again and again. It was some kind of message to me. But what did it mean?

I cleaned the flat in a daze, my mind veering between Torquay and America. Or why not both? But Jane is relying on me now, I think. We are becoming friends. I wanted that so much at first but now it does not seem to be important.

I worked at my writing until midnight. I think it is taking shape. I am beginning to believe in it. Maybe the *Telegraph* will be reporting my triumph in a year's time. Maybe.

I am still being paid to clean Mrs Settrington's house while she is away, but as it is no use pretending that it takes anything like three hours now no one is there I used two of the hours on my writing, before going up and cleaning Farmer Street. Once I would have used the extra time in looking into cupboards while I spring-cleaned them, but I do not want to know any more about Mrs Settrington. Enough is enough.

Amanda was away on Tuesday. No note, no message. I am paid up, so I cannot complain, but I do wonder where she was. The flat seemed curiously empty, more as though she were away than just out.

On Wednesday I found Lynda with unwashed hair, dirty clothes, staring eyes and no make-up. This from a woman who had once said, 'You know I can't even go to the post-box without my mascara on'. The flowers in the hall had shed their petals all over the floor, unwashed dishes were left in the sink. The dishwasher was full of dirty plates but had not been turned on. Unlike the unnatural tidy stillness of Amanda's flat the day before, here everything was awry. Lynda spoke and her voice was hoarse and as dry as her eyes.

'Randal's gone,' she said.

I did not mean to be obtuse, but I think her words put me into minor shock. 'Out?'

'No, gone. I don't know where. First the baby, and now him. I don't know what to do. He said he couldn't stand my self-pitying whining any longer. He said he would go to a hotel. He said he would send a cab round for some clothes.'

'Oh, Lynda—' I nearly confessed, told her of my folly, but the self-preservation that has kept me afloat for so long held me back. I pulled myself together. 'Did he say what he was going to do – next?'

She shook her head. 'No. He said I had to get my act together, he would give me time. He says if he ever hears the word baby again he'll sue for divorce. He says he didn't marry me to watch me drag myself around the house he provides as though life had dealt me an unfair hand. He said I should be grateful, the world is overpopulated, there are far too many babies born that no one wants.' She spoke dully, as though she had repeated the words to herself so often that they no longer had any meaning. There were no tears, just an awful submission. She has done everything her husband has asked of her for so long that she will even suffer this rupture without crying or bleeding.

'Is there – any reason?'

She did not understand me, perhaps deliberately. 'Reason? My "unreasonable behaviour" seems to be enough. I only wanted his child. All I wanted was his child.'

'He'll come back,' I said, although I almost believe it would be better for her if he does not. (Will that be a good thing? The end of that marriage? Not for him, I am sure, and Lynda does not think so on her account.)

'I'm sorry, Lynda, so sorry.' And I was. Sorry for her unhappiness (this kind of suffering touched me to the heart, much more than her earlier wails of loss), and sorry for the part I had played in bringing it about. (Although would it have made that much difference if she had not thought herself pregnant? She was obsessed already with a baby – one or two more periods down the line might have had much the same result as this 'loss'. And she would not have had those happy days of belief.)

'Oh well. He may come back. And if not I suppose he is right. It is all my fault. I should be thinking of Randal, who exists, not of a baby who does not.' I could not think of anything to say to comfort her.

I rang Nelly at the weekend, and arranged to meet her at the Uxbridge on Tuesday. She did not mention her letter and neither did I. I have not mentioned it to anyone else either. It is something I must work out on my own.

Amanda was back on Tuesday. Lying on the sofa with a fat novel, her eyes huge in her pale face. She put the book down as I came in and gestured to me to sit down. I sat awkwardly at her feet.

'How are you?'

'All right. I took your advice.'

'My advice?'

She managed a wan smile. 'Well, maybe you did not mean me to take it as advice. But I realised I could not go ahead. Not without – the father. I would look at it every day and think what a shit its father was. That would not be a very fair start in life, would it? Tears rolled silently down her cheeks. 'And I thought of your life and mine and knew that I would not be as good at coping as you are. I'm quite weak, really. Besides, he's married, I told you that. It wouldn't be fair on his wife. So, yes, I took your advice. I – terminated – the pregnancy. I think that's the right term at this stage. I'll have another baby one day, when it's wanted and loved. They tell me I'm bound to be weepy for a while, feel a little weak. But that's better than a lifetime of being bound, isn't it?'

I sat in horror looking at her white face and huge eyes. I had not advised her to have an abortion, not directly, not at all. I will not be responsible. 'But I wanted Tamsin, I love her!' I blurted out. I should not have. I did not mean to do it, but I could not bear her to think otherwise for one minute.

'Of course you love her,' she agreed, 'of course. I am sure I would have loved my baby, but . . .' and the big tears began rolling again.

'Excuse me,' I managed to mutter, and bolted to the bathroom and was sick. Why am I always sick in times of crisis? Why was this a time of crisis?

'Are you all right?' Amanda asked when I returned. 'Something you ate?' But she was not interested. She was thinking of nothing but herself and her dead baby.

'The father was not so bad,' she said. 'Paid for the op, came with me, took me away for a few days afterwards. And then he went back to his wife, where I suppose he belongs. I think that will be that. I don't think I could ever take up with him again. It would not be right, would it? Could you change my sheets for me, Cindy? Thank you. I'm afraid they're rather unpleasant.'

Maybe that was it. Maybe that polite apology for the mess that had been caused by the 'operation' was the element that finally made me realise what I had done – or to what I had contributed. I changed the sheets with tears pouring down my face, images of Tamsin through her life running across my mental video screen. I wondered if anybody could have persuaded me not to have her – my parents had tried and had not succeeded, but what would have happened if someone I trusted, someone my own age, had put the power of suggestion so deep into my head that I had aborted her? I would not have done, I think I can be sure of that. I was sorely tested and I passed. But, as Amanda said, I am stronger than she. For a brief moment I had not wanted Amanda to have that child, just as for a brief moment I had wanted Seth and Mr Nesbit to move in together. My passing whims had been gratified, one with a happy, one with an unhappy outcome.

When I went back out into the living-room I found Amanda fast asleep, a rosary clutched tight between her fingers. The last time I saw her with a rosary I found it comical, offensive, perhaps threatening. This time I found it very touching.

She had gone against her faith because she did not want to be a cleaning woman. Isn't that what it comes down to?

I left the flat quietly, and found myself on the street leaning against a tree trunk, crying noiselessly. My mind was a blank, I did not even know why I was weeping. I think that was deliberate at some level. I think the Cindy Martin self-preservation switch was well and truly tripped.

I do not remember much about the next week. I know I did not go to work, but that somehow I managed to feed Tamsin and make sure she arrived at school on time. Jane sent a note home one day with Tamsin. Lynda had rung her and wondered if I were ill. Would I be going to her flat on Friday? I remember Tamsin handing me the note and looking at me curiously as I read it. Then came a postcard from Nelly. I had stood her up, had I forgotten, was I all right? Was there anything that she could do?

I do not remember where I went or what I did, I was in some sort of mental limbo, some fugue state where I could just manage to function, but only just. I think I no longer cared about looking after myself, but had not lost myself so badly that I forgot Tamsin. I do remember snatches, though. Not of my actions, but of my thoughts. Mostly of Tamsin, of our life, of the love that bound us together. And I thought of Amanda's baby, the baby that I knew she would never quite be able to put aside or forget. I remember walking down a street (where? I think I did a lot of aimless wandering in that week) and seeing a mother pushing a new-born baby in a spanking new pram. I remember holding on to a post-box for support as I wept, really wept, howling like a dog in pain. The woman must have thought I was mad. Perhaps I was. You see, all these years I have congratulated myself on one thing – that I gave Tamsin life. That I had never doubted she had a right to that life. And then I had wilfully taken away the life of Amanda's baby. Because I was jealous of her. Because I had found myself in the habit of interfering in the lives of the people who paid me to clean their baths. I was as guilty as the doctor who took money to pull these living babies from their mother's bodies. As guilty as Randal with his cheque book, as Amanda with her horror of discomfort and inconvenience. More guilty than either, in a way, because I knew better. I had Tamsin.

It was Tamsin who brought me back to myself. As she always has, as she always will. She told me afterwards that she had taken herself to a telephone box and rung Liz, asking her to come and help. My first coherent memory is of the two of them standing over me as I lay on the settee. I remember seeing them first, then hearing them. These two faces I loved came into focus, their mouths moving in turn. Then came their voices, soft and persuasive.

'Come on Mum, you've got to get up. Let's go for a walk.' It made me smile. I always suggest a walk when Tamsin is out of sorts. I could hear my own tones in her voice, half-coaxing, half-authoritative.

'See, Liz, she's smiling. She *can* hear us.'

' 'Course she can, she's fine.' Liz was more brisk. 'Come on now, Cindy, there's been enough of this. Tamsin tells me you've barely spoken for a week. Sit up, girl, you're letting yourself down.'

Slowly, painfully, I pushed myself upright on the sofa. 'I feel awful. Can I have a cup of tea?' I croaked.

I noticed Tamsin and Liz exchange glances, saw Liz make a decision. 'I'll get it, love, you talk to your mam,' she said.

Tamsin sat on the sofa beside me. 'You've been ill, Mum, it was horrible,' she said. 'Miss Cox saw you after school when you came to get me and you didn't talk to her. She came and asked you what the matter was and you just looked at her and took me away. She asked me the next day if I'd been getting my tea.'

I looked dully at my daughter. 'Had you?' I asked. The answer interested me as an abstract question, rather than worrying me as a parent.

'Of course. You're my mum,' said Tamsin, then she burst into tears. Something – habit, love? – I don't know – made me put my arms out to her, and she came into them and clung to me, sobbing. 'Oh, Mum, what happened? You've been so odd. Liz wanted to take me home with her and call a doctor for you, but I wouldn't let her. I said I would look after you.'

Her last words finally pierced the fog of my self-absorption. 'But I'm meant to look after you,' I cried.

'I know, but I thought it was my turn. I didn't mind, Mum.'

'Well, it's all right now. I'm sorry, I'm so sorry.' I managed not to cry. I know how much Tamsin hates to see me cry and I had put her through enough in the last week. 'I'm better now, much better. I don't know what happened. I've been thinking too much, that's it. I've just got to think a tiny bit more, make some decisions.'

Tamsin looked alarmed, pulled away from my embrace. 'What do you mean?'

I took a deep breath. I think I had already made the decision, but I felt I should involve Tamsin in it in some way. After all, she was showing plenty of maturity. 'I think it's time we moved. What do you reckon?'

'Move? Where? I like it here. What about Liz and Ayesha? What about Miss Cox?'

'What about Torquay?'

'Torquay? You mean—' Her face changed, lit up. 'You mean the hotel? The sea?'

'Yes, Nelly suggested it – ages ago – and then she wrote to me . . .' I told her about the letter, painted the picture in the brightest colours, promised that we would come back and see Liz, would still see her grandparents. I hardly needed to speak. To her the hotel was the most glamorous place in the world, and the idea that I should work there utter heaven.

Liz came back in with the tea and sat for a while, listening. 'And what about Them?' she said after a while. 'Mrs Settrington, Amanda, all of Them? You'll miss them, won't you?'

I thought of Them for the first time. These people in whom my life had been so bound up for so many years. And I realised that I did not care. I have learned my lesson, it is time for my own life now. I want to shut the lid on all of them, on Lynda and her sterility, Amanda and her fertility, Mr Nesbit and his romantic urges, Mrs Settrington and her wilful malice. Even Jane and her kindness. I will be able to wish them goodbye with no regrets, even with some affection. I hope they will remember me as someone who was part of their lives, but know they will soon forget. Some other woman will come and do for them, someone who Knows Her Place and can Keep Herself to Herself.

And Fergus? He will always be Lynda's friend, he will never be Amanda's lover. He will never look at me unless, just possibly, he meets me again in a few years' time. My hair will be well cut, my clothes up to date, my head held high. 'Hello, do you remember me?' I'll say. 'Cindy Martin, I used to clean for you.'

And he will shake my hand and say, 'Well, who'd have believed it? Of course I remember you. I've read your books. Shall we have a drink?'

Yes, I will take up Nelly's offer. We will move to Torquay. And if the hotel does not work out, I am sure I will find some other people who need a cleaner. Until my book is published.